Blu's Boys

Aimee Stone

Copyright © 2020 Aimee Stone

All rights reserved. No part of this book may be reproduced in any form or by any electronic or mechanical means, including information storage and retrieval systems, without permission in writing from the publisher, except by reviewers, who may quote brief passages in a review.

ISBN-13 978-0-9824638-4-0

ISBN-10 0-9824638-4-7

Library of Congress Control Number: 2020916477

Printed in United States of America

Published by BookWorm Publications, LLC

102 W Rockingham Street, #334

Elkton, VA 22827 USA

Visit www.BookWormPublications.com

Blu's Boys

Aimee Stone

For my Family

I love you and all that you do for me, as a writer and as a wife and mother. All of you are greatly appreciated.

To my Editor

I am so happy to have found you. I am excited to be working with your company for my upcoming books.

To my fellow writers

You have inspired me to follow my dreams and continue writing, even when I was ready to give up.

Thank you all.

Chapter 1

The night was dark and stormy. The lightning was lighting up Blu's room with every bolt. The thunder was loud and rumbled through her body like a freight train on its tracks. All she could hear was the rain knocking on the window, like a stranger begging for entrance.

The lights in the house flickered off before coming back on with a displeased grinding noise. Blu lived in an old farmhouse and it never liked change. This storm did not seem to care about preferences this evening. Blu sunk in her bed, the covers pulled up around her neck, fending off the cool air that had joined the stormy night.

She closed her eyes, trying to find the sleep that the storm had chased away with all of its noise and flashing lights.

I am never going to be able to keep up tomorrow if I don't get a little sleep, she thought to herself as another crack of thunder rattled her windows, reminding her that sleep was not to be found.

Blu worked as a secretary in the city, for the CEO of Pascal Enterprises, that largest investment company on the East coast. It was never a job she aspired to do, but it paid the bills so that she could keep her family farm running.

"Please let me sleep," she said to no one in particular. For a young girl living alone, Blu never really felt lonely. Not until nights like this. She used to love storms when she was younger. Her parents tried to tell her about their dangers, but she never really understood their concerns. Not until she lost them in a car wreck just over a year ago, on a night much like this one.

Blu pulled the blankets up around her neck further, trying to drown out the noises that preyed on her very sanity as they continued to torment her.

STOP IT!!

Her thoughts continued to berate the Gods for continuing with this storm, even after she begged for it to stop. It took another half an hour for the rain to slow, the thunder to move on to torture another lost soul, and the lightning to no longer be lighting the shadows of her room.

She turned over, anxious to fall asleep. She needed rest to keep up at her job. Her boss was a nice enough man, very driven and successful, and with his success came her busy day. Pax Pascal was a handsome man. Most would say he was sexy. Blu would be one of those women, even though her busy days did not give her much opportunity to appreciate her daily view of the most sought-after bachelor in the city.

The next morning came too early for the few hours of sleep that the stormy night allowed for Blu. She woke with a slight headache and a large yawn.

I am not in the mood for another Monday morning, she thought as she stretched and threw the warmth of her covers back. She stepped out of bed and padded her way across the cool wooden floor of her bedroom. Only stopping when she reached the even cooler tile of her bathroom floor.

After her shower and a quick-drying off, she was able to feel almost human again as she dressed for the first day of the week.

Monday's were always busy. Busier than the rest of the week. It was undoubtedly the day that her bosses weekend fuck would try to reach out for another round. It was always her job to run interference between weekend fuck number... whatever... and her boss. They always tried to "land him" and he was never interested in being caught.

She wondered how he met these women as she finished her bagel and glass of tea. She shrugged her shoulders, conceding it wasn't her place to know how he met them, only to get rid of them. She grabbed her light sweater as she headed out into the wet and cool morning.

She pulled into the office building parking garage with

twenty minutes to spare. Plenty of time to say hello to her best friend, Zoe, before heading to her desk.

"Mornin' Zoe," she said as she stuck her head into Zoe's office door.

Zoe smiled and answered what she always did on Monday mornings, "Are you ready for hoe duty?"

"Maybe he didn't hook up this weekend." She laughed as she said it. He always did and she always got the call. "Where does he meet these women? Last week was a doozy."

The girls talked a few more minutes before Blu had to leave to get to her desk. She made it with plenty of time to spare.

Just as she was about to take her seat and read her emails, a deep voice rang through the office. "Blu, is that you?"

She didn't know why he asked that every morning, who else was he expecting to take the seat at her desk?

"Yes, sir," she answered as she made her way to his office door. He looked up from his desk, his dark hair disheveled for first thing in the morning. He looked as if he had been there a while.

Blu noticed how handsome he truly was when he had a bit of scruff on his face and his hair appeared to have had his hands run through it numerous times. For a moment, the thought crossed her mind that maybe it wasn't his hands that had been running through it. That made her smile disappear and her mind wander to her pulling his hair while his head was buried between her…

"I'm so glad you are here. I need your help."

"Of course, sir, what can I do to help you?" She asked as she stepped into his office. His cologne wafted into her nose as she got closer. The smile returned to her face at how delicious he smelled up close.

He ran his fingers through his hair as he looked over the papers inside a brown folder on top of his desk. "These numbers don't add up," he huffed as he stared at the papers.

Blu walked over to stand beside him as he sat in his chair. His cologne was not overpowering, it was just the right amount, but it always affected her. Blu wasn't immune to her boss or his animal magnetism that attracted every female within miles. However, he was her boss and she would have to keep that in mind, at least until she was at home, alone, and his image was what she used to pleasure herself.

Pax Pascal always seemed to be the star of her late-night fantasies. She looked down at his long, thick fingers as they laid out on his desk, on top of the folder. She imagined what other parts of his body were long and thick. She shook her head and cleared her throat before speaking.

"May I?" She asked as she leaned over his desk a little, getting a better view of the papers he was talking about.

He nodded and slid them closer to her, allowing her to read the numbers. She glanced at the papers and then at her boss. She swore that for a split second, she caught him looking at her chest. Her face felt warm and she was sure she was blushing. He must have noticed she caught him, as he cleared his throat and backed up a bit.

Blu brought her attention back to the numbers on the papers and studied them for a moment. She pointed to a line where there was a mistake. "Here. These two don't match," she announced with a smile. "This is your problem."

Pax looked where she had been pointing and he smiled up at her. "I would be lost without you, Blu."

She stepped back and gave him her friendliest smile. "You were just too close to it, sir. You would have found it."

Just as he was about to answer her, the phone rang. She excused herself and quickly got to her desk to answer it.

"Pascal Enterprises, you have reached the office of Mr. Pascal."

Blu was met with a screechy, whiny voice. No one she had ever heard before. This must be the dreaded booty call let down she expected. As she listened to the whiny voice asking for Pax, she wondered how he ever got through even a couple of hours with this one.

"I'm sorry, ma'am. I have strict orders…"

Before she could even finish her sentence the woman on the other end had started to yell at Blu about how they had a magical weekend, how he would be expecting her call, and to do her "damn job" and put him on the phone. Blu quickly put her on hold and went back to Pax's office. She quietly knocked on his door.

"Come in," he answered, sounding better than he had previously.

Blu entered his office and proceeded to tell him about the irate woman on the line. She explained who she said she was and had said she would continue to call over and over until she spoke to Pax himself. Pax rolled his eyes as he huffed, "Fuck."

Blu mumbled, "I believe fucking is what got you in this mess."

Pax looked up at her, giving her a glance from head to toe. He didn't acknowledge what she said, but she was sure he heard her. He advised her to put the call through, to which she did.

She closed the door behind her, but she still heard something heavy hit the wall beside the door, followed by a much louder, "FUCK!"

She wasn't sure if she should go back to his office or not. As she tried to decide what to do, he called for her. She immediately went to his office and entered his door.

"Yes, sir?" She muttered out as she noticed a shattered glass beside her feet.

"Do not ever put her through again."

Blu smiled. Another woman had been fucked and dumped by Pax Pascal, fuckery extraordinaire.

Blu excused herself from his office and got to work. The rest of the day went well. Whiny woman, as she would now be referred to as, didn't call again. She must have gotten the message, loud and clear.

As always, at the end of the day, Blu sat across from Pax. He always liked to meet with her at the end of each day to go over what had happened that day and what was needed for the next one. That part of this meeting was no different. It wasn't until the end that it changed completely.

"I have an event coming up this weekend," he announced like she didn't already know his schedule.

"Yes, sir," she responded sweetly, unsure of what he would be needing from her for this.

"I need a date." He said as his eyes traveled her body, for the second time today.

"Yes, sir. Is there someone you want me to phone for you?" She asked, hoping it wasn't whiny woman.

Pax shifted in his chair. His mouth was slightly open, his breath a little faster. Blu noticed that his glance had fallen to her breasts, which were also rising and falling quickly. Her heart thumped against her rib cage as he devoured her with his gaze, licking his lips like he was ready to taste her.

She wasn't sure what was happening but the look he was giving her would be making an appearance in her fantasy tonight. She felt her panties dampen at the thought of him touching her... of her touching herself.

It wasn't until his next sentence that she was brought back to the reality of where she was.

"No, I'd like for you to be my date."

Chapter 2

*B*lu looked like she was waiting for the food airplane to fill her mouth as babies did, as she sat with her mouth wide open.

Pax placed his hands behind his head and leaned back in his chair, clearly amused by his secretary's new-found surprise and lack of comment. It had been obvious, again, this morning that Blu Millar usually had a comment for everything.

The reaction he had caused by asking her to be his date to his weekend plans was a bit of a surprise to Pax. This was a rarity and he liked it. Enough that he wanted to do it again.

"You're catching flies, Miss Millar," Pax joked as he watched her slowly close her mouth.

"I must have heard you incorrectly," she finally responded. She was sure that she had done just that.

"I would like you to accompany me to the ball this weekend, as my date. Isn't that what you heard?" He teased.

"But… I…"

It seemed to Pax that blubbering Blu was back again. For some reason, Pax found this version of her attractive. He decided he wanted to see that again.

"You do know what a date is, do you not?" He pushed a little further. That must have been enough to snap her out of it, as she quickly and typically responded.

"Of course, sir. It's the women I constantly get rid of every Monday," she retorted.

As soon as it left her mouth, she slapped her hand to her lips. Trying to keep any more from coming out.

Pax chuckled as his smile grew bigger. "Not exactly. Those aren't dates as much as casual fucks."

"So, you don't take them on a date? You just fuck them?" She asked before she realized she did.

His smile turned into a smirk. "Yes. It's all we both want. No need to spend undesired time together when we both know what we want."

"Then why not take one of them? I'm sure any of them would say yes," she added, knowing that all of them would forgive his ignoring them for another shot at him. "Just not the one from this morning."

Pax's smirk became a full-blown laugh at her last declaration. "Why not her?" He asked, amused again.

"She's way too whiny. I guess during sex that's tolerable, but not for this ball."

Pax, once again, let his eyes roam her body, as he laughed out loud at her description of his latest conquest. How had he never noticed before? Her plump, round chest sits perfectly. Her flat stomach leads to what he had pictured today when her firm ass was pushed out, looking over his papers. If she only knew what that did to him.

He shook his head, trying to control the tent that was forming in his pants. She was his secretary. He never "fucked where he ate," so to speak. She was good for his business and he meant what he said earlier. He would be lost without her.

"I can assure you, Miss Millar, there will be no fucking… between us… this weekend."

"Why the Miss Millar all of a sudden?" She inquired.

"To show you I intend to keep it purely professional. You would be doing me a grand favor," he added, hoping to persuade her answer.

"Purely professional?" She asked, unsure of his intentions.

Pax adjusted himself in his seat, trying to will his erection away. He knew he wanted to keep it professional with her because he knew she was not the casual fuck kind of girl. Otherwise, he would have already had her bent over his desk, pounding what he imagined to be her tight pussy. "Yes."

"What do I wear?"

He smiled, knowing he was getting what he wanted. Well, at least part of what he wanted. His cock still wanted her to come around him. "Take Zoe tomorrow afternoon, after lunch. Both of you can get a dress, my treat. She will be going, as well."

Pax noticed her smile, that bit of news made her happy.

Blu gave him a slight nod, agreeing to his proposal. "Is that all, sir?"

Pax adjusted himself again. He loved it when a woman called him sir while he was fucking her. And for some reason, when Blu said it this time, he grew even harder. He was glad she said yes, but now he wondered how he was supposed to get through a whole night without tasting what was Blu Millar.

The next day went by faster than either of them expected. It was lunchtime and Blu was supposed to be taking Zoe to buy a dress this afternoon.

She was sitting at her desk, catching up on her final emails for the day as someone approached her. Blu looks up to see a beautiful red-haired woman standing in front of her. Blu took notice that like her, she had long red hair, but unlike her, this new woman wasn't covered in freckles that Blu always hated.

"Good afternoon," Blu said, greeting the woman with a smile.

The woman looked down at Blu, smiling at her like she held a secret that no one else was privy to.

"Is Pax in his office?" The other woman asked as if she already knew the answer.

Blu nodded, confirming he was. The woman smiled and turned to his door. Blu jumped up and blocked the doorway.

"I'm sorry, ma'am. No one is allowed in there without being announced," she informed the scowling woman. "May I have your name?"

The woman scowled at Blu and in her whiny voice, she gave her the name Veronica.

Blu immediately recognized her whiny voice as the woman from the phone yesterday. "You'll need to have a seat. I'll see if he is available," Blu said as she pointed to the waiting area.

The whiny woman reluctantly took a seat in the waiting area as Blu entered Pax's office.

"Sir? I'm sorry to barge in like this but…" Blu was stopped short when she saw Pax behind his desk with no shirt on. He had on a black pair of jeans and his boots with nothing else. Her voice stopped cold and her eyes roamed his body like the treat he was.

"What can I help you with?" He teased, noticing how she looked at him. Blu tried to speak but she couldn't take her eyes away from the muscled V that pointed into his dark jeans. "What can I help you with?" He asked again. This time he had a smile on his face as he flexed his muscles.

"Shit… I mean… Veronica."

"What about Veronica?"

Blu licked her lips, her gaze still feasting on his toned body. "She's here."

"Fucking hell. She's in the office?"

Blu nodded her head, "Waiting room."

Pax quickly grabbed a clean shirt and pulled it down over his head. Blu was disappointed that the show was over, but she had memorized enough of it to replay later. Pax stepped up to her as she stood and watched him. He leaned in so that his lips were being touched by her coconut scented hair. He took in a deep breath before slowly letting it out. "Did anyone ever tell you it isn't polite to stare?"

Instant flood to her panties as Pax's sweet breath licked at her neck. Her breath was coming faster, her breasts rising and falling in a quick cadence. "I wasn't…."

Pax touched her arm with a feather-light touch, his fingers brushed the outermost edge of her breast. "We both know you were." He leaned in a little closer, "and we both know what it did to your body."

Blu shuttered as he pulled away. How could he know what seeing him shirtless did to her? Did her face give that much away? Pax handed her his credit card from one hand, as his other brushed the loose hair from her shoulder.

"Get something sexy," he said as he turned to walk out the door.

Blu stood there for a minute, his card held tightly in her hand. She finally turned to leave his office so she could meet Zoe. When she walked out into the waiting room, she didn't see Pax or the whiny woman. She grabbed her things and quickly made her way to Zoe's office.

"Zoe, you ready?" She asked, hoping to get out of there before she ran into her boss and the whiny woman.

"Yeah." She grabbed her purse and they walked down the hall. "Who was that woman with Paxton?"

"This week's hoe."

"Oh," Zoe responded. Her smile getting bigger. "He didn't seem that happy to see her."

"You saw them?"

"Yes," Zoe shook her head. "He was walking her out and she was trying to get his attention. Something about the ball this weekend."

"Oh," was all she could muster out.

"So, we have the boss man's credit card, huh?" Zoe inquired with a large smile on her face. All Blu could do was give her a half-hearted smile back.

They made their way to the dress shop. It was the best one for what they would be looking for today. The woman behind the counter smiled as they walked in. "We're looking for two gowns for the Pascal ball this weekend," Blu announced as they looked around.

The older lady smiled at them as she spoke. "Ah, such a grand party. Special invitation, I hear."

"She's Mr. Pascal's date," Zoe boasted as she looked at Blu.

"Mr. Pascal has a date? I don't ever remember him having a date for this party."

"I can assure you it isn't a real date. I'm just doing him a favor," she assured the shop owner, as much as convincing herself.

"I don't know about that, dear. I have attended this very party every single year and not one time has Paxton Pascal ever attended with a woman on his arm."

The look that Zoe gave Blu was one that said "I told you so." Blu, however, was still not convinced. He asked her to do him a favor. She still wasn't sure why he asked her for this favor, but she decided she didn't need to know. At least not yet.

Zoe and Blu tried on only a few dresses before they found ones that the shop owner assured them would make them the two most gorgeous women in the whole place. Blu wasn't going for that reason, but Pax did say to dress in something sexy. Again, not sure why, but she did as he asked.

Blu picked a dress that was cut low in the front with a slight wisp of lace sticking out from the top. It was a medium shade of blue on top with small crystals darting out of the pleated fabric. It was form-fitting over her waist with a lace overlay, taming the dark bluish-purple that it had turned into under the dainty lace. The bottom of the dress was a bluish-purple color that was shiny and had a special quality to it. It was a little heavy, but it was the most beautiful dress she had ever had on before.

The shop owner said that she had to pair it with white gloves that came halfway up her forearm. She even had the perfect diamond look-a-like bracelet and large pearl ring to go with it. Even against her pale skin, red hair and freckles, the dress made Blu feel beautiful. She was sure that Pax would approve of the sexiness of the dress.

The rest of the week went by quickly. Zoe was over at Blu's house and they were getting ready together. Pax had informed her the day after she purchased her dress that he would be sending a car for her that evening. Because it was not a real date, Blu was okay with the informality of it all. Otherwise, she would have insisted upon a proper pick up for such an occasion.

"Are you excited about a date with Paxton?" Zoe asked as she watched her best friend slip on her shoes.

"It isn't a real date, Zoe. You know this already," she sighed, almost wishing it was.

Just as they finished, there was a knock at the door. Blu opened the door to find a handsome man in dark dress pants, a light blue buttoned-down shirt, and a black and white jacket, holding the most beautiful creamy roses.

"Blu."

"And you were saying?" Zoe whispered.

Chapter 3

Before her stood Paxton Pascal, holding a bouquet of the most beautiful roses she had ever seen. He reached out and handed them to her. She took them into her hands and instantly took a deep breath, inhaling the sweet, floral scent.

Zoe came up to where Blu was standing, unable to say anything to her "date." Zoe reached out and took the bouquet from Blu's hands. "Let me get these in some water."

Zoe disappeared into the kitchen and Blu opened the door a little more, allowing Pax to step inside of her home.

"I thought you were sending someone to pick us up?" Blu asked, still surprised that she was seeing him in her living room.

"I was going to, but I decided that you deserved to be picked up instead," he smiled.

Pax looked around Blu and saw Zoe come back into the living room, in her black gown. "You look pretty tonight, Zoe." Zoe is not the type to blush easily, but hearing Paxton Pascal call her beautiful made her face burn red.

Blu couldn't help but laugh at her friend's reaction to Pax. He had that effect on all women. Even her. Pax leaned in closer to Blu and pressed a short, quick kiss to her cheek. Just that small gesture was enough to make Blu's heart speed up, along with her breathing. "You are stunning," he whispered in her ear, only loud enough for her to hear. His lips just barely touching her skin.

Blu looked up to him with her bright green eyes. "Thank you." It wasn't much, but it was all she could manage to say. The smirk on his face told her he knew what he was doing to her and that he was enjoying it.

"Shall we?" He asked the two women as he slipped his hand

onto the small of Blu's back. Even though there was plenty of dress fabric in between her bare skin and his big hand, it didn't stop her from shivering at his touch.

The three of them rode in the back of a long, black limousine to the venue. It was a large country club that was known to have extravagant parties hosted there weekly. The old red brick and large white columns spoke of another time. The large chandelier that hung from the large porch was the perfect amount of old world and new to fit right in.

Once the limo was at the top of the circle drive, the driver got out and opened the door. Pax was the first to exit, taking Zoe's hand, helping her out next. He saved Blu for last. As soon as her feet hit the pavement, she stood, bumping into the large man standing in front of her. His hands immediately went to her waist to keep her from falling. "If I didn't know better, I would swear that was on purpose just for me to touch you again," he smirked.

Blu's face turned red, her gaze falling to the ground as he held her closer to him. "No, sir. I wouldn't."

He chuckled. "If you want me to touch you, all you have to do is ask. It would be my pleasure and yours."

"I..." Blu was unable to speak. She didn't have the words to tell him that she didn't want him to touch her, when all she could think of was how his hands would feel on her bare skin.

Pax took her hand in his and led them into the large room that was to hold their party tonight. The room was decorated in silver and gold, a splash of red every so often. Blu was fidgeting as they entered the room and everyone turned to see her with him. Her hand still intertwined with his. The whispers could be heard all over the room as he pulled her closer to his body.

"Wow, this is gorgeous," Zoe admired the room. Blu tried to appreciate the beauty of the room but with everyone staring at her, she was unable to notice more than that.

"Why is everyone staring?" She asked, stepping behind Pax a little.

Pax turned to face Blu. "Because you're the most beautiful woman in the room."

Blu giggled a nervous and short laugh. "And I just thought it was because you're never with a woman in public."

Pax laughed out loud at her joke. "That, too."

He leaned into her, his hands on her lower back, just barely above the place that would not be proper in public. He bunched up the fabric of her dress into his hands, pulling her closer to him. "Does it make you hot knowing that every man in here wishes he was me right now?"

"What?"

Pax smiled at her and pressed his lips to her cheek, just in front of her ear. His breath warm on her reddening skin. "Every man here wants to fuck you. Every single one of them is jealous that you are in my arms and not theirs."

Before she had the chance to respond, Pax backed up, taking her hand in his again. "Let's mingle."

Pax continued to hold her hand as the three of them mingled with the other guests. It was the job of the host to mingle with his guests. It was just that Blu didn't think she would be expected to accompany him during this tradition.

They made their way through the people, Zoe with them. "I have someone I would like you to meet, Zoe," Pax informed them as a handsome man turned to greet them. "Zoe, this is Owen. He is one of my business partners."

The new man smiled at Zoe and Blu could see that Zoe was attracted to him right away. The new man asked Zoe to dance. She excused herself as he took her to the dance floor.

"I knew he would like her," Pax stated, proud of what he had done.

Another couple had joined them and Pax was talking to them, not paying much attention to Blu. She was not upset about the lack of attention, she was relieved that not everyone was staring at her any longer. Blu loved to watch people and this was the perfect place to observe. Everyone was so engaged in their conversations and dancing, that they never even noticed they were being watched.

Pax was busy talking to the other couple and Blu was busy watching people. She never noticed that another man had joined their group until she heard him speak to her.

"So, you're here with Pax?"

Blu looked towards the stranger. She noticed right away that he was handsome. He had dark hair, a bit of a five o'clock shadow on his face and she could tell he was muscular under his suit.

"I am," she declared. Not wanting to give the wrong idea, but she did accompany him.

The man glanced over her body, licking his lips as his gaze traveled over her breasts. "Beautiful."

Blu was not sure she was comfortable with this man's stare. He looked at her like he was a starving man and she would be his next meal. "I don't believe I caught your name?"

He smirked, appearing to be happy that she was interested. "Everest Rinaldi. I am a *good* friend of Pax's."

Blu turned to get Pax's attention when she noticed he was no longer standing beside her.

"It seems as though your date has left you." His gaze traveled her body again, "not smart to leave such an incredible creature alone with the likes of these men."

Just when Blu was about to turn and leave the man, big strong arms wrapped around her waist from behind her. "Everest."

"Pax," he returned the gesture. "Such beauty you have with you tonight. Does she play?"

Blu looked at the new man with confusion in her eyes. She wasn't sure what he was asking but she was sure she didn't "play" whatever it was that he was inquiring about.

"Not now, Everest," Pax stopped the conversation quickly. Blu wasn't sure why, but she was happy that he showed up when he did. The feeling of his arms around her gave her all kinds of feelings that she wasn't used to having with Pax.

"Would you like to dance?" Pax asked as he rubbed his fingers along the front of her dress.

Blu didn't know why she wanted to dance with him right now, but she did. The thought of moving to the music playing, while being held in his arms was pleasing to her. She nodded. He took her hand in his and led her to the dance floor.

His hands around her waist, resting on her lower back. Her hands draped loosely around the back of his neck. "I don't bite, you know." He chuckled, "Unless you want me to."

He pulled her closer to him. So close that she could feel his muscular chest against hers. His hands began to rub up and down along her back, causing her to shiver with his touch.

They moved to the music for a little while in complete silence. Until Blu broke the comfortable silence. "What did he mean when he asked if I 'played'?"

Pax got a big smile on his face. His eyes became darker and his breath was ragged. "Sex. He wanted to know if you play with sex."

"You mean if I have had sex?"

Pax licked his bottom lip, his eyes watching Blu's chest rising and falling, faster than it had been. One of his hands caressed her face and his thumb rubbed over her cheek. "No. He wanted to know if I would be willing to share you."

"I don't know what that means? You mean if I would cheat on you... if we were together?"

The hand on her back grabbed onto some of her dress as he pulled her hips into his. "He wants to know if I would let him perform sexual acts on you... while I watch. He wants to make you wet." He paused, "he wants to make you come first before I fuck you."

"He wants to what?!?"

Pax leaned in, closer to Blu. His breath hot and wet on her

already flushed skin. He whispered in her ear. "We like to play. I like to watch him please a woman. Usually with his tongue and sometimes his fingers. It makes me hard to watch him playing with what only I can have. Wanting what is mine." Pax kissed on her ear making her moan barely audible. "I would watch him lick and suck on your wet pussy. He would make you come as you looked into my eyes. After you were worn out from as many orgasms as he could give you, it would be my turn." His large bulge pressed into her. "You would watch me stroke myself, while I watched him make you come for me. He would not be the one to fully have you. That would only be for me. He is only allowed to taste you… and only when I say he can. Otherwise, you would be all mine."

Blu gasped as she pulled back from him. "I need to go," she breathed out. She turned and all but ran out of the room. She found a bathroom and closed and locked the door behind her. She splashed cold water on her face, not caring it was ruining her makeup.

Knock. Knock.

"Open the door, Blu."

"I'm fine. I just need a minute," she spoke softly through the door.

"Please, Blu. Open the door," he begged.

She opened the door. Pax pushed it open and stepped inside. He closed and locked it behind him. He stepped forward, pushing her body against the sink. His hands on her face, his eyes on her lips. He licked his before leaning in and crashed his lips to hers. Blu only took a moment to kiss him back. His hands cupped her ass and lifted her to the counter.

He pushed her legs apart and stepped in between them, pressing his erection into her as much as he could. "I want to fuck you now."

Blu pulled away from him and shoved him back. He reached down and unfastened his pants. She could see how hard he was.

He untucked his shirt and took her hand in his. He placed her hand on himself and encouraged her to feel him, to touch him. "You make me so fucking hard."

She pulled her hand from his. He leaned in to kiss her again, but she turned her head. Pax lowered his head when she refused to kiss him. "No."

Pax was a dirty bastard. He loved getting off on watching what belonged to him be desired by someone else. Wanted by someone else. Even slightly pleased by someone else. But he was not one to force anything on anyone. He stepped back, his hands in the air.

"Okay," he resigned. "For now, I'll back off. I'll never force you to do something you aren't ready for. But don't think of this as me giving up. It isn't."

His fingers gently put the strap of her dress back up onto her shoulder. "When I know what I want, I don't stop until I get it." His gaze traveled her body.

"And I want you."

Chapter 4

*B*lu was unsure what was happening in this bathroom. She went in there to get away from what Pax was saying. Her boss was telling her that he wanted to fuck her. But he wasn't just saying that. He wanted to let this other man pleasure her first, while he watched before he took her. She couldn't take any more of this conversation.

"I'm not sure what you are saying to me, but you are my boss. And I am not interested in it… what did you call it? Playing?" She pushed him back further from her.

Pax stepped further away from Blu, giving her the space that she needed. Blu unlocked the door and rushed out of the much too small bathroom. Blu entered into the dance hall and went directly to the doors that led out onto the back patio. She needed some fresh air. She was only out there for a little while when she heard the door opening.

"I need to be alone," she said, not looking back to see who was joining her.

The other person didn't speak, instead she felt someone stand beside her. She heard the clearing of his throat before he spoke. "I take it you didn't know anything about our playtime?"

"What are you, twelve?"

He chuckled. "I'm sure you know that what we do isn't appropriate for a twelve-year-old."

Blu turned to look at the handsome man that stood beside her before she spoke again. "I'm not interested in whatever you call it."

He turned to glance at her, appreciating the moonlight shining on her pale skin. "Too bad, you would be… tasty."

Blu rolled her eyes at him. "Really? Tasty? You kiss your momma with that mouth?"

"Mmm, feisty. I like that. I could show you what I can do with this mouth," he glared at her, taking in her heaving chest.

"Asshole."

"Hmmm... I can play there, too, as long as Pax allows it."

"What part of I am not interested went over your head?" Blu asked, irritated.

He held his hands up in mock surrender. "Sorry. I guess I assumed that if Pax thought enough of you to bring you to this party, then you already knew about it... him... us."

"I didn't."

"Would you like to know more information?" He asked politely.

"More information? I don't think I need more information. The two of you share women, or he tells you what you can do and can't do, while he watches." Blu returned her glance out over the grounds.

"Something like that. Each time is different. I would only do it to you... with you... what you allowed me to do. Or what he said I could do. Most of the time there isn't much that he won't allow me to do." He paused, "But he just told me to back off. If we did this, he would not allow me to have you."

"To have me? The way you speak it's as if I don't have a choice."

"His exact words were, 'You are not fucking her', and you have all the choices. You decide what we can and cannot do."

"Well, neither is he," she added, quite frankly.

"I wouldn't be so sure about that. He always gets what he wants, and right now, that seems to be you."

"Do I look like I care?" She asked, turning to look at him again.

Everest glanced back at her, seeing the agitation in her face, "No, you don't. But you also look like you want him just as much as he wants you."

"Whatever."

"You may say no, but the flush on your chest that creeps up

your neck," he touched her neck with his fingers, "tells me that you were interested. Maybe even turned on thinking about him watching you and me."

"I can assure you, I'm not."

He chuckled. "Whatever you say." He lowered his hand from her neck, gently touching her chest as he passed it, "When you change your mind, it would be my pleasure to get you ready for him."

"What do you get out of this, anyway? If he doesn't let you fuck, what do you get?"

"Mmm, that's a good question."

He paused, thinking about how much he should tell her. He didn't want to scare her off because he wanted the chance to please her. He also didn't want to lie to her because he wanted her to know what she would be agreeing to when she agreed to have them both.

"It depends," he answered, honestly.

"Depends on what?" She didn't know why, but she was curious.

"Where we are. Who else is there with us and what they want me to do."

"So, you and Pax have sex with the same girl… at the same time?"

He shook his head. "No, never with him. With others that I have played with, yes. Pax never has been one to share that part."

"Do you get excited?"

He bit his bottom lip, "I'm excited right now."

"But if with him you don't get a release… why would you do it?"

Everest strokes his scruff with his fingers before answering. "I call someone that I know and I fuck the hell out of her."

Blu blushed at his honesty. Her heart was beating faster, her breath was hard to control. This handsome man was asking her to play with him, to let him make her come. And let her super hot boss watch them together so that he could then fuck her. She wasn't sure why, but the thought of the two of them pleasing her was making her wet.

"If we are at a club, there are no shortages of women waiting to be properly fucked. I have my favorites."

She looked at him with even more curiosity in her eyes, "Club?"

"Maybe you should be asking him these questions," he paused. He wasn't against answering her questions, but he didn't want to step over any boundaries that Pax wasn't ready for her to know.

"I'm asking you," she pleaded with him with her eyes. He could see that she wanted to know more and he wanted to tell her everything. Not to scare her, but to convince her to say yes to their proposal. He wanted her the minute he saw her. His only regret was that she would not be his.

"There are clubs. Clubs that are safe for this kind of thing. Everyone there is either participating or curious about it. Everyone there is safe and knows what we are there for."

"You're there for sex?"

He nodded. "We are there to play. It isn't always sex. Sometimes it is to watch others having sex. Sometimes it is to experiment with other partners, while your partner does the same. Shit, some couples just like to have others watch them and never even touch another person. With Pax and I, when we team up, I get to have a taste of what is his. I get to please you, doing what I love to do and he likes knowing that I want what he has. Knowing I cannot have what I want gets him…"

"He gets off on knowing you want her and can't have her?"

He nodded again. "Yes, and he likes watching his woman be pleasured before he gets her."

"And that doesn't seem weird to you?" She asked, again curious.

"No. I have plenty of women that I can have any time I want and he never goes near them."

Everest turned Blu to look at him, her hands in his.

"He would never do anything to make you uncomfortable. The women seem to like pleasing him. They like watching him get excited by watching what I am doing to you."

"Does he ever join in with you?"

"You mean does he touch you at the same time?"

She nodded, wanting to know more, even though she knew she shouldn't.

"Not usually. When he's ready to touch you, he'll tell me that it's enough."

"And you just leave?"

"Yes," he answered, looking at her body again. "Sometimes that's hard to do, I would imagine it would be difficult to leave you. I would want to make you mine, claim you."

She let go of his hands. "Would you kiss me?"

He smiled, knowing that she was interested. "No, it's too personal."

"No?"

"Not your mouth, anyway," he winked at her.

She flushed, her heart sped up with the thought of him touching her. She never thought she would ever consider such a thing, but for some reason he made her want him to touch her.

"I would not kiss your mouth, neither would Pax. I would kiss your breasts, I would kiss every other part of your body, I may even touch you with my hands. I would never be allowed to have sex with you, I would remain clothed from the waist down at all times. I may be allowed to touch you with my fingers but no penetration of any kind."

She was confused by him saying that Pax wouldn't kiss her, either. It was only a little while ago, in the bathroom, that he kissed her.

"And those are your rules?"

"No, they are his rules." Everest smiled at her as the door to the patio opened. She glanced over to see Pax joining them. "Speak of the devil."

Pax walked over to stand beside them, his eyes still on Blu. "I was wondering what was taking so long," he glanced at Everest, "I was wondering if you were trying to start without me."

Everest let out a full belly laugh. "As if that would ever happen."

"May we have a moment?" Pax asked as his gaze went back to Blu.

Everest smiled at Blu as he answered Pax, "Sure."

Moments later Blu found herself on the patio alone with Pax.

"How was your conversation?"

"Very informative," she answered, giving him a nervous smile.

"Is that all, informative?"

"What else would it be?"

Pax stepped closer to Blu, her breathing speeding up to match her quickening heartbeat. "You tell me, Blu. I can see the way your body is reacting to me. I've seen it many times over the last year you have been in my office."

"I," she tried to speak but he was right. She had been watching him for over a year. Imagining what it would be like to be one of his weekend women. The problem with that was she wasn't sure she was the type to be just a casual fuck.

"It's okay to admit it, I have been watching you, too." He stepped closer to her, causing her breath to hitch. He ran his hands up both of her arms. "Wondering just how you would feel in my arms." His hands grazed over her shoulders. "How you would feel underneath me," he murmured as he took her face into his hands. "How you would taste," he whispered as he leaned in closer. He pressed his lips to hers, moving gently over them. She moaned into his kiss, allowing him to take charge. He slipped his hands into her hair, deepening the kiss at the same time.

She allowed it. She even wanted it. But she knew this wasn't right. She knew that she needed to stop it, no matter how much she wanted him. She was not the type of girl he was looking for and to pretend like she was would only break her heart in the end.

Blu pushed away from him, her mouth still tingled from his kiss. His hands remained around her waist. His eyes gazed into hers, looking for something she couldn't give him.

"I can't… we should go back inside," she sighed. She didn't want to do anything other than stand right here and let him kiss her until her lips fell off. She knew that was a bad idea and someone had to stop this before it went too far.

He groaned, lowering his head to her shoulder. "I know you want it," he whispered as he kissed her shoulder. "What I don't know is why you're fighting this so much."

Blu took his hands into hers and pulled them from her sides. "Because…"

Just as she was about to tell him she was not the kind of girl he wanted, the patio doors swung open and whiny woman made her presence known.

"There you are, Pax baby. We need you…" She didn't finish her thought as she noticed Blu standing in front of Pax, his hands still in hers. She immediately dropped his hands and backed away from him.

"I'll leave you two alone," Blu spoke softly as she turned and walked away, leaving Pax with the whiny woman. As she walked through the patio doors she heard the whiny woman speak to Pax.

"I have been looking forward to tonight all week."

Chapter 5

*B*lu rolled her eyes as she entered the dance hall. She didn't want to leave Pax with that woman, but Blu knew that whiny woman was much better suited for him than she was.

Once inside she quickly found Zoe. She was at their table with Owen. Blu sat down beside her, out of breath from the time spent with Pax.

"Are you okay?" Zoe asked, concerned about her friend.

Before Blu could answer, there was a commotion from the patio. She turned in time to see Veronica and Pax coming through the door. Veronica was hanging all over Pax as they walked into the room.

Blu turned back to Zoe, "I think I'm going to go home."

"I'll come with you," Zoe said as she stood to leave with her friend. Blu watched her friend lean over to tell Owen that they were leaving.

Owen stood, as well, "I'll take both of you home," he insisted. Blu was so anxious to leave she didn't object.

Zoe had planned on staying over at Blu's house tonight since it was going to be late when they got home. Dinner hadn't been served at the party, so the three of them decided to pick up a pizza on their way to Blu's house.

"He isn't with that woman," Owen offered, trying to console Blu.

"It's okay if he is, I'm not with him."

"Didn't you come with him?" Owen asked trying to make sense of what happened.

"I'm his assistant, it was a work thing."

Owen looked perplexed. "He's never brought any woman to this party, not even one of his assistants for a work thing."

Blu wasn't sure what she was supposed to say to that. Instead of speaking she looked out the window.

Owen stopped and went in to get their food. Blu's phone started ringing. She pushed the silence button so that it would go to voicemail.

"You gonna answer that?"

Blu shook her head. She didn't want to answer his calls. Nothing he could say mattered to her. She did him a favor and he found someone better. End of story. She would go back to work as if nothing happened.

Her voicemail notification popped up on her screen as her phone started to ring again. She silenced it and tossed it back into her purse.

"You should get that."

"Nope, I have nothing to say," Blu huffed as she looked out the window.

Owen got back in the car with their dinner as her phone notified her of a text.

Owen noticed she didn't look at her phone.

"Pax," he guessed. Zoe nodded, confirming it was him.

A few more text notifications went off.

"Maybe you should get that," Owen offered.

Blu shook her head no. She wasn't going to answer it, nor was she going to read them. No use.

The phone continued to beep to her house. They went inside and she tossed her bag on the front table and went to her room. Zoe followed, excusing them to change their clothes.

"What the hell, Blu?"

"I don't want to talk about it," she tried to shut it down.

"What's got our boss in a tailspin?"

"He kissed me, twice. Then she came out and she was all over him when they came back in. I know it was just as a favor, but why did he kiss me and then… never mind. Can we just forget it?"

As they were changing clothes, they heard a pounding on the

door. It soon stopped and started again on her bedroom door. When she didn't answer, the door flung open. Zoe had just put on her shirt and Blu was still in her underwear.

"Can we have a minute, Zoe?" Pax demanded more than asked.

Zoe nodded and left the room, after smiling at her friend. Pax slammed the door shut and locked it behind him. He stormed over to stand in front of Blu, his eyes taking in every last curve of her body. "What the fuck happened to you?"

"We left," she answered swiftly.

"No shit, but why?"

"I was tired," she lied.

"So, you left with someone else?"

"I did, didn't you?" Blu could see he was getting angry. But she didn't care, she was already angry. "I was only there as a favor and it looked like you didn't need me any longer."

Pax stepped closer to her, taking her hips into his hands. "You are the most stubborn, infuriating, sexy woman I have ever known. You make me fucking crazy." His hands cupped her bare ass, pulling her into him. "I want to put you over my knee and spank you for leaving me there."

Blu gulped, her head spinning. "You want to spank me?"

Pax squeezed her ass in his hands. "And I want to bite this ass."

Blu grabbed onto his jacket and pulled him to her. His lips crashed onto hers so fast it took her breath away. He lifted her and carried her to her bed. He laid her down and was over her body in an instant. His jacket was in a heap on her floor. Her hands were in his hair, tugging, causing him to groan into her mouth.

"I'm not going to fuck you," she announced between kisses.

"I'm not going to fuck you... tonight," he added with a smirk on his face.

He leaned down and kissed her again. His hardness pressed into her. She knew it wouldn't take much for him to convince her to have sex. He was already making her wet and with a little more friction she would come for him, but she needed to calm herself.

"We need to stop."

"Yes, we do," he agreed. "If we don't, I'll say to hell with it and I'll take you right now."

He kissed her again but kept it calm. He rolled off her body and let out a deep sigh. "I don't know what you are doing to me, but I like it."

She sighed, "We were about to eat, would you care to join us?"

"I'm guessing eating you is off the table for tonight?"

Blu blushed a deep shade of red as she smacked him on his chest. "It is."

He sighed, "Okay, dinner it is."

He gave her one more quick kiss, swatted her on the ass as she stood and watched her get dressed.

"Why are you watching me?" She asked as she pulled her shirt over her black lace bra.

"Because I can't seem to keep my eyes off you," he answered honestly.

She walked to her bed, grabbed his hand, and pulled him up. "Let's go eat."

He grabbed her around the waist and into his body. He left open-mouthed kisses on her neck. "I would much rather eat you," he said between kisses.

"Too bad, you're having pizza."

She pulled him out of her room and into the living room. Zoe and Owen already had their plates full of pizza and the open boxes were on the coffee table. Blu made a plate and handed it to Pax. He sat down on one end of the small couch while she made her plate. She went to sit down on the couch, and Pax laid his plate down beside him, reached up and grabbed her arm and pulled her down onto his lap.

She gasped, "What are you doing?"

"Having dinner," he said as he grabbed a piece of pizza from his plate and took a big bite. His other hand around Blu's waist, resting on her hip.

Zoe laughed as Pax pulled Blu into him, chewing on his pizza. "This is a new development," Zoe teased as she watched her best friend sitting on their boss's lap, eating pizza.

Blu shrugged her shoulders. "He has a hard time with the word no."

"No isn't acceptable," he chided. "I will get a yes from you."

"What is the question?" Zoe asked the two, curious about what was going on.

"Nothing," Blu spoke before Pax had a chance. Blu slid off his lap so she could eat her pizza.

Dinner went by quickly. Zoe continued to watch Pax and Blu. She wasn't sure what was going on between the two, but she was sure that something was.

Pax stole glances at Blu. He wondered why she was having this effect on him. He had never worked this hard for some random pussy before. He knew she wasn't some random like all the others. He knew her. He liked her. But it was always just sex, just a good time. No feelings were there other than pleasure. Why was she different?

After they cleaned up the living room, Owen and Zoe had decided to watch a movie. It was still early and neither of them was ready to say goodbye yet. "You two wanna watch with us?" Zoe asked as she smiled at her best friend, being ogled by their boss.

"I was thinking I may just head on to bed," she hinted, hoping he would take the hint and leave.

Pax grabbed her around the waist and pulled her back into his lap. "Is that any way to treat your date for the evening? Cutting the night short?"

Blu squirmed in his lap, causing him to harden beneath her. As soon as she felt it, she stopped moving. "I..."

Pax pulled her into him, pressing into her with his hardness.

He leaned in so he could whisper in her ear, "If you keep squirming like that on my dick, I am going to take you to that room of yours and fuck you into next week." He lightly licked her neck as he let out a deep breath. "Or we could just do it here. You know I don't mind if someone else watches."

"Then let me off your lap," she responded with a breathy tone.

"I will let you off my lap on one condition," he teased as he ran his hand up the back of her shirt.

"What's that?" She was curious about what he wanted so that he would let her up.

"Come to the club with me tomorrow night?"

Blu's eyes got as big as saucers. Her breathing stopped and her heart pounded. "Club?" She asked. "The sex club?"

He nodded. "Yes. Come with me to the club tomorrow night and I will let you off my lap."

Blu wasn't sure which was worse. Feeling him underneath her, making her wet, or going to a sex club with him. She decided she would make the choice that let her off the hook for right now. She nodded her head and he smirked.

"I can't wait to see you there. You are going to love it," he bragged.

Blu wasn't sure what she had just agreed to, but she was happy that she had put an end to their little game tonight. Pax kissed on her neck before letting go of her hips. "I am still not going to fuck you, Mr. Pascal."

Pax laughed at her attempt to remain professional. The lights were low and Owen and Zoe were making out, not paying any attention to the two of them. Before she slid off his lap again, he ran his hand up her inner thigh. Blue took in a deep breath at the sensation of his fingers on her bare leg. His fingers only stopped when they reached her panties.

"Just a little bit more and I could make you come. I know you want me to. I can feel your breathing and your leg is wet." Pax pushed his finger just a little more, touching her warm center over her soaked panties. "Goddamn, you are wet." He licked up her neck. "Mmm, I want to lick your pussy."

His finger dipped in the side of her panties, making one circle around her clit as he sucked on her neck. For a brief second, she let him touch her. She quickly came to her senses and pushed his hand from her aching core. "You need to stop," she managed to say.

He smiled at her as he removed his hand from her panties. He took the finger he had inside and placed it in his mouth. His lips closing around it as he closed his eyes. "Mmm, you taste good," he said after he removed his finger from his mouth. "Everest is going to love eating this… if I let him. I may just have to keep your tasty kitty all for myself."

Blu slid off his lap. Her breath shallow and her heart racing. She needed a release and she needed him to leave so she could get it. He stood and offered her his hand. "Walk me out?"

She nodded, taking his hand and walking him to the door. Once out of sight, he pinned her up against the wall, his body and hands holding her in place. "Never have I worked this hard to get a woman to fuck. But something tells me you are going to be worth every single time I have already had to stroke one out thinking of you."

Blu didn't answer him. She just smiled at the thought of him pleasuring himself thinking of her.

"Think of my tongue licking you, tasting your sweetness as you come for me when you have your fingers working that incredible pussy tonight. I can't wait to have you and do it for you."

Blu moaned as Pax leaned in to kiss her again. One hand on the wall beside her head, the other between her legs, rubbing over her pants. She spread her legs a little, letting him get a better angle.

He smirked. "Mmm." His kisses moved to her neck, his fingers rubbed quicker. "Come for me, Blu. I want to see your face as I make you come with your best friend in the other room.

If you make any noise she will hear us. She will know what we are doing."

Blu grabbed onto Pax's shirt with both fists. Holding on so she wouldn't fall when her climax hit. Pax's finger dipped into her panties again. She never even realized he was that close. "Pax..." she moaned his name.

He bit on her neck as he dipped his fingers inside of her. "You are so tight. You will strangle my cock with this tight pussy." He praised her as he continued working her body. She wasn't able to fight him off any longer. He had won this time. He had his fingers inside of her, working her body to the edge of insanity. "I am going to have to watch Everest with you, he is going to want you for himself."

Her orgasm ripped through her body like a freight train that was off its tracks hearing how much Everest was going to want what he couldn't have. She bit on his shoulder to keep from screaming out. He worked her until he got every aftershock from her before he pulled his fingers out. He held her limp body up against the wall as he kissed her hard. "That was just the first of many, my dear. I will be here to pick you up at six o'clock tomorrow evening. Be ready to play, baby, because I have more of those to give you." He kissed her again before he let her body go. "See you tomorrow, Blu."

With that, he turned and left her holding onto the wall for balance after what he just did to her. She brought her fingers to her lips. They tingled still from the kiss he had just given her. She walked back into the living room and went straight to her bathroom. She took a nice shower and climbed into her bed. She looked at her phone screen as it lit up with a text message.

"*See you tomorrow evening, beautiful. Now that I have had a taste, I don't know how I will ever get enough of you. Sweet dreams.*" She smiled at the text from Pax. She didn't want to, but she already liked him. She had always appreciated and been attracted to the way he looked and now she was attracted to his confidence and arrogance. Not something she had ever liked before.

The next morning Blu was lying in bed, trying to figure out a way to get out of going to the club tonight. *Maybe if I just don't answer him, he will go without me,* she thought. For some reason, she didn't like the idea of him going to the club without her. Was this jealousy? But why now? She had been getting rid of his hookups for the last year. Why was this so different? Why did the thought of him with another woman bother her all of a sudden?

"Ugh… stupid man," she said to the empty room.

Her phone buzzed with a new text message. *"Good morning, beautiful. Can't wait to see you tonight. I can still taste you on my lips and I need more."*

Blu looked at the message, her heart sped up remembering last night. If she was being honest with herself, she wanted to see him. What she was unsure of was that she would be okay at the club with him. She was sure she was going to see things she had never seen before. But she was sure that she was not going to do the things he wanted.

She was lying in the bed, deciding how she could get out of going to the club when the phone beeped again. Another text message. *"Don't even think about trying to stand me up tonight. I know where you live and I am not afraid to show up there, sling you over my shoulder and make good on our deal, baby."*

She quickly sent one back. *"I think I am getting sick. Maybe I should stay at home."*

It was immediately returned. *"Good try, dear. But if you need your temperature taken, I have something we could use for that."*

Ugh, she huffed. He was not going to let her out of this deal. *"Fine. See you at six."*

"Good girl."

Chapter 6

The day had gone by much faster than Blu had hoped. It was time for Pax to be there and she was nervous. She didn't know what to expect. He had already told her that she did not have to do anything that she was uncomfortable with. She didn't know if that meant that he would leave her and take part in the activities or what any of this meant.

"He's here," Zoe yelled through the house after opening the door.

Blu stood from the side of her bed where she had been sitting and went to the living room. As soon as she saw Pax, she felt her heart speed up. He was dressed in a leather jacket with no shirt underneath. Her gaze traveled his body. This was the first time that she was seeing so much of him and she liked what she saw.

"Blu," he smirked.

Blu took in a deep breath, still trying to bring her eyes from his bare chest.

"Mr. Pascal," she answered, her gaze on his eyes, finally.

He chuckled. "Mr. Pascal? I think we are beyond that, Blu."

"I think we are exactly there, Mr. Pascal."

He smirked at her, enjoying her sassiness. "You ready to go?"

She shook her head no, causing him to smile at her. He reached his hand out, taking hers in his. "Come on, little one. We are going to have a great night."

She took his hand and let him lead her to his fancy car. He opened the door and let her into the passenger side. She buckled up and waited for him to enter the car. After about half an hour's drive, they arrived at their destination. It was a large, red-brick mansion. There were a lot of cars parked outside, but other than that, you would never know anyone was here. Pax parked the car and turned to Blu. "You have been quiet." It was true. She had only answered his questions with few words at a time until he finally gave up asking.

"I'm not sure what you expect from this tonight," she answered as she looked out to the rolling hills surrounding the mansion.

"Nothing. Everest said he thought you would benefit from knowing more about this lifestyle than we could give you by just explaining it."

"Me coming here was his idea?"

"It was both of us." Pax held her hand in his and she felt better, more at ease. "I don't expect you to do anything you aren't comfortable with. No one will bother you while you are with me."

"And what happens when you go off to play with someone and I'm left alone?" She asked, fearful of being left alone in this house.

He leaned in closer to her, his breath on her cheek. "If you aren't playing, neither am I. I will not leave you alone tonight, not at all."

"I thought you would be here to play."

"If you want to try something, let me know. If not, that's okay, too. The only person I have any desire to do anything with tonight is you."

Somehow, she knew he was telling the truth. She wasn't sure what she was going to see in there but with him by her side, she could do it.

"Okay." He leaned in and kissed her lips.

"You are going to see things here that you have never seen before. If at any time you want to try something, I will be the only one you try it with."

"No one like Everest?" She asked, smiling.

"Tonight, no. He will be here, and I am sure he would be more than willing to play with you tonight, but no. Tonight there will be no one else allowed to touch you." He smirked. "Maybe next time."

Before she could answer him, he was out of the car, walking to her side. He opened her door and took her hand, helping her out of the car. He did as he promised, he held her hand to the front doors.

"You ready?"

She nodded, unable to speak. She wasn't sure her voice would come out if she tried. Pax knocked on the door and he gave a code to the gentleman that answered from the other side. The doors opened and Pax stepped inside. Blu followed behind him. The gentleman on the inside spoke to Pax. Blu was too busy looking around to pay attention to what was being said. "Blu?"

She looked around to see Pax smiling at her. "Blu, this is Jerome. This is my girl, Blu." The look across Jerome's face was pure and utter shock.

"Damn, Pax. You brought a girl tonight?"

Pax nodded to the handsome man. "I did."

Jerome looked over her body shamelessly. "Everest going to be with you tonight?" He asked, appreciating the woman on Pax's arm. "Or are you in need of a third for the evening?"

"No," Pax's response caused Jerome to smile. "We will not be needing anyone tonight."

"What the fuck did you do with Pax? You brought a woman and you aren't looking to play? Are you sick?"

Pax shook his head at the man. "Just not feeling like sharing tonight."

The conversation ended with those words. Pax squeezed her hand in his as they entered further into the house. The foyer was large with a large winding staircase to the second floor. There was music playing through the speakers that were in the ceilings of each room.

Pax led her into a room that had dark colored walls. There were couches against every wall. If it wasn't for the people making out on them, it would look like a normal living room. Blu noticed that one woman was in a black lace corset that came down just above her hips. She had on black stockings that fastened to circle her waist, being held up by elastic bands. She had on nothing else. The man that she was making out with was taking full advantage of her exposed center. His fingers were buried deep inside of her, making her moan out as his lips attacked her neck.

Pax must have noticed that she was a little uncomfortable watching this display. He put his arm around her and pulled her close to him. His other hand on her chin, lifting her face to look at him. "Does that turn you on?"

She nodded slightly. Truth was, it did. She could still hear the woman moaning as the man pleasured her with his hand. Pax leaned in and pressed a kiss to her lips. His tongue entered her mouth as she moaned out. He pulled back quicker than she had wanted him to. She enjoyed his kiss and didn't want him to stop. He took her hand in his again. "Come on, much more to see."

He led her into the next room. The room was similar in color but there were different pieces of wood throughout the room. One of them was a large X and had four chains connected to each end of it. Attached to them was a leather band with a metal buckle. "What is that?" She asked, staring at the large piece.

"That is for many things. Someone gets strapped into it, usually naked, and either gets whipped or fucked, or both." Blu gasped at the thought of being fastened spread apart like that and whipped.

"No way."

He chuckled. "How about this one?"

She looked over to see another piece of wood. It was two pieces standing straight up and on one side two other boards were sticking straight back. Directly opposite of them were two smaller pieces that looked big enough for a hand to rest on. There were two leather cuffs at the end of the long boards and two more on the shorter ones. "What is that for?"

He led her over to the wooden statue. He helped her to place her legs on the longer boards, her body between the two upright boards, and her hands rested on the small ones. This put her on all fours. Pax stepped up behind her, still fully clothed, and ran his hand down her back. "How does this one feel?" He asked, pressing against her ass.

"I feel vulnerable in this position," she answered honestly.

Pax leaned forward, his hard cock pressing into her. He ran his hands around her sides and cupped her breasts. "This one puts you at the perfect height for me to enter you all the way." He leaned over her back, kneading her breast with one hand, his other he slid down her stomach. "And I can play with your pussy while I fucked you from here." His hand cupped over her hot and wet center, causing her to gasp. His hips ground into her as he rubbed her center with his long finger. He was happy that she had worn a skirt because it allowed him easier access to her.

She moaned as he continued rubbing her wet center. "Don't pay any attention to the other people here." That did it. She pulled away from him. He chuckled and helped her stand. He spun her to face him, his hands on her hips. "Let's see another room."

She nodded. He took her hand in his and led her around the corner and into a third room. This room was full of people. Some were half dressed. Some were completely naked.

She noticed a woman was moaning out as a man's head was between her legs. Another couple was having sex on the other couch. The rest were in different stages of making out, one even had two women with one man.

"Anything here you want to try?"

She shook her head. He chuckled at her embarrassment. He found her innocence in this situation adorable. He took her to the staircase that was in the back of the house. "Let's go upstairs."

She followed behind him. As they reached the top, Blu heard a voice she was familiar with. "Pax. Blu." Everest was standing in the hall, in only his boxers.

"Everest, you been here long?" Pax asked his friend.

"No, just a little while. Not long enough to even get my tongue or dick wet."

Pax chuckled. Blu was uncomfortable. As Everest was talking, he was staring at her.

"You two want to play? I wouldn't mind getting her ready for you, Pax." Everest winked at Blu. She stepped behind Pax, keeping him from leering at her more.

"No. I am not sharing tonight."

"Whatever," he chuckled. "If you change your mind, let me know." Everest opened the first door and walked inside. They heard a woman call out to him, "Come here, big boy." Blu giggled at the woman.

"This room here is a bondage room."

"Like handcuffs?"

"I'm sure there are some. But there is a lot more to it than that." They continued walking and there was a glass window. Pax stopped at the window and turned Blu to look inside. He pressed his body up against hers, causing her to press up against the glass. "See anything in there you want to try?"

Blu looked into the room. There was a woman that was tied to a bed. Her hands were tied to the two corner posts at the head of the bed. Her feet were in some kind of cuffs that had a pole between her feet, causing them to be spread apart. "What's that?"

"The spreader?"

"Is that what is on her feet?" Blu clarified what it was that had interested her.

"Yes. You want to try it?"

Blu nodded before she could stop herself. Pax chuckled in her ear. "I have one."

She pushed her ass back into his groin. "Of course, you do."

Pax growled in her ear as he sucked on her neck. "I would love to spread your legs apart for me. I can finally get my tongue on you and you won't be able to push me away when I make you come over and over again."

Blu took a deep breath as she noticed his hands were on her breasts again. He ground his hips into her ass. "We have one more to see. This will be our last room. This room is ours."

"What do you mean, ours?"

"I mean this is the room that you and I are going to. We will be completely alone."

"Is there a window like in this room?"

"No. There isn't. But if you want someone to watch us, that can be arranged."

"What do you plan on doing to me in this room?"

He slid his hands down her stomach and into the top of her skirt and panties. His long fingers spread her apart as he circled her clit with his fingers. "I love playing with this pussy." He dipped a finger inside of her. "I want to please you more, with my tongue." He pulled her hips back into his hardness again. "I want to bury myself inside of you and let you strangle me with how tight you are."

"Pax," she moaned as he worked her body like he knew she liked. He removed his fingers from her and took her hand in his.

"Come with me." He led her to the end of the hall. He pulled a key out of his pocket and unlocked the door. He ushered her inside, closing and locking the door behind him.

Chapter 7

"Is this your room?"

He nodded, "Yes, it is."

She looked around. The walls were a deep shade of burgundy, but not so dark as to make the room appear dark. There was a large bed on one wall with a metal bar at the head of the bed. Attached to both ends of the bar, was a white, furry handcuff. A couch was against the wall to the left and windows to the outside on the right.

Blu walked over to the bed and ran her fingers up the soft bedspread. It was a striking white contrast to the dark walls. Pax stood just inside the door, letting her explore the room. He watched her, enthralled with her curiosity. Blu explored the room with a childlike curiosity. Feeling each item that interested her. There was a large wooden cabinet against the window wall, in between the two windows that let in a small amount of light. "What's in here?" She asked, curious as to what was behind the thick wooden doors.

"Toys."

"What kind of toys?" She asked, wanting to see inside.

"Adult toys," he smirked.

"No shit. I wasn't expecting an X-box," she sassed.

He chuckled. Most women that would have sassed him like that would have been punished. He wanted to spank her, but not to punish her. He wanted to do so many things to her. Things that he usually watched being done to the woman he was going to fuck.

"You do know that your sassy mouth is going to get you in trouble, don't you?"

Blu turned to face Pax. She looked at him through her eyelashes, showing her true innocence. "What kind of trouble?"

His smile took over as he thought of all the ways he could punish her. All the ways he wanted to punish her. "Are you asking or do you want me to show you?"

"Asking," she mumbled. She wanted to know what he was thinking about when he said he was going to punish her, but she wasn't sure she wanted him to do it.

Pax took a few steps over to her side, unlocking the wooden doors. He opened them and pulled out a spreader, similar to the one that she saw being used down the hall. He handed it to her. She opened her hand and took the spreader from him.

"Your spreader?" She asked as she ran her hands up and down the cool metal.

"Yes." He watched her hands soothing the cool metal. He could imagine what it would feel like to have himself in her hands as she stroked him.

"And this goes on my ankles?" She asked as she handled the leather straps.

"Do you want me to show you?"

She nodded. He took her hand and led her to the bed.

"You will want to be lying down for this. Lay down on the bed," he instructed.

She did as he asked. She laid on the bed, on top of the perfectly white comforter. Pax climbed on the bed at her feet. He removed one shoe and sock, then the other. He ran his hands up her inner legs until he reached where her skirt stopped.

"Relax. I won't do anything that you don't want me to do. Okay?"

She nodded. She took in a deep breath and enjoyed his hands on her body. She felt him place one of the leather cuffs around her ankle. He tightened up the metal buckles and repeated the process on the other side. The spreader was not very far apart. It wasn't as bad as she imagined.

"This isn't so bad," she observed.

He smirked at her as he grabbed the metal bar between her feet. He moved his arms out from his body, the bar extending outward and her feet were further apart. No matter how much she tried, she could not bring her feet back together. Her center was on full display to him.

She felt embarrassed and wanted to close her legs, but the spreader kept her from moving. His eyes traveled up her body, stopping at her exposed black lace underwear. "Damn, you're sexy."

"I'm ready to take it off now," she said, embarrassed that she was so exposed before him.

He smiled at her, taking one of her ankles in his hand. He unfastened the metal buckle, freeing one leg. She closed her legs immediately, feeling better now that she was covered again. She wasn't sure if it was because of him or the fact that she was sure there had been many women in here before her.

He unfastened the other ankle, closing the spreader to put back in the cabinet. "Is there anything else you would like to try?" He asked, putting the spreader back in its place.

She shook her head. She sat up on the side of the bed, watching him close the cabinet. He walked over to where she sat and sat beside her. "What are you thinking?"

"I'm not sure you want to know that."

"I do. If this is going to work, I need you to be completely honest with me."

"Will you be honest with me?" She asked, wondering if he would be willing to be honest with her.

"Yes, I will," he agreed.

"I am wondering how many women you have had in this room."

The smile that had previously been on his face fell. He looked down at his hands in his lap. "Many."

It wasn't a shock to her for him to answer that way. She already knew he was not an innocent man. Not only because of what she and Everest had talked about on the patio, but also because she had been the one to get rid of all those women the day after their weekends together. She just didn't think he would be so honest about it.

He took her hand in his. "I know you already knew the answer to that question. I know that many of them call the office and you are the one that gets rid of them." He kissed the back of her hand. "You are different than those women."

"How? Here I sit, in the room where you have those weekends. The only difference I see is that I will be in the office on Monday, not calling trying to reach you for another hookup."

"I don't think of you like that."

Blu laughed. "Are you saying you want a relationship with me?"

He looked at their intertwined hands. He shook his head. "I wouldn't be any good at it."

"And if I were to sleep with you, even though I know it would be just sex, it would hurt my feelings to get rid of your other hookups every week."

Pax placed his hand on her cheek, turning her face to look at him. "I wouldn't mean to hurt you."

Blu closed her eyes. "I know."

Pax leaned in and pressed his lips to hers. He didn't try to make the kiss into something that would lead somewhere. He held her face like she was fragile and he had to handle her with care. His lips were soft on hers, not asking for more than she was willing to give him. His hands didn't roam her body, asking to give him even more access.

"I don't want this to be over." He mumbled into her lips.

Blu placed her hand on the hand that was holding her face. She looked directly into his eyes. "We both know where this would end. I don't want to hate you, Pax."

He closed his eyes. "I don't want that, either."

Blu smiled at how vulnerable he was being with her at that moment. He showed her a side of him that she was sure no one else ever got to see. Too bad that it wasn't enough.

He leaned in and kissed her lips again. This time she pulled him into her. If this was going to be the last time she ever kissed the lips of Paxton Pascal, by God, she was going to make it count.

He took over the kiss, gently pushing her back onto the bed. She pulled him into the kiss even more. His lips moved to her jaw, sliding down her neck to her shoulder. He sucked and nipped at her exposed skin. Her head leaned back, giving him access to make this one count. His hand tickled her side as he found her hip and pulled her leg over his hips. His hands continued its journey down her thigh, pulling her closer to his body.

He sucked harder on her neck, marking her pale skin with his kiss. She groaned at the pain from his mark. "Pax."

He groaned into her ear as he separated his body from hers. "I can't help wanting you."

Blu smiled at the confession of want from Pax. She wanted him just as much. Saying no to him was one of the hardest things she ever had to do. She knew it was the right decision. She knew she would only get hurt when she wanted more than he was capable of giving her. Pax kissed her lips one more time.

"Shall we get you home?"

"I can call Zoe or get a ride. You don't have to leave." She said, hoping that she wouldn't have to leave him here alone.

"Absolutely not. I will take you home." He stood and held his hand out to her. She took it and smiled. She knew that he was not going to swear off all women forever, but at least she didn't have to leave him with someone tonight.

The drive back to her house was mostly quiet. It wasn't an uncomfortable silence. He held her hand, leaving kisses to the back every so often. The way he was being with her was making her doubt her decision. She knew if she was with Paxton it would be for one night and one night only. She also knew that she would not be satisfied with one night with him.

When they got to her house, he walked her to the door.

"Are we going to be okay?"

She smiled at his concern for her feelings. She nodded, "Of course, Pax. We are good."

He smiled at her. "I'm glad, I certainly don't want to lose you at the office. I seriously could not make it there without you anymore."

"I will be there on Monday morning, I promise."

He leaned in and placed his hands on her hips. He pulled her body to his, closing the small gap between them. He pressed his lips to hers. She wrapped her hands around his neck, his around her lower back.

How was it possible to have a goodbye kiss when there was nothing to say goodbye to?

One thing that this whole week had taught her, was that somewhere over the last year she had developed feelings for her boss. She wasn't in love with him, but she cared. Sleeping with him would only intensify those feelings for her and she knew she would end up broken-hearted the next time she had to get rid of one of his hookups.

What she didn't realize was it was already too late for that.

Chapter 8

Monday morning came way too quickly for Blu. She laid in bed when her alarm went off. She had a strong desire to call off sick this morning, but she remembered she had promised to be there today. What was causing her to have butterflies in her stomach was the dreaded hookup call. She knew that he took her home and didn't stay at the club, but she wasn't so deluded that she thought he was home alone all weekend.

She made herself get out of bed and shower. She was dressed and ready to head to work when her phone pinged with a text message.

"Good morning, beautiful. See you soon."

She smiled at his message. She wasn't expecting to get a message from him this morning. She arrived at the office early like always. She was nervous about getting his hookup call today but hiding out at home wasn't going to help the situation.

She stopped by Zoe's office, as usual. Zoe had a big smile on her face when she saw her best friend. "You ready for hoe duty?" Zoe started laughing, "Oh wait, that's you!"

Blu stuck her tongue out at her best friend. "You know that I didn't sleep with him."

"I know, but something sure as shit happened."

Blu told her that she was going somewhere with Pax Saturday night, but she didn't tell her they went to a sex club, or that he fingered her while they watched someone else having sex. Or in the hallway with her in the next room. She knew her friend wouldn't judge her, but she wasn't sure it was something she was ready to share. Besides, it was only that one time… or the second time. Whatever.

Blu quickly changed the subject to Owen and their make-out session during the movie. Blu enjoyed seeing her friend happy and Owen seemed like a nice guy. Zoe was happy that he didn't try to stay with her all night. Maybe they have a shot at something.

After their morning banter, Blu decided it was time to face the music and head to her desk. It was quiet when she arrived. Pax's door was shut and she was glad he wouldn't be calling her in right away.

Several hours passed before Pax even made her aware he was in the office. Finally, his door opened and he stood in the door frame, arms crossed, and a smirk across his face. "Morning, beautiful."

"Mr. Pascal," she smiled.

Pax stepped forward and leaned down where his face was beside her ear. "I think we are past Mr. Pascal, Blu," he spoke into her ear, his breath on her pebbled skin. "I have had my fingers inside your body, and I know what you look like when you come. I think you can call me Pax."

"Yes, sir," she teased. His lips brushed her ear causing her to shiver.

He backed up, leaving her with her thoughts and desires. A smirk on his face, knowing what he caused. "You know what that does to me, Blu. Are you trying to get me to bend you over this desk?"

Before Blu had a chance to answer him, the phone on her desk rang, taking her attention from their flirting. Blu transferred the call to Pax and she attempted to cool herself off from the previous interactions. It was getting close to lunch and Blu was thinking about calling Zoe to see if she wanted to grab something. She was finishing up an email when she heard a voice that she recognized.

"Don't you look beautiful today," he smirked. Blu looked up from her computer screen and smiled at the handsome man standing in front of her.

"What are you doing here?" Her question came out a little more dumbfounded than she meant it to be. He just smiled back at her, letting her surprise go unnoticed.

"I would like to take you to lunch," he paused, looking over to Pax's closed door. "If your boss won't mind."

Blu glanced back to Pax's door. He had not left her side but a few minutes before to take his call, when Everest showed up in front of her desk. She smiled thinking about the interaction they had just before the phone rang. Blu turned her gaze back to a smiling Everest. "I don't know. I was supposed to have lunch with Zoe," she answered honestly.

Everest sat on the edge of her desk, smirking down at her. "I'm sure she would be okay if you canceled."

"I don't think it would be a good idea," Blu answered as she glanced back to Pax's door again. She wasn't sure what was going on with them at this point. He wasn't looking for a relationship and she wasn't wanting a casual hookup with him.

She couldn't deny how handsome Everest was and how she was attracted to him, but he was nothing compared to Paxton Pascal. She turned back to Everest, considering his offer when Pax's door opened. Everest remained seated on her desk and looked up to smile at Pax. "Pax," he greeted his friend.

"Did we have a meeting today?" Pax asked, looking between Blu and Everest.

Everest smiled bigger as he answered his friend, "No. I'm here to take Blu for lunch."

"Oh?" Pax glanced between Blu and Everest again. Blu's phone began ringing again. She decided to let the boys figure this out while she answered the phone.

As soon as she finished her practiced phone greeting, she heard it. Whiny woman. "Can I please talk to Paxton?"

"Can I ask who's calling?" she asked, already knowing it was the same woman from before.

"This is Veronica, the woman that Pax spent this past weekend with," she sneered.

Blu didn't give her a chance to continue her thought. "Please hold," Blu said as she pushed the hold button, the handset still in her hand. She looked up to Pax, who appeared to be in a silent conversation with Everest. "It's for you." She handed Pax the headset and looked directly at Everest. "Are we ready?"

Everest smiled, standing from the edge of her desk and reached out to take her hand. "Yes, ma'am. Do you like Italian?"

"I love it," she answered, smiling at Pax and standing to take Everest's hand. "I will be back after lunch, Mr. Pascal," she stated as she turned to leave with Everest. As they were getting in the elevator, she heard Pax answer the phone and quickly slam the receiver down. "Fuck!"

The elevator doors closed and Everest smiled at Blu. "Seems like your boss is a little upset about something." Blu continued to stare at the doors. "You wouldn't know anything about that, would you?"

Blu turned to look at Everest and returned the smile. "No. Why would I?"

"I'm not sure I believe you, but I'll pretend that I do."

She giggled, "That's wise."

They rode the elevator to the first floor in silence. As they stepped out into the lobby her cell phone pinged with a message. She glanced at the screen and quickly silenced her phone and shoved it back into her pocket.

"Pax?" Everest asked, sure that he didn't need an answer. Blu nodded. "So, you do know why he's so mad?" Blu nodded again. "But you aren't going to tell me?" Blu shook her head no. She knew he would be mad when he picked up the phone and heard Veronica's voice, but at the moment she didn't care. She was upset herself after the part of the weekend he spent with her, to only hear he spent the rest of it with her. It was more than she could stand in the moment.

Everest's hand on her lower back brought her back from her thoughts. Everest chuckled. "It looks like we aren't the only two who like to play." That wasn't completely true. She wasn't playing when she gave him the phone. She was pissed and jealous. She found herself wishing she could be what he wanted, but she knew it wasn't in her genes. Sex meant something to Blu. She would fall in love with him and he would break her heart.

Her phone pinged again. This time she took the time to read the message. *"You want to play, do you? I can play your games if you want. But I won't lose."*

Blu huffed as she typed back her response. *"I'm not playing with you. That's what you have Veronica for. Go call her and play your games with her, PAX."* She hit the send button before she had a chance to think about it or chicken out. Within seconds her phone pinged again.

"You are the only one I want to play with, and the only woman I was with this weekend."

She smirked as she wrote back. *"Don't care who you play with. We aren't together. I have no control over what or who you do. I am going to enjoy my lunch. See you when we get back."* She made sure of her wording, knowing that she meant herself and Everest.

Blu looked over to Everest as he laughed at their exchange. "Damn, I have never seen him so bent out of shape over a woman before. What happened with the two of you this weekend?"

Blu shrugged her shoulders. "Nothing."

"There is no way that nothing happened between the two of you with the way he's acting."

"I didn't sleep with him, if that's what you are thinking."

"Fuck. This is a first."

"What? A woman telling him no?"

Everest shook his head. "Not that you told him no, but that he is so pissed at whoever was on that phone and whatever they said to you."

"She just said they spent the weekend together. Nothing I haven't heard before."

"Well, shit. You have it as bad for him as he does for you." Everest led them into a restaurant.

"No, he doesn't."

"Can I ask you a question?" Everest asked as he led them to a table in the back.

Blu nodded.

"Have you kissed him?"

Blu's face deepened in the red it already was. Telling him her answer without speaking.

"Well, shit. You have kissed him."

"I didn't kiss him. He kissed me."

Everest chuckled. "Kissing and no sex." He shook his head. "No wonder he stared at me like that."

"Like what?"

"Like he wanted to kill me for asking you to lunch."

Blu shrugged her shoulders. "He's just being an ass thinking he can do whatever he wants and it doesn't matter."

"What happened with the two of you this weekend? You already said he kissed you and you didn't have sex."

Blu told Everest about the night of the party and how Veronica came out to the patio, talking about thinking about their weekend all week long. How she was the one he was with the previous weekend and about how she left him there. That caused Everest to laugh out loud.

"You left him there? With her?" He laughed.

"Yes."

"And she was the one that was just on the phone?"

Blu nodded.

"No wonder he was so pissed."

Blu and Everest placed their lunch orders and she continued to tell him about the night at the club. How they went to his room and how he kissed her, how they did not have sex and how he took her home when she asked to leave.

"You should know something."

"What is that?"

"Paxton did not come back to the club that night and he was not with her at any time this weekend."

"And how do you know that?"

"Because I know the guy that she was with, and she was away with him all weekend."

Chapter 9

*E*verest and Blu had a good lunch. She was comfortable being around him. She found him attractive and easy to talk to. They didn't talk any more about Pax or Veronica. He was a nice guy. There was no more talk about the club or what they had talked about the night on the patio.

The waitress brought the check and was openly flirting with Everest. Blu tried hard not to laugh at her open flirting and how Everest seemed not to notice. After she left the check on the table, she said she would be back to get the bill and his payment. Blu glanced down and noticed that she had written her phone number on the bill.

"You going to use that phone number?" Her laughter was no longer able to be held back.

"This number?" He held up the bill to show her the number.

Blu nodded, smiling at him.

He shook his head. "I would never call someone like that."

"You mean a waitress?" Blu asked, surprised by his answer.

Everest got up from his chair and took the chair closer to Blu, scooting it over to be directly beside hers. "No, the kind of woman that would give me her number while I am on a date with another woman."

"But I thought you didn't mind sharing."

Blu noticed the look that Everest had in his eyes as his hand grazed her arm. "I don't, but she doesn't know that. She thinks she can get me to call her behind your back." He leaned in closer to Blu, taking a deep breath to take in the fresh coconut smell of her shampoo. "But if you like, I would let her watch what I want to do to you."

Blu swallowed hard, her face hot with red. "You want her to watch?"

Everest kissed the side of Blu's neck, just below her ear. "I said I would let her watch, not that I wanted her to."

Blu backed up a little from him, causing him to chuckle. "There's a difference?"

"There is." His finger traced a line down her arm. "I would let her watch because I get off on it. Not because I want her, but because I want you."

"Is that how you are all the time?"

"Not all the time. I have time alone with a woman, but I like being watched. I especially would like to have Pax watch what I want to do to you."

His eyes darkened with desire, his breath heavy, and his pants tight with his growing erection. His finger continued down her arm and onto her thigh. "I can see why Pax is so enamored with you."

"You just had to ruin a good time by bringing him up, didn't you?"

Everest laughed as he shook his head. "He would never let me have you without him there, you know?"

"Last I checked, he wasn't in charge of me or who I spend my time with."

Everest groaned as he leaned in closer to her again. "What are you doing tonight?"

Blu sighed, feeling him this close to her was making her think of the things he said he wanted to do to her while Pax watched. She closed her eyes, letting her desire wash over her like a warm blanket.

As she imagined his lips on her she heard the waitress speak. "Thank you, sir."

Blu opened her eyes long enough to see Everest hand the woman his credit card and her to glance at how close the two of them were. Blu pushed Everest's hand from her thigh. "Not this."

"Please, hurry back with my card. I have something that I'm afraid I can no longer wait to do to my girl here." He glanced around the restaurant. "And even though we are in the back, I'm sure it will not be appropriate to fuck her in public."

The waitress looked down to the ground, took his card, with the bill that had her phone number on it, and left them.

"What the hell was that?" Blu asked, only half-embarrassed at what he was insinuating.

"What? I just told her that I wanted you for my dessert."

"Both of you are trouble, you know that?"

He nodded. "Yes, we are." His lips grazed her neck again before he whispered in her ear. "But I would be willing to bet that a little trouble is just what you need."

Blu backed up from Everest, smiling at him. "I should be getting back to work."

Everest looked down at the table. He took a drink of his water. "Let's get you back to work. He will be upset I kept you this long."

Everest walked Blu back to work, not touching her until they got to the front door of the office. He placed his hand on her lower back as he led her through front door. They took the elevators up to the top floor and Everest walked her to her desk. Pax's door was shut and no one else was around.

"Thank you for lunch, Everest," Blu said as she sat down at her desk.

"It was my pleasure, maybe next time we meet it will be yours." Everest sat on the corner of her desk, where he had been before. He reached his hand out, gently cupping her chin in his hands. "He likes you."

Blu tried to glance away from Everest, but he wouldn't let her. "It's more complicated than that."

"It isn't. He likes you and you like him." Everest let go of her chin. "I'm telling you right now, I like you, Blu. There is nothing I would like to do more than to play with you. Anything that you and he would allow me to do. I don't do relationships. Hell, I barely have time to play anymore." He smiled at her, looking past her to Pax's door. "But Pax, he's different."

"I don't see how. He is there with you, for the sex and that is all."

"Yeah, he has been. But you are different. Think about it. Let him show you his world, our world. Then, maybe you can show him yours." He smiled at her. "He has his reasons."

Everest leaned in and gave Blu a kiss on the cheek. As he was pulling away from her, they heard Pax's door open behind her. "Blu, I need to see you in my office."

Blu rolled her eyes. "Yes, sir." Everest stood from the side of her desk, smiled at Pax, and said his goodbyes. After Everest made the corner and was out of sight, Blu turned to face Pax.

"What is it that you need, sir?" She teased, seeing the look of desire on his face.

"In my office. Now."

Blu stood and walked past Pax as he continued to stand in his office door. As soon as Blu was inside his office, Pax slammed the door shut, clicking the lock on the handle. His frame towered over her from behind. His hand on her shoulder, moving her hair from her neck.

"Did you have a good lunch, Blu?" He asked, his breath on her shoulder.

Blu nodded, taking a deep breath before speaking. "We did."

As soon as Pax heard her say "we," he growled into her neck. He grabbed her by the arm and turned her to face him. "Did he touch you, Blu?" He asked, his eyes burning into hers. "Tell me why I shouldn't bend you over that desk and fuck you until you can't walk."

Blu swallowed. "I didn't ask you to."

His hands on her face, holding her gaze with his. "But you want me to."

Blu's breath hitched as she trembled in his hands. "I don't," she whimpered.

"Did he touch you, Blu?" His body was closer to hers. "Don't lie to me, Blu. Liars get punished."

Blu licked her bottom lip, thinking of what he would do to punish her. "How would you punish me if I lie to you?"

Pax growled at her, lifting her off the ground. Her legs wrapped around his waist as he carried her to the couch in his office. He tossed her down, his body on top of her in an instant. His lips and teeth on her neck, kissing, sucking, and biting at her skin. "Did he touch you?" He demanded as his hand found her silk-covered breast under her shirt.

Blu moaned out as he sucked her skin, leaving his mark on her. "Pax…"

His other hand found her leg, wrapping it around him so he could grind his erection into her. Another moan escaped her lips. She grabbed his ass, pulling his hardness into her more. "Please… Pax…"

Pax leaned up on his elbow, a smile on his face. "Did he touch you?"

"He kissed my neck after we ate lunch." Pax pushed into her hot, wet center again.

"What else?" His lips on her neck, his hand under her bra, pinching her nipple in between his fingers.

"His fingers touched…" Pax bit her neck. She couldn't continue what she was saying.

"What else? Where did his fingers touch you?"

His hand left her breast and was now under her skirt and at the edge of her panties. "Pax…"

"Answer me, Blu. Where did his fingers touch you?" His fingers slid past the edge of her panties and were at her entrance. He coated his fingers in her wetness.

"My leg," she breathed out.

Pleased with her answer, he shoved two fingers inside of her. "Did he touch you here, Blu? Did he touch my pussy?"

Blu shook her head. "No," she mumbled.

"Good. He is not allowed to touch this pussy if I'm not watching." He thrust his fingers in and out of her, causing her to raise her hips to meet his fingers. "You hear me? He is not allowed to touch this pussy unless I'm there. Only if I'm there."

He curled his fingers inside of her, hitting the spot that he knew would send her over the edge. "This is my pussy and he can only touch it when, how, and if I say he can."

Blu nodded as Pax made her scream out. Her orgasm came over her body like a wave. Her body shivered underneath his touch. His body still on top of hers, his kisses gentle on her neck. "Pax," she started to say.

Pax's lips were on hers in a second. His kiss was rough and hard. His fingers started to move again. Curling inside of her, bringing her to the brink of her second orgasm. Just as she was about to scream out, he stopped. "Say yes, Blu. Tell me you understand that he can't have you without me there."

He moved his fingers again, bringing her back to the tipping point before he stopped again. "Say it, Blu."

"He can't have this pussy without you there."

Pax curled his fingers inside of her again, his mouth on hers, taking her breath. Blu only pulled away long enough to catch her breath as her orgasm shot through her body.

"Good girl."

Chapter 10

Pax kissed Blu as he pulled his fingers from her body. He pulled back, looked her right in the eyes, and stuck his fingers inside of his mouth. He sucked them clean as she watched, embarrassed by what they had just done. "God, you taste good."

"Why did you just do that?"

"Which part, make you come with my fingers or need to taste you?"

"All of it," she whispered, wanting his hands on her again.

"I can't seem to stay away from you."

Blu grabbed his cheeks and pulled his face to hers, kissing his lips. Her tongue shot into his mouth where she could taste herself. He kissed her with everything that he had in him, while her hands roamed his body, under the shirt she had pulled from his pants.

Blu unfasted his belt and slipped her hand inside his boxers. She found what she was searching for and took him into her hand. His breath caught as she rubbed the wet tip. "You don't have to…"

"Shut up, Paxton, and kiss me." He smiled as his lips devoured hers again. Her hand moved up and down his long, thick shaft, lubricated with what was coming from his tip. He thrust his hips into her hand, helping her to get the rhythm that he wanted. The one he needed to find his release.

"You are going to make me come if you keep doing that," he murmured against her lips.

"Good. That's the plan," she mumbled back as she sucked his bottom lip into her mouth.

"Oh… Fffuuuccckkk," he growled as he thrust into her hand harder and faster. She tightened her grip on him as she felt him pulse. She increased her speed to match his thrusting. His breath came faster as he sucked on her neck, shoving his pants down his thighs.

"It's your turn to come for me, sir."

"Fuck…" His head dropped into the crook of her neck as his shaft pulsed in her hand. He reached for the back of the couch and grabbed onto a small throw blanket that was lying on it. He leaned up, onto his knees on the couch, between her legs. Her hand continued to stroke him as he spread out the blanket on her lap. He placed his hand on top of hers and they stroked him together. "Just like that, baby."

She liked him calling her baby. It made her want to please him even more than she already did.

He placed both of his hands on the couch, one on each side of her head. Both sets of eyes watching what she was doing to him. Pax leaned his head back and groaned as he came onto the blanket that he had laid out to catch his orgasm. Blu continued to work his body until she was sure that there was nothing left.

He quickly grabbed the blanket, tossing it to the floor beside them before he laid back on top of Blu. Her skirt was up around her waist so that all that was between his still semi-hard erection and her dripping core was her thin panties.

"I have never come that fast from a hand job."

Blu turned her head away from him. Thinking of him with another woman wasn't something she wanted to think about right now. He pulled her head back to look at him.

"What's wrong, baby?"

"Nothing."

"Oh… I shouldn't have… I didn't mean… shit. I told you I wasn't good at this stuff."

Blu could see the look on his face. He was sorry that he had made that comment, but it wasn't something he could take back. She knew he wasn't innocent, she was the one that had taken the calls over the last year, after all, but hearing that hurt her feelings. It was the reason that she knew she should not get involved with Paxton Pascal.

"I'm sorry."

"It's okay. I know you aren't exactly a virgin, Pax." She smiled, trying to be convincing.

"Don't do that," he nuzzled his face into her neck. His hips still in between hers.

"Don't do what?" She asked, feeling him hardening again.

"Look so God damned sexy."

He kissed on her neck, rubbing his hardening shaft on her wet panties.

"We are going to have to get dressed." He mumbled into her neck.

Blu ran her fingernails down the exposed skin on his back. "Why is that?"

He sucked on her neck. "Because if we don't, I am going to fuck you, Blu." Blu pulled his face to meet hers, smiling at him as she pulled him closer.

"Kiss me, Pax."

Pax smiled at her as he took her lips in another hot and steamy kiss. His hardening shaft in his hand as he rubbed the tip up and down her wetness.

"Tell me what you want, Blu." His fingers moved her panties to the side so that his bare tip was rubbing her wet slit.

"What do you want, Blu?"

She knew the answer to that. She wanted him. All of him. But she didn't want him here, in his office. If she would have had her mind with her, she wouldn't have done what they already did in his office. She also knew it was futile to continue to deny what she wanted, what she needed.

His tip was at her entrance, pushing just a little. "I want to be inside of you. What do you want, Blu?"

He pushed just a little bit and she could feel the pressure of him starting to stretch her. "Tell me what you want, Blu. Do you want me as much as I want you?"

His lips on hers, he kissed her softly. "I can't, Pax." He pulled back from her and she missed him as soon as the contact was gone.

"Okay."

"I'm sorry." She didn't have to pretend this time. She was sorry. She wanted him at this moment as much as he wanted her. She knew she might have been about to get her heart crushed by agreeing to this, but she knew she was going to.

She felt bad right away. She pulled his body back to hers, craving his touch, his weight on top of her. "We shouldn't do this here."

He glanced over to his desk and the rest of his office. "Okay."

She pulled his face to hers, kissing his lips with everything she had. "I want you just as much, Pax." He smiled against her lips. "Just not here."

"Not here."

Blu pulled him to her for one last kiss before they got fixed up and ready to go back to work. He had fastened his pants and she was combing through her hair with her fingers. She reached under her skirt and pulled off her panties. "You have a trash can I put these in?"

He smiled and took them in his hand. He shoved them in his pocket. "They are staying with me."

She rolled her eyes at him as he stepped closer to her. He took her into his arms, one hand on her lower back, the other on her cheek. "You are beautiful."

"I bet you say that to all the girls," she teased, trying to lighten the mood.

"I don't. I don't have to."

He leaned closer to her, his breath against her lips. "I will always tell you the truth, Blu. I promise."

"You promise?"

"I do. I want you and I can barely wait to have you. But I will. Because it is what you need." He touched his lips to hers. "This weekend? What are you doing?"

She shrugged her shoulders. "I don't know. I don't have any plans."

He smiled against her lips. "You do now."

"Do I?"

He nodded. "You do. Everest and I have a project to work on this weekend, but I would like for you to come to my house."

"With you and Everest?"

"Yes," he smirked at her. "Not for that… unless you want to." He winked at her.

She smacked his chest playfully. "Pax."

"What? We will all three be there… just saying."

"You are trouble."

He leaned in and kissed her again. "I can't help it when I'm with you."

"So I've heard."

He kissed down her neck, pulling her body to his again. "Bring an overnight bag, I have a feeling that one night isn't going to be enough with you."

"You want me to stay the night?"

"No," he looked her in the eye. "I want you to stay for the whole weekend."

They were dressed and Blu was ready to go back to her desk and try to get some work done. As she was about to unlock his door, she felt his body press up against hers, pressing her into the door. He swept her hair off her neck, trailing his lips up the side. "This weekend, you are mine."

She nodded, pressing her ass into his groin. "This weekend."

He grabbed onto her hips, pulling her back into him. "You had better go." She turned to look at him with a smile on her face. He quickly kissed her lips before he let her leave his office. Blu sat at her desk with a smile on her face.

Her phone lit up with a text message. *"Shame on you leaving me all hard and horny."*

Blu giggled at his text while she messaged him back. *"Maybe you should take matters into your own hands."*

Her phone pinged right away with another message. *"I would much rather your hand... or your mouth... or your tight little... ugh. Fuck it. Let's go to my house now."*

"Get back to work, Mr. Pascal."

Blu's phone rang at her desk. She picked it up and heard Pax's voice on the other end. "Come back to my office."

"What do you need?" She asked, smiling.

"You." Before she could answer him back, her other line started ringing. "I hear it... go ahead and do your job, I can wait." He pouted. She laughed as she answered the other line.

Her laughter quit as soon as she heard the whiny voice she had grown to loathe. "I need to talk to Pax."

"Sorry, ma'am. He's tied up at the moment," Blu lied. She knew he wasn't doing anything important, he had just been talking to her. But she wasn't going to transfer this whiny woman to him anymore. She was done with that.

"Just put him on the phone." She whined.

"I told you. He's busy."

"And I told you, put him on the phone. If you don't, I will make sure he fires you."

Blu tried to be nice, she tried to be polite and courteous like her momma taught her, but even Blu had her limit. She was so angry, she didn't hear the door open behind her.

"Pax is cleaning up from the amazing sex we just had in his office. His couch is quite comfortable. You'll have to try back later, dear." Blu snarked at her, hanging up the phone on the whiny woman.

Blu turned around quickly when she heard Pax chuckle behind her. "That was an interesting conversation. And I don't remember us having sex... but if you want to it would be my pleasure," he teased as he walked up behind Blu's chair.

"Just shut up, Pax."

Pax placed both of his hands on her shoulders as he leaned down to kiss her neck. "Were you jealous, baby?" He kissed on her neck and up to her ear. "I have an idea on how we can keep my mouth busy."

"I am sure you do. Go back to your office and get to work."

"Yes, dear," he whispered into her ear, giving it a small kiss before standing back up. "I'm only going back to my office because I want to."

"Whatever gets you out of my hair." Pax laughed as he walked back into his office, leaving the door open this time.

The rest of the day went quickly. Veronica didn't call again, but Blu was sure she hadn't seen the last of her yet.

Chapter 11

*E*very day that week, Blu and Pax had lunch in Pax's office. There was always kissing and a little heavy petting. She refused to let him go too far. She told him he needed to wait for Friday. The truth was she didn't want to make him wait until Friday, but she knew she wouldn't be able to say no to him once they got started.

It was Friday afternoon and they were just finishing lunch. Pax had thrown away their trash and they were sitting on his couch. "Do you want to ride to my house with me tonight?" He asked, holding her hand in his.

"I don't want you to have to bring me back to my car."

Pax kissed her hand. "I could bring you back on Monday."

"Are you saying I would be stuck with you all weekend?"

He laughed, "Yes, or I could bring you back whenever you want."

Blu smiled at him as he cuddled her to his chest. She liked the way things had been this past week. He was sweet and caring, as well as hot and steamy. She was seeing sides of him she didn't expect to see.

"I will follow you if that's okay." She wanted to ride with him, but she also felt like she needed an out in case things got to be too much for her. She knew that Everest was going to be around for at least part of the weekend and that made her a little nervous.

"Whatever makes you more comfortable," he kissed the top of her head as she laid on his chest.

At the end of the day, Pax walked Blu to her car and quickly kissed her lips before she got in. "You are going to follow me, right?"

She nodded at how cute he was being. She got in her car and

watched as he went to his and got inside. He pulled out first and she followed behind him. She knew what his address was and had to go to his house to pick up something for him before, but she had only been in the living room, kitchen, and home office.

Once they arrived at his house, he pulled up into the carport and motioned for her to take the other spot under the covered parking. She pulled her car into the other spot and opened her door. Before she could get out, Pax was already getting her bag out of the car.

After she closed her door, he stood in front of her, her bag in one hand and his other on her waist. "Are you nervous?"

Blu shook her head. She wasn't nervous. They had spent enough time together over the last week that she was becoming comfortable with the attention that he was showing her.

"Good. No need to be. Nothing will happen this weekend that you don't want to happen, okay?" She nodded and he leaned in to give her a small kiss. "Let's go inside and we will figure out something for dinner."

"Are you cooking?" She asked, surprised that he could cook.

He took her hand in his and led her into the house. "Not tonight, but tomorrow night I will if you want me to."

"Hmmm, Paxton Pascal can cook?" She teased as they walked into the kitchen from the outside. Paxton lived in a large house, but it wouldn't be considered a mansion. It was a three-story brick house with a full basement. She knew it had a basement because she had heard him talking about a theatre room in there.

"I can, I just don't get to very often." Pax laid her bag on the floor beside the staircase that led up to the bedrooms. "I will put this here and we can take it up later."

He grabbed some take-out menus from a drawer and spread them out on the island. "Take your pick and I will order."

Blu looked through the menus and picked out one that had diner food. She told him that she wanted an old-fashioned burger and fries. He placed the order and fixed them something to drink. He ran upstairs and took a quick shower and changed into a T-shirt and some shorts before coming back to join Blu.

They sat on the large couch in the living room and Pax turned on the TV. He sat close to Blu, pulling her feet up into his lap. He took her shoes off and rubbed her feet and legs while they watched some TV. A little while later there was a knock on the door and then the kitchen door opened.

"Hey, asshole… whose car is outside?" They heard Everest enter the house, yelling about Blu's car parked outside.

"Shut up, man. We're in here," Pax yelled back. Blu went to remove her feet from his lap, but Pax grabbed onto them, keeping her in her place. "Stay." Blu smiled and left her feet in his lap.

Everest walked into the living room and chuckled when he saw Pax and Blu on the couch. "Well, well, well. What do we have here?" He asked as he took a seat on the other chair in the room.

"We are just waiting for dinner. You want anything?" Pax gave Everest the number of the place they ordered from and he was able to add on his meal to their order to be delivered.

Everest pointed to Pax rubbing on Blu's legs and smiled. "I didn't realize that you were here."

Before Blu answered, Pax did. "She's staying this weekend."

"The whole weekend?" Everest asked, smiling at his friend and Blu. He shifted in his seat, excited at the thought of her being here and what he wanted to do with her.

Blu nodded. "Looks like it."

There was a knock at the door and Pax excused himself to answer it. He came back a few minutes later with the food in hand. They spread it out on the table and started eating. Pax and Everest were talking about the project that Pax had mentioned they would be working on this weekend. "After dinner, we can go into my office and work for a little while," Pax offered.

"Sounds like a plan." Everest smiled at Blu, again thinking about pleasing her.

"We will need to work a little while, is that okay?" Pax asked Blu as they ate.

"Of course, I will just get a shower and watch some TV while you guys do that."

After they finished eating, Pax took Blu's bag upstairs and showed her where the master room was. "My room is here, and the bathroom is just in there," he pointed to the door on the other side of the room. "I was hoping that you would stay in here, with me."

Blu nodded. She hadn't given much thought as to where she would be sleeping while she was here. He kissed her lips and left her to shower and change. Blu explored his room, sitting on his king-size bed. It was not like she had imagined. She was remembering the room at the club. This room was nothing like that.

This room was brightly colored with dark blue tints throughout. The bathroom had a bathtub and a separate shower in the corner. She decided that she wanted the Jacuzzi tub. She filled up the tub with hot water, stripped naked, and climbed inside.

She enjoyed her bath in the big tub. She got out and dried off. Standing in front of the mirror, she looked at herself. *Can I do this?* She thought to herself. She knew that she was going to be with Pax tonight, what she hadn't planned on was Everest being here, as well. She had thought a lot about the two of them over the last week. She knew that neither of them would do anything that she didn't want and would stop as soon as she said to.

She grabbed her sexiest, red lace underwear, and put them on. She dried her hair and put on some lip gloss. She gave herself one more look and smiled at what she saw. As she went to open the door to the bathroom, she saw a Navy blue robe hanging on the back of the door. She enjoyed the silky feel to the robe as she ran her hands over it. She took it down from the hook and placed it on her back and over her shoulders. The cool material helped to cool her body from the hot bath.

She fastened the robe shut around her waist and walked back into his room. She placed her clothes back in her suitcase and left

Pax's room. She entered the living room and there was no one there. *They must still be in the office*, she thought, looking around the room. She found his Bluetooth radio and she turned it on. She found the song that she wanted to play and started the music. She knew if she turned it up they would be able to hear it...

Meanwhile in the office...

"She's staying all weekend?" Everest asked, curious about Blu's presence.

"She is," Pax smiled, thinking about what he had been waiting for all week.

"And you two are going to..." Everest prodded.

"We are going to do whatever she is comfortable with."

Everest smiled at his friend. "You like her."

Pax smiled back. Truth was, he did like her. He wasn't sure where it was going, but he knew that he wanted her here all weekend. He knew that one night with her was not going to be enough to tame his desire for her. He wasn't sure how much he would need to get enough. "She's different."

"Is she off-limits for playtime, Pax?" Everest asked, hoping that he wouldn't say yes.

"That's up to her. I won't ask her for more than she's willing to give. She knows about it and if she wants it, she'll ask for it." Pax gave his friend a serious look. "Otherwise, she's off-limits." Everest nodded, hoping she would ask for it.

As they talked, they heard some music start to play in the living room. "Is that?" Everest asked, smiling.

"That's Marvin Gaye..." Pax smiled, hearing the music play. They both stood from their seats and made their way into the living room.

As soon as they walked into the room, they looked at each other and smiled. "I'll be damned," Everest sputtered out.

"Fuck me," Pax breathed out.

• • •

Blu turned on "Let's Get it On" by Marvin Gaye, not too loud. She walked around the room and lit all the candles that she could find. She turned off all the lights and the whole room was lit by candles only. She turned the music back to the beginning and turned it up, loud enough that they could hear it.

She was facing away from where she knew they would walk into the room. She allowed her body to feel the music, her hips swaying in time with the beat, her hands exploring her body over the silk robe.

She heard the office door open and their footsteps as they entered the room. She even heard what they mumbled when they saw her dancing in Pax's robe. She didn't turn around to look at them. She was afraid she would lose her nerve if she looked at them right away.

She felt two hands come around her waist from behind her, his breath on her exposed shoulder where the robe had slid off. "My robe looks good on you, baby." She knew it was Pax before he said a word. Not just from his familiar scent but his hands felt different on her body than anyone else's. He kissed on her neck as his hands cupped her breasts from behind. "My God, you are beautiful," he mumbled into her neck as he sucked the pink skin in between his teeth.

He turned her to face him so he could kiss her lips. His desire for her was off the charts and he had to taste her. As his hands continued their path down the front of the robe, untying it as they went, she felt another set of hands on her hips and a hard body press against her back. His kisses on her shoulder were light as his hands cupped her ass.

Blu kissed Pax back with all she had as Everest kissed on her shoulder. One hand around Pax's neck to pull him into the kiss, her other hand grabbed for Everest to pull his body into hers.

Pax pulled back from the kiss long enough to look her in the eyes and make sure she was asking for this.

Blu smiled up at him, licked her lips, and said, "Took you boys long enough…"

Chapter 12

Blu was sandwiched in between the two men that had been turning her on for over two weeks. She had only ever kissed Pax and she wasn't interested in changing that fact tonight. She wasn't sure what was going to happen, but she was sure that the only person she wanted to kiss or have sex with was Pax. The rest would be decided as they went.

She felt Everest pressed into her ass, his hard body against hers. She took her left hand from his hips, where she had been pulling him closer to her and rubbed him over his jeans. He hissed and bit into the shoulder he had been kissing. "Fuck."

She giggled as she did the same to Pax. She looked up into Pax's eyes as she slid her hand into his shorts, past the waistband of his underwear, and found what she was searching for. The look on his face was one of desire, surprise, and pure lust. She took him into her hand and gave him one long stroke, wetting her hand with what was already leaking from his tip.

"Baby, don't make me come yet," he moaned into her lips as he kissed her again. His tongue demanding entrance into her mouth. She loved his kisses. He kissed her like no one ever had and like she wanted from no other man.

She felt Everest's hands slide around her waist as she continued to rub him through his jeans. His hands stopped at the top of her panties. He was asking permission. This is how she knew she would be safe with them. They would both take care of her. Not just her physical needs, but her emotional ones, as well. He looked up to Pax and asked, "What am I allowed to do?"

Pax looked at Blu and smiled. "Baby, he wants to play. Do you feel his hands on your stomach?" Blu nodded. She felt them and they felt good on her body. Not as good as Pax's felt any time he touched her, but they felt good. "If at any time we do anything you don't want, tell us to stop. Do you understand?"

"I understand." Blu agreed. Her heart thundered in her chest, her breathing became more and more ragged as they touched her.

Pax glanced over her shoulder to look at Everest. "No sex and no kissing. Those are only for me, understood?"

Everest nodded. "Yes."

"The rest is up to her. She will tell you what you are allowed to do and not to do." Pax looked to Blu for conformation, she nodded her approval.

Everest slipped his hand into her panties, coating his fingers in her wetness. "You are so wet. Do you know how wet she gets, Pax?"

"I do. Wait until you taste her. She is fucking delicious," Pax boasted knowing he had already had a taste and couldn't wait to have more of her.

Everest removed his hand from her panties, placing his fingers into his mouth, sucking them clean while he moaned his approval of her taste. "Fucking delicious," he mumbled into her ear as he placed his fingers back into her panties. He found her clit right away, circling it with his middle finger. "Is she tight?" He asked Pax as he continued to rub her like she was rubbing him.

"She is," Pax boasted again, as he pulled her panties down, allowing room for his fingers to enter her. His other hand pulled her red lace bra down over a breast so that he could take her erect nipple into his mouth. She relaxed, her head tossed back onto Everest's shoulder, allowing him access to suck on her neck. His other hand released the hook on her bra, giving Pax better access to her breast.

"Come on my fingers, baby," Pax demanded as their fingers worked her body. It only took a few minutes for her to follow his order and let herself go, both of them working her body into a frenzy.

She cried out as her orgasm took over her body, still standing on the living room floor. "I want to taste you," Everest moaned into her neck as they worked her through her high.

"Is that okay, baby?" Pax asked as he led her to the room at the other end of the living room. She nodded. He opened the door and ushered her inside. Somewhere between the living room and this room, Everest had lost his jeans. He was only in his boxers and she could see how hard he was.

"Lie down, Blu," Everest demanded. Blu looked up to Pax for approval, he nodded. She climbed up onto the bed, naked. Everest climbed up onto the bed, his body over hers. He laid down on top of her, his hardness pressing into her wet center. He kissed on her neck, down to her breast and took her erect nipple into his mouth, his fingers playing in her wetness. His kisses continued down her stomach, just above the spot he wanted. "May I?" She nodded and he shoved his tongue into her wetness, lapping up everything that they had just caused. His fingers traced her sensitive bud, asking for entrance into her body.

"I want to feel how tight you are," Everest said after he licked her clean. Blu looked over to Pax. He was on the chair to the side of the bed. He had his hardness in his hand, through his boxers; his shorts on the floor. He nodded at her.

"Yes," she moaned out as Everest slid his fingers inside of her.

Everest moaned into her as his tongue and fingers both worked her body. "You are tight," he moaned his approval against her wet center. "Come for me, Blu. He's watching us and I want him to see me make you come like he just did." Blu turned her head on the bed to see Pax watching them, eyes half-closed. He had taken himself out of his boxers and was stroking himself, slowly.

She reached down and pulled Everest up closer to her. "I want to feel you in my hand while you lick me." She looked at

Pax and smiled. "I want him to see me stroke you like he is doing."

"Fuck this girl and her dirty mouth," Everest grinned, moving up on the bed to grant her what she asked for.

"That's my girl," Pax smiled as Everest moved so that she could reach him. He leaned back down between her legs, his erection within arm's reach. Blu reached inside his boxers, freeing his hardness. She slowly stroked him up and down, using his own wetness for lubrication. He was impressive in size, but not as big as Pax.

She bit her bottom lip and she stroked Everest, looking into Pax's eyes. She saw the desire building in them. The same eyes that were darting between her hand stroking Everest and watching Everest lick and finger her throbbing pussy. She knew he was getting close watching her please his friend and his friend pleasing her. She wanted to drive him wild, so she sped up her stroking of Everest, matching the rhythm that Pax was doing on his own. She only closed her eyes when she was ready to have her second orgasm of the night. Everest cleaned her up with his tongue as he felt Pax tap him on the shoulder. "Enough."

Everest stood beside the bed and Pax took his place between her legs. His tongue explored her slit as his fingers curled inside of her. "Shall we go for number three, baby?" Just having his hands and mouth on her like that was enough. She came for the third time tonight, quickly, as Pax dove into her pussy with his tongue and his fingers at the same time.

She glanced over to see Everest on the chair that Pax had claimed only minutes ago. He was stroking himself, faster than she had done, bringing on his orgasm as he watched Pax lick her, as he had just moments before.

Her attention was brought back to Pax immediately when his body laid on hers, his hardness pressing against her entrance. "He is going to watch me claim what is mine. He is going to watch me fuck you and he is going to wish it was his cock that was buried inside of this perfect pussy." Pax had already placed a condom on himself and was ready to enter her. She didn't have to answer him, instead, she pulled him to her, his lips crashed into her and his hardness slid into her.

She heard Everest speak. "God damn, I want to fuck that pussy. Oh… God."

She moaned out, "Yes… Pax… please…"

He answered her by thrusting into her all the way. She gasped as he stretched her around him. She glanced over to see Everest stroking himself faster.

Pax kissed her again, keeping her attention on him. She faintly heard Everest moaning as he stroked himself, watching Pax take her. Paxton's hands and lips were all over her body, sending her senses into overdrive. Orgasm number four was quickly approaching. Pax could feel her starting to shake again. "Come with me, baby."

And… she did. She screamed out as her most intense orgasm of the night took over her body, feeling him pulsing inside of her as they came together. He made sure every last drop was milked from his body as he helped her get all her aftershocks out. He laid on top of her, still inside of her, and kissed her lips. Softly, gently as they came down from their high. She wasn't sure how long he kissed her, while still being inside of her. She just knew she didn't want him to stop.

She glanced over to the chair to find it empty. Everest had left them alone at some point and she had no idea when. She looked back to Pax with a smile on her face. He leaned down and kissed her.

"You are incredible, Blu Millar…"

He kissed her again.

"And you're mine."

Chapter 13

*B*lu laid there, in Pax's arms with a smile on her face. He had just told her that she was his. Her heart skipped a beat when she heard those words pass from his lips, but it was too good to be true. Her? Belong to Pax? That couldn't be. "For this weekend, I guess I am."

He slid out of her and disposed of the condom. He walked back to the bed and picked Blu up, bridal style, and kissed her lips. "You most certainly are," he whispered to her as he carried her exhausted body upstairs and to his room. He laid her on his bed and walked to the other side. He climbed under the covers, both of them still naked. He pulled the covers up over their naked bodies and he nuzzled his face into her hair.

His arms wrapped around her as she laid her head onto his chest. "Are you sleepy?" He asked as he stroked her hair.

"I'm exhausted," she mumbled into his chest.

He held her just like that until she relaxed and fell asleep, his hand continued stroking her hair. Pax had never felt the urge to hold someone while they slept before. Usually, after sex, he was the first to dress and leave. He had also never told someone that they were his before. He didn't dare correct her when she mentioned she was his for only this weekend.

He slept cuddled up to her all night. He was glad that when they came down from their last high of the night that Everest was already gone. Pax knew Everest would be back to the house today to continue their work, but he was thankful for the time alone with Blu.

That wasn't something he was used to, either. He never craved time alone with a woman before. He never minded sharing a woman, but with Blu, he wasn't so inclined to share her. His rule was he never kissed. It was too personal. Too confusing. He knew that Everest never kissed the women they were with, either, but Blu was different. He loved kissing her, her lips felt like heaven to him. Every part of her felt like heaven to him.

Last night was hot and he was getting excited again thinking about how she looked laying in that bed, being pleased by Everest. But what he loved more than that was how she kept looking at him. Making sure he was enjoying himself. Asking for permission to continue. Looking to him for direction. He knew if she wanted it again, he would do it. He would give her anything she wanted… well, almost anything.

"Good morning," she sleepily muttered as she started to stir.

"The best. How did you sleep?" He asked as he rubbed her back.

She stretched, causing the blanket to fall and expose her bare breasts to Pax's hungry eyes. "Wonderfully," she teased as she stretched further.

Pax's eyes drifted to her exposed upper half. He licked his lips as he rolled his body over hers. His lips captured hers in a heated battle. Her hands in his hair, tugging at the ends. His hands slid down her body until they found her wet center. "Hmmm, so wet for me this morning."

"Maybe for you… maybe not…" she smiled at him, his eyes glimmered with jealousy.

He reached over to the bedside table, pulled out a condom, and rolled it on quickly. "I'll show you who you are wet for," he groaned as he slid inside of her aching center.

"Pax…" she moaned as he thrust deep inside of her.

"Now who are you wet for, baby?"

"Oh… God…."

He stopped his movement, his lips touching hers. "Who does this wet pussy belong to, Blu?" He thrust forward again, going as far as he could. "Answer me Blu, who makes you this wet?"

"You… Pax… Oh, God…. Only you," she screamed out as he pulled out and slammed back into her.

"That's right... only me..." he thrust into her hard, feeling her tighten around him. "You and this magnificent pussy belong to me," he demanded as they both came together.

As they came down from their high together, he kissed her again. "Wow, that was amazing," she panted between breaths.

"Yeah, it was," he agreed as he leaned down to kiss her again.

He pulled out of her and discarded the condom. When he came back into the room, he saw her standing beside the bed. "Dammit woman, cover that sexy ass before I have to have you again." He smirked as his eyes traveled her naked body.

Blu smiled at him as she met him halfway across the bedroom floor. Her hands ran up his chest and over his shoulders, she pressed her breasts up against his bare chest. He cupped her ass in his large hands, his lips on her neck. "I think we should go shower."

She pulled back, giving him her most innocent look. "Together?"

He chuckled. "Don't give me those innocent doe eyes after last night." He kissed her neck again as he kneaded her ass in his hands.

"What about that shower?" She teased as she pulled back from his hold. She walked past him and into the bathroom. He chuckled as he followed behind her. She already had the water on and was stepping into it when he entered the bathroom. He quickly joined her under the water.

Blu washed her hair as Pax watched her with amazement. He soaped up his hands and ran them down the front of her body. Making sure to go slow as he approached her breasts. "These are incredible," he mumbled before taking her breast into his mouth. She held onto his shoulders to steady herself on her shaky legs.

Pax slid a soapy finger into her slit so he could get her wet and ready for him. As he sucked on her breast and was preparing her for him there was a loud banging on his door.

"Get the fuck up. We got work to do." Everest yelled through Pax's bedroom door.

Pax groaned as he sucked harder. There was another knock on the door. "If you don't answer, I'm coming in," he yelled again.

"He'll go away," Pax replied as he sunk his finger into Blu.

There was a knock on the bathroom door before it opened and Everest came walking into the bathroom. "Fuck, I didn't know the party was in here," he smirked as he watched them.

"Out!" Pax demanded as he worked Blu's body.

Everest chuckled. "Maybe she wants me to stay." Everest looked at Blu and saw that she was looking at him as he watched them. Growing harder by the second.

"Do you want him to stay?" Pax asked as he sucked on her neck. Blu nodded. Pax smiled as he removed his fingers from her wetness. "Do you want to play or let him watch me take what's mine, Blu?"

Blu glanced at Everest and then back to Pax. "I want him to play," she said as she smiled at Pax. Pax turned off the water and opened the shower door. They both stepped out and he grabbed their towels. They dried off as Everest watched them, adjusting himself in his jeans.

"You want to play?" Pax asked her as he took her towel and tossed it over the rack on the shower. She nodded. "Okay."

Pax pulled Blu to stand in front of him, her back against his chest. She looked up to Everest as she stood in front of him, naked. Everest removed his shirt and his jeans as he walked closer to her. "You are a lucky man, Pax."

"I know," he agreed as he cupped her breasts from behind. His hardness slid between her thighs, warm and wet.

Everest took a breast in his hand and brought his lips to the nipple. "Same rules as last night?" He asked to confirm.

"You cannot kiss her lips and your cock will not enter her sweet pussy. You want to add anything, baby?" Blu could feel Pax sliding back and forth against her wet center. She wanted him inside her.

Her head fell back onto Pax's shoulder as he sucked on her neck. "I like it that you won't let him fuck me," she moaned.

Pax chuckled and Everest growled. Everest reached down and took himself into his hand. He stepped forward and rubbed himself through her wet center. "I may not be able to fuck this pussy, but I can feel it." He stroked himself as he rubbed the tip of his hardness on her clit. "I can still make you come with my hard cock," he breathed on her neck.

Pax slid back and angled her just right so he could slide inside of her. "Does it make you wet knowing how much he wants to fuck you?" Pax asked as he slammed inside of her, Everest rubbing her clit as he stroked himself. Blu nodded.

"But I only want you to fuck me," she added.

"Do you want to suck him off?" Pax asked with some jealousy in his tone.

"Oh, shit. I want her to suck me off," Everest chimed in.

Blu shook her head. "I want to suck you, Pax."

Pax pulled out of her and took her hand. He led her to the room down the hall. He laid on his back on the bed, his legs hanging off. His hardness in his hand. "You sure?" Blu nodded. She stood between his legs and leaned over, her ass in the air. She placed her hand at the base of his shaft and licked his tip. He moaned out as she took him into her mouth. "Oh, shit."

She felt Everest behind her, his fingers playing in the wetness. "Dammit, I want to fuck you," he growled. He took himself in his hand and rubbed around in her wetness. "Please let me slide it in," he begged. Blu pushed her ass into him, causing him to growl again. He was stroking himself harder and faster as he circled her ass with his wet tip. "Let me fuck this ass," he begged again.

Blu continued her work on Pax. Sucking him in and out her mouth. Pax reached over beside the bed and grabbed a long rubber vibrator. He handed it to Everest. "You can fuck her with this." Blu pushed into him again, craving contact. Everest took what Pax handed him and slid it inside of Blu. He turned on the vibration and he could feel her tighten around it. He rubbed against the vibrating wand and he could feel the pulsing that she was feeling.

He stroked himself harder as she moved with his movements. "Oh, baby... I am going to.... Oh.... Fuuuccckkk..." Pax moaned as he started to come. Blu took it all and never stopped. Everest pushed against her as his hand went around to rub her clit. He rubbed her until he felt her coming undone, stroking himself until he was at his breaking point. "Can I come on your ass?"

Pax pulled her closer to him so he could kiss her lips. He replaced Everest's fingers on her throbbing clit as she came again. "He's going to come, can he come on your ass?" Blu nodded as she rode her aftershocks out with Pax's fingers. She heard Everest groan as she felt a warm liquid shoot out onto her ass. "God damn, I want this fucking woman."

Pax chuckled as he kissed her again. "She's mine."

Everest leaned over onto Blu's back and kissed her shoulders. "That was the hottest fucking thing I have ever done." He looked up at Pax. "When are you going to let me fuck her with you?"

"I told you, that's my pussy," he smirked at Everest.

"Then you fuck her pussy and I'll fuck this ass," he said as he rubbed himself along her ass again. "Climb on up there and let him in and I will take this ass," Everest suggested. "We can both have you at the same time." Pax pulled Blu up to him so she straddled him. He eased her down onto him as he stretched her out around him. He tipped his head back as she lowered down onto him. His hands placed on her ass guided her hips to move just right.

"Fuck, that's hot," Everest said as he moved closer to her, his hardness in his hand. He stepped in closer, coating his hardness with her last orgasm. "Our girl riding that big cock." Everest smiled.

"That's MY girl riding this big cock, letting you fuck that ass," Pax moaned in approval of their double teaming.

She leaned forward and felt Everest place his tip just inside of her. "Oh, God, this ass is even tighter than your pussy," he smirked at Pax.

Blu felt her body shake as he entered her. Her body began to tremble.

"Baby?" She heard Pax call for her. "Hey, babe?" Her body trembled again. "Babe? Wake up, Everest will be here soon."

Blu opened her eyes and looked up. She saw Pax smiling at her as he held her close to him. "Pax?" She asked sleepily.

"Good morning babe. We need to get up, Everest will be here soon." Pax kissed her lips. "Go shower and come down when you're ready. I will make us breakfast."

Pax kissed her again and climbed out of the bed. She sighed realizing it was only a dream. That she dreamed of having them both again this morning. "Everest isn't here this morning?"

"No. He left before we were done last night and he hasn't been back since, why?"

Blu giggled. "Last night was real?" She asked, unsure if it was real or not.

"Yes, baby. It was real. You came out in my robe… and well… he made you come while I watched and then I took what is mine and he left before we were done."

"Okay…"

Pax sat beside her naked body in the bed. He traced his fingers along where the blanket met her skin, just above her breasts. He gently pulled the blanket down, exposing one breast. "You were moaning in your sleep," he smiled at her, his finger circling her erect nipple.

"I was dreaming." She smiled at him. She was taken aback by how handsome he was.

"Hmmm… a good one, I take it?" His hand pulled back the covers further.

Blu nodded as his hand continued to her stomach. "Are you

wet, Blu?" She nodded again. "If you don't stop me, I am going to find out how wet you are."

Blu spread her legs apart, giving him access. "I'm not going to stop you," she smirked. Pax kissed her lips as his hand slid down further.

"Hey, asshole!!! Get up!! Stop fucking my girl!" They heard Everest yell from downstairs.

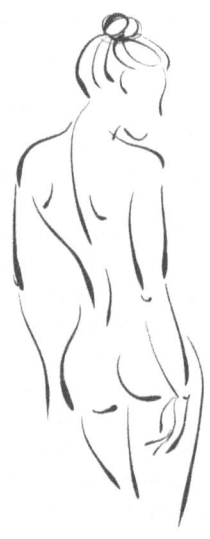

Pax groaned into the kiss, stopping his hand before he reached her wetness. "My girl," he mumbled into her lips. "You're MY girl," he reiterated as he kissed her lips again. "Go shower or else I am going to be buried so deep inside of you I may never come out," he said as he pulled the covers over her again.

"I wouldn't mind," she teased, wanting him again.

Pax smirked at her before he kissed her again. "Shower and dress and come down. I promised my girl breakfast." He stood from the bed, adjusted himself, and walked to the door. He looked back and saw her walking to the shower, naked.

Pax yelled down to Everest, "Get breakfast started, I will be down in a little while." Pax chuckled as he ran into the bathroom behind Blu, only stopping to grab a condom from his table.

Chapter 14

Pax caught up to Blu as she was stepping into the shower. He grabbed her around the waist and held her body close to his. "Where do you think you are going, baby girl?"

Blu reached behind her and grabbed onto Pax's hips. "I'm going to shower… unless you have other plans?" She smirked as she rubbed her ass against him.

"Get in that shower," he demanded as he stepped in behind her. "I can't wait any longer to have you again."

Blu stepped into the shower, under the hot water. Pax was right behind her, his hands on her naked and wet body. Pax placed his hand on the middle of her back and pushed her forward a little bit until she reached her hands out to support her upper body. He pushed one foot to the side, to spread her legs.

"I know you were dreaming about being fucked. You moaned the same as you did last night. What I want to know is… who was fucking you?" His other hand slid around her waist to find her wetness.

"I… Ohhh…"

Pax lined up with her entrance and teased her opening with his tip. "Tell me, Blu. Who was fucking you?"

"You were… I was on top of you… and…" She gasped as he pushed inside her just about halfway.

"And what, Blu? Who else was there?"

"Everest was there."

Pax bit her shoulder and then sucked the same skin between his teeth. "What was he doing, Blu? Was he fucking my perfect pussy?"

"No," she yelled out. "He was… oh God," Pax slammed inside her. "He was fucking my ass."

"Goddamn," he muttered out in a deep voice. "You let him fuck this ass?" He pulled back out before slamming back inside.

"He… Pax… Please. I need to come." She begged him for her release as his hand continued to work her sensitive bud while he buried himself deep inside of her, over and over again.

That was by far the best sex that Pax had ever had. He knew it was going to be impossible for him to let her go. His body slammed into hers until she clamped down onto him, making him ache with need. He never felt anything with any woman that he had been with. Blu was different. She had already given him the most explosive orgasms of his life.

"What am I going to do with you?" He mumbled into her neck as he pulled out of her.

She giggled her answer, "Feed me."

He turned her to face him, the warm water massaging her back. He cupped her face in his hands as he leaned down to kiss her. "I don't like him having what's mine," he groaned.

"He was just playing. Like last night," she reminded him of their time together.

"I'm a greedy bastard, Blu. I don't share what's mine. I won't."

"But you always share?" She asked confused.

"None of those women were mine." He pulled her face to his. He kissed her rough and she loved it.

She was confused. "Are you saying you don't want to play with me anymore?"

"I'm saying what we did last night was fine. I loved watching him please you like that. I loved how you watched me as he licked my pussy," he smiled as he said my.

"Do you want to watch that again?"

"Yes. I do," he answered decisively. He knew he did. He got off on the fact that he was the one that got to have her. The only one that got to have her, completely.

"And you wouldn't like it for him to … say… fuck my ass while you were in my…"

"No!" They stepped out of the shower and dried off. "He can eat you all he wants, I will even let him use his fingers inside of you, but that is all. You are mine and that I won't compromise on, I'm sorry."

Blu smiled at Pax. "Okay."

"Good, now get dressed, and let's go downstairs. I smell food cooking."

They finished getting dressed and headed to the kitchen. Everest was standing at the stove frying bacon. "Juice is on the table, I'm almost done here," he announced as he heard them enter.

"Thank you, Everest," she said as she sat down at the bar.

Everest placed the plate of bacon and eggs on the counter and joined Pax and Blu, sitting on the other side of Blu. He leaned in and kissed her cheek. "Morning, beautiful." He smiled at her and Pax. "Asshole," he greeted Pax.

"Fuck off," Pax snarled. He didn't like how close Everest and Blu were becoming. Pax had never been jealous before and he didn't like the feeling at all.

They ate breakfast, the two men talking about work. Pax looked at Blu and smiled. He knew he was experiencing something he had never experienced before. She smiled back at him as he brushed some crumbs from her chin with his thumb.

The guys decided they needed to start working right after breakfast since they had playtime last night instead. Blu said she was going to go swimming while they worked.

They were done with breakfast and Everest placed all the dishes in the sink. Pax spun Blu around so he could stand between her legs as she sat on the barstool. "Are you sure you're okay with me working?"

Blu smiled at how considerate he was being. "I'm fine. I'm going to go swimming. I'm sure I can find something to get into."

He leaned in and kissed her lips. The kiss was short and sweet. Pax liked how comfortable they had become with each other already. Everest stood behind Blu and Pax. He placed his hands on her hips and kissed her on the side of her neck. "Hmmm, I should've had you for breakfast." He kissed her neck again. "Every part of you is delicious."

Pax took Blu's bottom lip into his mouth and sucked hard. Blu moaned. He pulled back and smiled at her as Everest cupped her breasts in his hands from behind her. "I want to fuck you again," Pax moaned as he pressed his hard shaft against her wet center, begging to be let inside.

Everest mumbled on her skin, "Let's take her into your room."

Blu pulled away from them. "You boys have work to do and I am going swimming."

They laughed and pulled back. "Okay, baby. We will go to work... for now. However, I can't promise that we won't steal you soon... for some playtime."

She winked at Pax. "You know where I'll be, baby." Pax groaned as he sucked on one side of her neck while Everest got her other. "How are we supposed to work with hard dicks?"

"Sounds like a personal problem," she teased as she headed up the stairs to change.

Everest and Pax watched her go up the stairs. "How do you not stay buried in that all the time?" Everest asked Pax as he adjusted himself in his jeans.

Pax chuckled as he did the same. "I want to, trust me."

The boys went to the office to work. Blu decided she wanted to play with the boys when they were done, so she put on the skimpiest bikini she could find. It barely covered her. She made her way to the pool. She rubbed some sunscreen on her body and laid out on the recliner until she was warm. It was then she went into the cool water.

A few hours later... in the office...

"I am serious, if she were mine, I would walk around with a fucking hard-on all the time," Everest confessed as he sat at the side table where they had the plans laid out.

"I practically do and have for the last year. I couldn't stand it any longer seeing her in the office every day. All those other women... they were to try to forget that I had a hard-on for my assistant."

"Did it work?" Everest asked as he tried to see her out the window.

"What do you think? You've seen her naked and tasted that perfect pussy. Not to mention the fact that I am spending as much time as I can this weekend, buried as deep inside of her as I can be."

"I have and I have to say, I want more."

"I think she will let you play again."

"I hope so, but I mean I want... more. I want to be inside her."

"She dreamed about us last night."

"She did?" Everest asked, intrigued.

Pax chuckled, thinking about her moaning in her sleep. "She did. She rode me while you fucked her ass."

"Man, you can't say shit like that to me. I want her."

"I don't know, man, I'm not sure I am okay with that."

"I don't mean try to steal her from you, I just... I don't know. I want her," he paused. "Would you let me have her if she said yes?"

"I don't know."

"I wouldn't do it without you there. I would make sure you watch as I pounded the hell out of her. It isn't like you two are a couple or something."

Pax adjusted himself in his seat. For some reason since this morning when she told him about her dream, he had considered if he would let Everest be with her. The thought of watching Everest fuck her was making him hard. He already knew he liked watching her being pleased by him when he had his tongue buried inside her. Would it be that hard to let him please her more?

"Man, we gotta work, and talking about fucking my woman is making me want to fuck my woman."

Everest chuckled. "Then let's go fuck her." He stood up and grabbed his hard length in his pants and adjusted it for more room.

Pax stood and walked out of the office and to the sliding glass doors. He stopped as soon as he saw her wet body in the shallow end of the pool. Everest ran into his back. "Why'd you stop?"

Pax pointed to Blu. "Look."

Everest looked at her beautiful body in her small suit. "God damn, please let me fuck that. I will wear a condom, I promise."

The boys walked out to the pool where Blu was. She looked up and smiled at them as they stripped to their underwear. They both jumped into the pool, Pax behind her and Everest standing in front of her. Pax ran his hand into her panties from behind, circling her ass with his finger. He kissed her neck. "Do you want him to take you here, baby?"

Everest kissed her neck as his fingers found her wetness, two fingers slipped inside her. "And Pax will fuck you here?" She moaned as Pax stuck a finger in her ass, slowly stretching her out to prepare her for what was to come if she said yes.

"You said no sex," she moaned.

"Maybe I would let him if you wanted it, but you don't have to if you don't want to."

"You'd still be his girl… and I would never do anything with you when he wasn't around, but I want you so bad. I want to bury myself into your body." He bit her neck. "But still no kissing."

"You would watch everything?" She asked Pax.

He nodded as he continued to move his finger inside her,

adding a second one to stretch her more, "Everything, baby. He won't do anything you don't want. I promise I won't leave your side."

She reached down between Pax and herself, she could feel how hard he was. Everest was, too. They both wanted this. She pulled Pax and Everest out of their underwear and began stroking them. They both removed their fingers and Pax turned her to face them. He kissed her hard. His hands were on her ass as Everest ran his tip through her wetness from behind her.

"You don't have to do this, baby. If you want he can…"

"I want to try," she confessed. Since her dream, she had wondered if she would want them both at the same time.

Pax lifted her and lowered her down onto his hardness, filling her up with his long thick shaft. She leaned her head back as he entered her. She felt Everest push against her ass. He had jumped out and gotten a condom when Pax picked her up. Everest whispered in her ear, "I will go slow and if you need me to stop, just say so and I will, okay?" She nodded.

He pressed a little further as his tip entered her. "Can you feel that baby? I can feel him inside your tight ass."

She nodded, feeling him push in more.

"Holy fuck, she's tight back here. I may come as soon as I get inside."

"Oh God…" she screamed out.

Everest stopped. "Are you okay?"

Blu was breathing heavily as he filled her up. They both filled her completely. Pax held her like that for a few moments, letting her adjust to them both inside her. She had never had someone do that… there before. She dug her nails into Pax's shoulder, causing him to thrust his hips. "I can't control myself when you do that."

"Then don't… I need you to fuck me. I need you to kiss me, Pax."

Pax started to move, lifting Blu up and down, allowing her to move up and down on Everest as he kissed her hard. "Fuck, this feels good," Everest said as he moved in and out of her. "I am not going to last long, Blu. Can I come in this ass?"

She nodded. "I want Pax to come in my pussy."

"You mean in my pussy. This pussy belongs to me, isn't that right, Ev?"

"Fuck yeah, I want this fucking ass." She felt Everest start to pump erratically. Pax was, too, and she knew he was close. Everest helped hold her up as Pax dropped his hand between them, rubbing her clit to make her come again.

"Come for us, baby. Come all over us," Pax growled as he pumped her hard.

"Holy shit, I am going to come," Everest announced just before he thrust one last time, hard inside her ass, his orgasm spilling out around him.

"Oh…" she moaned out as Pax filled her up while she came all around him. "I'm coming… Pax… please."

One last thrust and her body felt like it was on fire. Everest pulled out of her, as Pax lowered her on himself harder. Making sure every last drop was hers. After all, everything he had belonged to her. No matter how hard he tried to fight it, he belonged to her.

Blu was finally coming down from her high as Pax held her body close to his, kissing alongside her neck. She was wrapped around him so tight she wasn't sure where her body began and where his ended. She had never felt so desired and wanted in all her life.

She didn't know it was possible to feel what she was feeling right now. "Pax…"

"Yes, baby?"

"I…" she started. She wanted to tell him so many things. Things she wasn't ready to say and she was sure he wasn't ready to hear. This was only for the weekend, after all. That was what he said, she was his for the weekend. Monday she would go back to being his assistant and try to forget how good it felt to be in his arms and his bed.

"Yes, baby? What is it?" He asked as he kissed on her neck.

"I... That was..."

Pax kissed her lips, soft and sweet. His tongue slowly found its way into her mouth. She sucked his tongue as he pulled back. "You better stop kissing me like that or I am going to need you again."

She giggled as she lowered her legs to stand in front of him. He wrapped her in his arms and kissed the top of her head. "Did you get any work done?"

He shook his head. "Not all of it, we needed my girl," he laughed.

She looked around. She didn't see Everest. "Where's Ev?"

"He's inside. I need to get back to work."

She nodded. "I know. It's okay. I'll go shower and watch some TV, and make you some lunch."

He kissed her and headed back inside. He needed to get some of his work done, but he would much rather be with her. He never had an issue concentrating on work but having Blu in his house was making him only want to be with her.

Chapter 15

*B*lu slipped out of the pool and put a towel around her naked body. She went and took another shower, both to get the chlorine off her body and to soothe her sore muscles. After her shower, she went to the kitchen to find something to fix the boys for lunch.

In Pax's large kitchen she found the ingredients for a seafood salad and some soup. She put lunch together and placed everything on the bar. She walked to the office and knocked on the door.

"Come in," Pax spoke from behind the closed door. Everest and Pax were both at the table where they had lots of papers strewn about. They both smiled when she came into the room. "Come here babe," he patted his leg. Blu stood beside him as he pulled her into his lap. "Hi," he smiled before he kissed her.

Everest cleared his throat as Pax and Blu kissed, harder than he had planned. Pax had a hard time controlling himself when she was around and her in his lap was more than he could handle. "I have lunch ready when you guys get to where you can take a break."

Pax nuzzled into her neck, kissing and biting as he mumbled, "Take off your shorts and lay on the table and I will be a happy, well-fed man."

Blu playfully smacked his chest. "I am talking about real food, Paxton." He loved it when she called him by his full name. "You can have that later," she winked.

"Can I?" She heard Everest ask as he stood behind her. "I would like to be a well-fed, happy man, too."

Blu looked to Pax and he smiled at her. "What are you asking, Everest?" She teased.

"I am asking if I can have a taste, too." He smirked at her.

Pax pulled her further into his lap, his hardness sticking her in the leg. "I think he wants to play tonight, baby." Pax looked at Everest and smiled. "Isn't that right, Ev? You wanna taste my girl again?"

"Fuck yeah. I didn't get to earlier."

"You did something I said you wouldn't be able to do. Don't get greedy, Ev," Pax scolded Everest. Everest just smiled back at Pax and his jealous outburst.

Blu moved on Pax's lap, causing him to pull her in closer. "What are we having for lunch since you aren't currently on the menu?"

Blu stood and took Pax's hand in hers. "Come on, I'll show you." She led them to the kitchen where the three of them sat and ate their lunch, talking about the project that they were working on.

"Are you almost done?" Blu asked.

"Almost. Another couple of hours and we should be done," Pax added as he took his last bite.

"I should probably go home tonight, I don't want to keep you from your work."

Pax turned her to look at him, cupping her face with his hands. "Don't leave. We can finish this later."

"I just don't want to get in the way of your work. I should just go home. I can see you on Monday."

"Don't leave on my account. We don't have to get this done this weekend," Everest offered.

"Are you sure?" She asked, looking at Pax hoping that he didn't want her to leave. She didn't want this weekend to be over yet. She wasn't ready to go back to being just his assistant just yet.

"I'm sure, baby. I am not nearly done with you yet," he smirked at her before taking her lips with his. She moaned into the kiss. "You keep moaning like that and I won't be able to wait until later."

She laughed. "You need to work and stop thinking about sex,

Paxton."

"How can I think about anything other than sex when I have this gorgeous woman staying with me all weekend, letting my best friend play with us and making us both want her all the fucking time?"

"Sounds to me like you need to kick her out," Blu giggled as he kissed her again.

"Hell no, that is not happening," he kissed her neck and mumbled, "I don't know how I am ever supposed to let her go." Pax kissed the side of her neck, causing her to moan again.

"Pax... ah... that... feels so good," she moaned.

"I can make you feel even better," Pax informed her as he sucked on her neck.

"We can make you feel better," Everest added as he rubbed her back.

Blu giggled as she pulled away from the two men that were getting her heated up again. "Go, work. Playtime will be later."

Pax groaned into her neck as Everest kissed the other side. "Woman, you are driving us crazy," Everest hissed as he nibbled her neck.

Blu pulled the rest of the way from them and stood from her chair. "Go, work. I have things to do."

"What? What do you have to do?" Pax asked, curious as to what she would want to do more than to be loved by them.

"I am going to the store to get something for dinner. You two need to work tonight and get this done. I will cook for you both tonight, and if you want..." She smiled at the two of them. "I will get something for dessert."

"We want you for dessert," Pax informed as he stood, causing her to take another step back.

Blu playfully swatted his hands as he reached for her hips. "No. Go, now."

"When did she get so fucking bossy?" Everest asked as he laughed at how Blu handled Pax.

"Both of you, go get your work done and after dinner, we can play if you want to," she added innocently, knowing they did.

"If? If? What if? I want to now," Pax stepped towards her again, this time she allowed him to grab hold of her.

"I have to go shopping, Paxton, and you need to work." She melted into his arms, his lips on hers, demanding entrance.

Everest was pressed up against her back, rubbing her ass with his hands, biting on her shoulder. "Can't we play first?" She could feel how excited they both were getting with both of their erections pressing into her body from both sides.

She pulled away from them and took a deep breath. "Enough. You two need to work and I need to get something for dinner."

Pax smiled at her as he touched her face with his hand. "You promise you're coming back?"

"I promise."

It took some convincing for Pax to allow her to leave. She assured him that she would be coming back.

Blu left the boys to go shopping for dinner and a surprise that she would let them in on later tonight. Pax and Everest went back to his office to attempt to get the project completed before dinner was ready.

Blu was at the store and Pax and Everest were working. Or at least they were trying to work. "Can you concentrate?" Everest asked, trying to concentrate on work.

"Not on work. I can't stop thinking about Blu and what I want to do to her when she gets back."

"What's wrong with us? I have never had it this bad for a woman before," Everest admitted to Pax.

"Me either. I don't know what is happening to me."

"I have always loved sex and sharing has always been fun… but this woman takes it to another level. How the fuck are you going to be able to go back to her just being your assistant on Monday?"

"Honestly, I don't know. I can't make it without her in the

office. She is too valuable to lose. But I don't know how to not kiss her every time I see her."

"Maybe it's time to have a real relationship with her?" Everest smiled at his friend, knowing they both were feeling something for her. He wanted something with her but he wasn't sure how much Pax would let him have, especially when he realized he had feelings for her.

They smelled food cooking and headed out to the kitchen. They both saw Blu at the stove, finishing up dinner in a small black dress. Pax went up to her and spun her around to him. "My God, you are gorgeous." He praised her before he crashed his lips to hers.

Everest let them have a moment. He was feeling things for this woman and he wanted to devour her as much as Pax was doing. As soon as Pax pulled away, he took his place in front of her. His hands roamed her body, settling on her ass. "I hope I can make it through dinner before I have to have a taste of you," he praised her as he kissed on her neck. His hands pulled her into his hardness that wanted to be buried deep inside her.

She giggled as she pulled away from him. "Eat your dinner," she ordered.

"And then I can eat you?" Her face flushed red and he bit at her neck.

"Everest. Eat your dinner." She turned away from him as he slapped her on the ass.

He turned to look at Pax. "That was a yes, wasn't it?"

"It wasn't a no," he teased.

She served them their dinner of homemade lasagna. They all ate dinner as they talked. Everest was a little more quiet than usual.

Pax cleaned up the dishes as Blu sat with Everest. "What's wrong, Ev?"

He smiled at her that she knew something was bothering him. "I was just thinking."

"About what?" She asked as she placed her hand on his.

"About how much this weekend has meant to me and how I want to bury myself so deep inside of you that I may never find my way out."

"Everest..." she breathed out.

"I know Pax and you have this thing. I don't want to try to come between you, not that I could, but I can't help what I am feeling. I don't want to stop seeing you after this weekend." They sat on the couch.

"Do you have to?" She asked curiously as to what would happen after this weekend. Would she want to see one of them still if the other wasn't involved? Would the three of them still play together? Or would she just go back to being his assistant that got rid of his weekend hookups again?

He smiled at her. "I don't know. I just know I don't want to. I guess that is something we all need to discuss. But tonight I would like to have you as I did in the pool, if that is okay with you and Pax."

"If what is okay with me?" Pax asked as he finished the dishes and joined them again.

Blu slid over on the couch beside Everest, Pax taking the seat on her other side. "Ev wants to play like in the pool."

"Oh, does he?" Pax asked, raising an eyebrow at his friend.

Everest placed a hand between Blu's legs as he pulled up her short skirt. "Yes. If I can't have this pussy, I would like to have this ass again tonight." He looked at Pax as he slid his fingers into her panties, finding her soaking wet clit right away. "If this is my last night with her, I want to fuck her ass again."

"And what do you want, Blu?" Pax asked as his fingers joined Everest's, sliding inside her wetness, curling to hit her spot.

"I think I want you both tonight," she moaned as her head laid back onto the couch, her eyes closed, her legs open.

Pax turned her head to face him and took her lips with his. Everest nibbled on her shoulder, making his way to her breast. He found a front zipper on her dress and unzipped it, finding a barely-there lace set underneath. He pulled her bra down and took her breast into his mouth and she moaned.

He grabbed her hips and spun her so she was lying in Pax's lap. One of Pax's hands found her exposed breast, as the other continued to play in her wetness. "Lie back, Blu. I want to taste you."

She laid back into Pax's lap, opening her legs for Everest. He pulled her panties from her body and spread her open for him. He could see her glistening as he got close to her. His tongue darted out to flick at her clit. She lifted her hips to meet his mouth. "Ahhh, a greedy pussy tonight," he mumbled against her flesh.

Pax spread open her lips for Everest between his two fingers. "Does she taste good?" He asked Everest as he watched him lick her.

Everest moaned, "She always tastes fantastic." He lapped at her again, sticking his fingers inside her. When Everest pulled his tongue back a little, Pax flicked her clit with his fingers.

"Do you like him eating my pussy, baby?" Pax asked as he flicked her again.

She nodded. "I do," she moaned her response.

"Do you want him to fuck this ass again tonight?"

She nodded as she moved a little off Pax's lap so she could free his hardness from his underwear. "Let me suck you while he licks *your* pussy." Pax groaned as she took him into her mouth, her tongue flicking the end like he had done with his fingers to her sensitive bud.

"Holy shit, your mouth feels good wrapped around me." He looked at Everest, licking and sucking her clit. "Eat *my* pussy good, Ev. Her fucking mouth feels so good." Everest sped up his tongue and fingers, making Blu come undone all over him. He lapped her up like he was a starved man.

Everest pulled her to a sitting position, Pax's hardness popping out of her mouth. "Come here, sexy, lets give Pax a taste." Everest slipped on a condom and laid back on the couch, pulling Blu on top of him, onto her back. She spread her legs for Pax as he licked her all the way.

"Goddamn, she's good," he praised as he stuck his fingers inside her, coating them with her wetness. He pulled them out and circled her ass. Making sure she was well coated. He slid a finger inside as he lapped at her again. "This ass is tight, Ev. I see why you want to fuck it again," he smiled as he licked her again. His tongue flicked quickly on her bud, her hips rising to meet him. His finger moved in and out of her ass, stretching her for Everest.

"Can I have it now?" Everest asked as he moved under her.

Pax looked up to Blu, she nodded at him. Everest lifted her hips and positioned himself at her entrance. He slowly let her down, Pax still rubbed her bud with his fingers as he watched Everest's cock disappear inside her ass. Everest didn't move as Pax reached down and quickly flicked her clit with his tongue one time.

"Oh my God, she feels good," Everest praised as he moved inside of her. Blu moaned out as Pax inserted his fingers inside her, filling her holes again. His other hand stroked himself as he watched his friend fuck her ass. He got on his knees between their legs as he stroked himself. Blu watched him as she licked her lips.

Everest leaned her back so her pussy was fully exposed to Pax. His hips gyrated in and out of her. Pax leaned in, his hardness in his hand. "I am going to fuck *my* pussy, Blu." She nodded and he smiled. He leaned more and slid inside of her. She screamed out as Everest held her legs open so he could go all the way inside her ass, while Pax claimed her pussy again.

They both moved and she screamed out in ecstasy. "God… you both… I'm going to…"

"That's right baby, come all over me." Pax leaned forward to kiss her lips then her breast as she laid back onto Everest, his hand trailed down to her clit. He rubbed her while they both fucked her hard. "I love this pussy," Pax moaned as he came inside of her.

Everest quickly came, as well, followed by Blu. The three of them rode out their high as Blu collapsed back onto Everest. Pax pulled out first as he sat back on the couch. Everest kissed her shoulder from below her. "And I love that ass," he kissed her shoulder again.

He helped her to sit up as he pulled out of her. Pax grabbed onto her and pulled her onto his lap. He cradled her like a baby across his lap. "I can't let you go after this weekend," he mumbled into her hair as her body laid limp in his arms.

"I don't want you to," she replied quietly. She looked up at him, he gently kissed her lips.

Chapter 16

*E*verest didn't say a word. He heard them speak to each other and he wanted to say he wanted to keep her, too, but he didn't. He knew that he was walking a fine line with them. He knew that they had feelings for each other and that he was attracted to Blu, but he wasn't sure he would be able to commit to her. He knew that he would never promise to do that if he couldn't.

Everest had never wanted to commit to a woman before and he wasn't sure he could with her, either, no matter how badly he wanted her. It just wasn't what he had ever wanted. He loved being single and able to do whatever he wanted, whenever he wanted. He wasn't sure that, even as much as he enjoyed his time with Pax and Blu, that he could only be with them.

"I am taking her to bed," Pax told Everest as he cuddled her into his body. Everest stood and placed a blanket over her, Pax tucked it around her.

"Thank you, Everest." Everest leaned in and kissed her cheek.

"You're welcome, sweetheart," Everest watched as Pax carried Blu to his room. For the first time in his life, Everest thought he may want something more than the life he had been leading.

Pax pulled the covers back on his bed and laid Blu in his bed, covering her naked body with the blankets. He crawled in on the other side, pulling the covers over his naked body. Blu curled up against Pax, his arms around her and her head on his chest.

"Did you mean it?" She asked as he rubbed her back.

"Did I mean what?"

"That you don't want to let me go after this weekend."

"I did. I don't want this to be the only weekend that I spend with you," he whispered as he kissed the top of her head.

"Mmmm," she acknowledged that she heard him. She was just too tired to talk about it right now.

Pax kissed her head again. "Go to sleep, baby. We have all day tomorrow together, just us."

"Just us?"

"Yeah, baby, just us."

"Okay," she whispered before falling asleep in Pax's arms. Pax laid in his bed, holding her. When he started this whole thing with her, he had no plans on ever being with her more than just to play. He knew that Everest would like her and that he would be interested in making her a regular in their playtime.

They had not had that many women together. None like they have had Blu. Everest was always into the threesome scene more than Pax had been. He didn't mind watching and then being with the woman, but to have the same woman, at the same time, wasn't something he had ever been into before.

As he laid in bed, holding the woman that was quickly becoming his addiction, he couldn't help but wonder what the future would bring them. He knew that he wasn't ready to let her go, but he also knew that he was not the type of man that would be good at a relationship.

"I hope you will forgive me," he whispered into the room just before he fell asleep.

He woke up the next morning with Blu in the bed beside him. She was still asleep and she looked so beautiful. He couldn't help but stare at her, wondering how he was ever going to be able to let her go.

Pax went to shower and get dressed. He was going to fix breakfast for them this morning. He planned on spoiling her today before their weekend was over. He knew that she would need a good day when she thought back on their time together.

He was almost done cooking when Blu came into the kitchen.

"Good morning," she said as she sat at the bar. Pax turned to smile at her. His breath caught in his chest when he saw her. She had her overnight bag in her hand and laid it on the floor beside the island.

"Morning, why the bag?"

She smiled at him, but he could tell it wasn't a happy smile. "I'm going home," she took a drink of the water that he had put on the bar beside her plate.

"You're leaving? Now?"

She nodded. "I am."

Pax walked to stand in front of her, taking her face in his hands. "Why are you leaving?"

Blu smiled at him, trying not to let her emotions show. She was ready to cry and she was determined not to cry in front of him. She was not going to let him see how affected she was leaving him. "I have had a really good time with you this weekend. I never thought being with you would be like this. I…" she paused, willing the tears not to fall. "I can see why women want more than just one weekend with you, Pax."

"Blu," he wiped the tear that fell from her eye with his thumb.

"It's okay, Paxton. I knew what this was going into it, you don't have to worry about me. I will be fine, I promise."

Pax slid his hands around to the back of her neck and pulled her into a kiss. The sweetest, softest, and most incredible kiss that Blu experienced in her whole life. When he pulled back, he placed his forehead on hers. "You don't have to leave, we can spend all day together, just you and me."

She smiled at him, "That sounds like a lot of fun, Pax. But I should get ready for work tomorrow."

"I was hoping to spend tonight with you," he kissed her lips again, taking her bottom lip into his mouth, lightly sucking on it. "I don't want you to go."

Another tear fell from her eyes. She didn't want to go, either, but the more time she spent with him, the more she was going to feel for him. She was already on the verge of falling for him and she needed to distance herself.

Pax wiped the tears from her eyes and sweetly kissed her lips again. "Please, don't go. Stay with me tonight. Let me make love to you."

She took in a deep breath. That would have been exactly what she wanted to hear any other time. But that couldn't erase what she heard last night. When he thought she was sound asleep, he said, "I hope you can forgive me" She heard him.

"You are a really sweet man, Paxton Pascal. Don't let anyone ever tell you any different."

"Blu."

She stood and picked up her bag. "I will see you tomorrow at the office."

Pax reached out and grabbed onto her. He pulled her body into his. His lips crashed into hers, kissing her with everything he had. Every bit of emotion that he had ever felt, he put into that kiss. Everything he wanted to tell her but couldn't find the courage to say was in that one kiss. Every time he had imagined what it would be like to kiss her, to make love to her, to make her belong to him was in that kiss.

"I will see you tomorrow, okay?" She smiled at him as he held her in his arms.

"Don't leave," he begged. He had never begged a woman for anything. Not sex, not attention, and certainly not to spend time with him. But here he was, begging Blu Millar to stay with him. What he wasn't sure of was if he was asking her to stay for today or forever. He knew that until he knew what it was that he wanted from her, he would need to let her go.

"I have to," she hugged him to her. He kissed her neck as he held her tight.

"Okay," he reluctantly agreed. He knew it was for the best, even if he didn't want her to go.

He kissed her lips one more time before she pulled away and left through his front door. He stood, looking at the door, hoping she would come back inside. When she didn't, he picked up the pot that was still on the stove and slung it against the wall. "FUCK!!!!"

He walked to his liquor cabinet and poured himself a large glass of whiskey. He downed it and poured himself another one, gulping that one, too. After repeating that a few more times, he called Everest.

After three rings, he picked up. "Hey, asshole."

"I fucked up, Ev."

"Oh, shit. What did you do? Have you been drinking... at 9 am?"

"I'm fucking drinking now... I... She left."

"What do you mean, she left? You were supposed to spend the day with her, just you and her."

"I know. I fucked that up."

"What did you do?" Everest asked as he grabbed his keys. He knew that if Pax was already this drunk this time of the morning, he was going to need someone there.

"I fucked... it... up." He slurred his words, already drunk from the repeated shots of whiskey.

"You are an idiot, aren't you?"

"Why do you say that?" Paxton mumbled.

"You were supposed to spend the day with her and figure out that you were falling for her, you jackass. Just as much as she has fallen for you."

Pax thought about what Everest said. "I've fallen for her?"

"Do you go to sleep thinking about her?" Everest asked as he pulled out of his driveway.

"Yes."

"And wake up thinking about her?"

Pax nodded his head.

"Are you nodding your head?" He chuckled.

"Yes. I think about her all the time."

"Even once this weekend, have you thought about being with another woman?"

"Fuck no. I just wanted to be with her." Pax downed another shot.

"Are you miserable?"

"What kind of question is that? I'm drunk," he answered honestly.

"But are you miserable since she left?" Everest pulled into Pax's driveway.

Pax thought about his question for a minute. He was miserable. Watching her walk out of his house was hard for him. He had never missed a woman before and he was missing her.

Everest walked into the house. He walked over to Pax and took away the glass in his hand. "I think you have had enough."

Pax sat down on the couch, his head in his hands. "What am I going to do?"

"You are going to get your shit together and tell her how you feel."

"But I don't know what I'm feeling." Pax sat back on the couch, looking to his friend for answers.

"She's a great girl, Pax."

"I know."

"Then straighten up and get her back. I saw the way she looked at you this weekend. The girl is in love."

"I'm drunk, I can't go after her."

"She'll be in the office tomorrow, right?"

"She said she would." Pax smiled thinking about seeing her again.

"Then you'll talk to her tomorrow."

Pax looked at his friend. "What do I say?"

"You tell her that you want her. You tell her how you are feeling. You tell her anything you have to for her to forgive your dumb ass and give you another shot." Everest paused. "Because if you don't, I will."

"You are going to tell her I want her?"

Everest looked at his friend, for the first time he felt bad for Paxton. Paxton had feelings for only one other woman in his life. She was only after his money and what he could do for her. She stole from him, she cheated on him and she was a royal bitch. Everyone but Pax saw it. "No, Pax. I am going to tell her that I want her."

Chapter 17

As soon as Blu got into her car she called Zoe. After a few rings, she answered. "Blu? Are you okay?"

When she heard Zoe's voice, Blu lost it. She started to cry. "No… I… I think I love him, Zoe." She admitted for the very first time to anyone. Including herself.

"Where are you?" Zoe asked, now more awake.

"I'm on the way home," she wiped the tears from her eyes.

"Come here, you don't need to be alone."

Blu agreed to drive to Zoe's house instead. Once there, Zoe already had breakfast started. She hugged her friend as soon as Blu walked in the door. "What happened?"

Blu followed Zoe into the kitchen. She sat at the table with her head in her hands. "I don't know where to start."

"How about you start where you finally admitted that you are in love with Paxton and what he did to make you cry."

Blu started telling her about the night at the dance. How whiny woman hung all over him. She told her about what Everest told her about on the patio. Not leaving out any detail.

Zoe remained caring, even when Blu told her about what he did to her at the front door. She told her about the sex club and how she wanted to let him have all of her that night but couldn't in the room where she knew he had been with so many others.

Zoe reached out her hand to Blu. "Why didn't you tell me?"

"I was embarrassed."

"Of the sex club?"

Blu shook her head. "No, of loving a man that will only want me for sex."

Zoe reached out and pulled her in for a hug. Blu mumbled in her shoulder. "There's more."

Zoe let go and continued to listen. Blu took a deep breath and told her about staying at his house. About how she asked for it... for both of them. How good she felt when Everest pleased her and Pax watched. She told her friend how much she loved it when they both took her at the same time. Something she never imagined she would ever want.

She even told her about what he said last night and this morning. "Oh, Blu. He has feelings, too. Do you have feelings for Everest?"

Blu smiled, thinking about what she felt for Everest. "He's a sweet man and I would love to play with him more, he's sexy as hell and very good with his tongue," she giggled, "but I love Pax."

Zoe smiled at her friend, knowing she had been through a lot these last few weeks. "I say... it's time for a makeover. We need to show Pax what a hot and sexy girl you are. Make him beg you to stay."

Blu smiled at the thought. "Okay, let's do it." Zoe got on the phone and called her friend Mary. She was an excellent hairstylist and owed her a huge favor. Mary agreed to come over and work her magic on Blu. A few hours later Mary had come and gone. She deepened the red of Blu's hair and gave her a very layered cut. She kept the length and even showed her how to style it to get it to look like she did.

"Holy fuck!" Zoe said as she looked at the final product. "Now, I want to do you." They both laughed.

"Don't tell Pax that, he might agree." They laughed again.

Zoe grabbed her purse. "Now we go shopping."

Zoe and Blu went shopping for the perfect outfit. They found a couple they liked and Blu bought them all, but this one in particular, was what she was going to wear tomorrow. They found a short black skirt, a cream-colored silk blouse that had buttons to leave undone, and a black jacket to go over it with a button at the waist. She was ready for tomorrow.

They were back at Zoe's and were eating pizza when Blu's

phone pinged with a message. She picked it up and saw a message from an unknown number.

"Lunch tomorrow?"

"Who is this?"

"It's Ev. Have lunch with me tomorrow?"

"Everest?"

"Yes, sweetheart. It's me. I would like to take you to lunch tomorrow. Say yes."

Blu giggled at his message. Zoe looked at her, curious if it was Pax.

She shrugged her shoulders.

"Okay."

"Great. I will pick you up at the office. See you soon, beautiful."

Blu handed Zoe the phone and let her read it. "Do you have a picture of him?" Blu pulled up his Instagram and showed her a picture of him.

Zoe laughed as she stared at the picture. "You were with Paxton and this guy this weekend?"

"Yeah, why?"

"Good lord, girl. You hit the jackpot with these two. You sure you don't wanna keep them both?"

"What do you mean? Everest was just for fun."

"Maybe so, but he's also hot and clearly into you if he is asking you to lunch."

"I don't think it's like that."

Zoe wiggled her eyebrows at Blu. "He's going to want you after he sees the new you."

They spent the rest of the evening laughing and eating junk food. Blu stayed over at Zoe's house. She had her clothes for work tomorrow and she hadn't planned on being home this weekend anyway. She had a hard time falling asleep. She kept thinking about seeing Pax tomorrow and about her lunch with Everest.

She dreamed about Paxton and Everest. She knew she was in love with Paxton, but she was also very attracted to Everest. She got up and showered and did her hair the same as Mary showed her yesterday. She put on her short black skirt, her silk shirt and covered it with the black jacket. She headed out to work, her stomach in knots.

She stopped in Zoe's office like always. It was the first time Zoe didn't ask her if she was ready for hoe duty on a Monday morning. Zoe had to be in the office an hour earlier than Blu did, so she missed her this morning. "Damn girl, you are hot."

"I'm feeling a little nervous."

"Don't be nervous. If he doesn't see what he's giving up, then give Everest a chance. He seems to want one."

"I doubt that. I just hope today goes well."

Zoe got up and hugged Blu. She went to her desk and saw that Pax's door was closed. She was happy about that. She knew she would have to talk to him eventually, but she was hoping it would be later in the day.

She read her email and answered her phone as it rang. She worked on Pax's schedule and watched the clock. It was almost time for lunch when his door finally opened. "I need you to make copies of these and send them out as soon as possible," he said as he handed her a stack of papers.

Blu reached out to take the papers and set them on her desk. She noticed his eyes travel her body as she smiled up at him. She was not going to bring up the weekend if he didn't and it seemed like he was not going to. "Anything else, sir?" She asked, knowing what it did to him when she called him sir.

Pax ran his fingers through his hair and rubbed the back of his neck. "Can we talk?"

"I'm afraid that's going to have to wait," Everest walked in and kissed Blu on her cheek. "We are going to lunch."

Blu saw a look cross Pax's face. It looked to be a mixture of hurt, jealousy, and something she hadn't seen before. "You're early," she said as she smiled at Everest.

He chuckled, "What can I say? I was anxious to have you… I mean, take you to lunch."

"Is it warm outside?" She asked, trying to ignore his sexual innuendo.

"It is. I don't think you will need your jacket." Everest added, looking over her body. "You could probably get rid of a lot of those clothes."

Blu unbuttoned her jacket and took it off, tossing it on the desktop. She fluffed up her hair and smiled at Pax as he gave Everest a dirty look. "Is that all, sir?" His lips were parted as he stared at her chest. She made sure to wear her push up bra so that her cleavage would show in her silk blouse. It was cool in the office and she knew that her nipples would show through the shirt and Pax couldn't take his eyes off her.

She stepped closer to him, bringing his attention to her lips. "Is that all, sir? Can these copies wait until I get back?"

"Uh... yeah... they can wait," he stammered.

Everest interrupted the moment, "I'll wait for you in the lobby." Blu nodded at him.

"Let me just get my purse and I'll be right there." Everest smiled at her as he turned and walked down the hall.

Blu went to walk past Pax to grab her purse from the cabinet behind him when he grabbed her arm. "Don't go," he whispered into her neck. Her breath hitched at the feeling of his breath on her neck. She closed her eyes and took a deep breath.

The effect that he had on her body was beyond her control. No matter how much she tried to ignore his touch, how good his hands felt on her body, she couldn't. She wanted more.

"I can't cancel, Pax. It's only lunch." She felt him breathe out against her neck. His arm slipped around her waist as he kissed on her neck.

"Please, don't go," he whispered again. She dipped her head to the side, letting him kiss her neck again. She loved the feeling of his lips on her body. He pulled her body close to his, his tongue licked up her neck to her ear. "I don't... I can't lose you."

"It's only lunch, Paxton. I have to go or I'm going to be late getting back."

He growled in her ear as she pulled away from him. It was true, it was only lunch. She wasn't going to be with Everest like that. There was going to be no sex. She turned away from Pax, he grabbed her and pulled her back into him, her back against his chest. His hands rested on her stomach, pulling her hips into his. "You're not his, Blu." She closed her eyes for a second as he kissed her neck. "You're mine."

Pax let go of her and she walked out of the office. She found Everest at the elevators. He smiled at her as she walked up to him. "You okay?" He asked, concerned.

"I'm fine, thanks."

Everest took her hand in his and led her inside the elevator. He took her to the restaurant on the first floor of the building. It wasn't fancy but it was close and the food was good. "You sure? You look flushed."

They ordered their food and sat down at a table. "Can I ask you something, Ev?"

He smiled at her before answering, "Anything. I think after this past weekend, we are close enough to be honest with each other."

Blu's face turned a dark shade of red remembering their weekend together. The last time that she was with Pax was also with Everest. That night she thought she was happier than she had ever been. Pax carried her to bed and held her while she fell asleep. It was also the night that he told her he hoped she could forgive him.

"Yeah, I think we are."

He smirked at her as he took a bite of his food. "What do you want to know?"

"This past weekend was not at all what I expected."

"I hope it was better."

She took a drink of her tea and smiled at him. "It was so much better than I could have ever imagined."

Everest reached over and took her hand in his. "You love him, don't you?"

Blu took a deep breath and closed her eyes. She had just admitted that fact to herself and Zoe, she wasn't sure that she could tell him, too.

"Can I be honest with you?" He asked as he pulled his hand from hers. She nodded. "I have never wanted to be with a woman more than I wanted you this weekend." Blu smiled at him. "I would take you right now if you would let me."

"Ev," Blu blushed at his honesty.

"But…" his smile faded. "It would only be sex with me. I would be happy to fuck you every day for the rest of my life. I would even have feelings for you, I already do." He got up from his seat and took the seat beside Blu. He put his arm around her back. "But I would not commit to you, and only you. At least not anytime soon."

She laughed at his confession. "Are you saying you wouldn't be faithful to me, Ev?"

He chuckled. "I'm saying I would not agree to be with you and only you. I have no interest in it and to say I did would be a lie. But if I did, it would be with you."

Blu leaned over and put her head on Everest's shoulder. "Being with you this weekend was really good… and I would play with you again… but…"

"You love him." Blu didn't say anything, she couldn't. Everest pulled her closer to him and kissed the top of her head. "Just to let you know, when the two of you figure things out and he finally admits that he loves you as much as you love him, and you want to play…"

"You're our guy?"

"Yes. I will always push his buttons and ask for more with you. Even though I know there are things he would never give in and let me have." He kissed her head again. "And if you weren't in love with the asshole, I would take you home with me tonight and fuck you as I wanted to all weekend."

"You sure know how to sweet talk a woman, don't you?" They both laughed.

"That is sweet talking when you know what I can do with my tongue," he winked at her.

They finished their lunch and Everest walked her back up to her desk. "Thanks for lunch, Ev."

"Thank you for agreeing to go. I had to know how you felt about the asshole and see if I had a chance."

"You always have a chance," she winked at him. He leaned over and kissed her on the cheek and hugged her. He was pulling back when Pax's door opened. At lunch, Blu decided it was time to talk to Pax when she got back. She looked up, ready to talk to him when a woman walked out of his office, adjusting her clothes.

Chapter 18

The woman was tucking her shirt into her skirt as she walked out of Pax's door. She looked up and saw Everest and Blu watching her. She smiled at Everest as she spoke to him, "Hello Everest." She glanced back into Pax's door. "He's certainly in a mood today. Looks like he needs more fucking to feel better."

Pax appeared in the doorway. "I don't think anyone asked you, Laura."

Blu felt a tear ready to fall at seeing the woman coming from Pax's office. "I need to freshen up from lunch." She muttered as she turned to go to the bathroom.

Everest glared at Pax. "Really? You gonna fuck this hoe while Blu is at lunch?"

"Fuck her? I didn't fuck her."

Laura huffed. "I think it's broken, he wouldn't even try and I was completely naked when he came back."

Everest laughed, "I can assure you it isn't. I happen to know he fucked his girl all weekend."

Pax groaned, "I... wait, what? My girl?" He looked at Everest with hope in his eyes.

"If you go fix..." he pointed at Laura, "this shit before she smartens up, realizes it isn't you that she loves and leaves your stupid ass for good."

"She loves me? Fuck!"

Blu washed her face with cool water, trying to cover up that she cried again over Paxton Pascal. She was drying her face off when the bathroom door opened. She looked up to see Pax walk into the women's bathroom.

"You can't be in here, Pax."

"I own this company, I can go anywhere I want."

"This is the women's bathroom."

He pushed on the three-stall doors and they all opened, showing no one else was in there with them. "It's just you and I, Blu."

"Then I should leave so you can ask Laura to come in with you."

Blu was standing in front of the sink, looking at him in the mirror. He smiled at her as he walked up behind her. He placed each of his hands on the counter, pushing his body up against hers.

"What do you want, Pax?" She asked, aggravated that he was still having this effect on her.

He moved her hair from one side of her neck with his hand, brushing his fingers over her shoulder. "What do I want?"

"That's what I said, you can't hear now?"

"You, Blu. I want you."

"You sure have a funny way of showing it."

He kissed on her shoulder. "You are all that I want, Blu."

His hands moved to her stomach, rubbing the silk fabric of her blouse. "I can't keep doing this."

"Doing what?" He kissed her neck, just under her ear.

"This back and forth stuff. My heart can't take it." She closed her eyes as his lips grazed her ear.

"There is no back and forth, I know what I want. I want you."

"What about her?"

Pax turned Blu around to face him. He lifted her to sit on the counter and stepped up in between her legs. "After you went to lunch with Everest, I left the office. I went to get something to eat. I was going to interrupt you and Everest, but I was too upset. I just ordered my food and took it back to my office." He held her face in his hands, holding her gaze with his. "I came back to my office to find her... half-naked. I didn't touch her, I swear."

"You didn't?"

He shook his head. "No, I want you."

He leaned forward. He pressed his lips to hers, his hands moved down her back, grabbing onto her hips. He pulled her into him, rubbing her back while he kissed her. Her hands ran up his arms and into his hair, tugging it lightly.

He pulled back from the kiss, leaving both of them breathless. "Do you love me, Blu?" He asked, his forehead resting on hers.

She shook her head, "No, I hate you."

He smiled at her, taking a deep breath in. He leaned in to kiss her again, whispering on her lips, "Good, I hate you, too."

His lips crashed into hers. Their kiss was hot and hard. His tongue didn't ask permission to enter her mouth, he took what he wanted. He knew she would gladly give it to him. His hands cupped her ass, her legs wrapped around him. He picked her up from the counter and walked out of the bathroom door. The bathroom was only a few doors down from his office and he was taking her there. He didn't care who saw them. He was claiming her and soon enough everyone would know it anyway.

He carried her down the hall, kissing her the whole time. Once he got to his office door he heard someone clear their throat. "About damn time."

Blu giggled against Pax's lips and he bit her bottom lip. "We'll see you later, Ev."

"Yeah, just remember when you want to play that I am the one that got you two together."

"Bye, Ev," Pax yelled out from his office as he slammed the door shut, locking it immediately.

They heard Everest yell from the other side of the door, "Tell her how you feel, asshole." Pax chuckled as he sat Blu onto her feet.

"Do you want to talk?" He asked as she backed up a step.

She shook her head.

"What do you want to do?" Pax asked as he stepped closer to her.

She smiled at him as she took another step back.

"Have you sent out those letters yet?"

"No."

Blu unbuttoned the first button of her blouse as she stepped back again.

Pax stepped forward until the backs of her legs were pinned up against his desk.

"Don't you think you should get back to work?"

She smirked at him. "I could… or I could do this." She teased, undoing another couple buttons on her shirt.

"Mmm," he moaned, unbuttoning his buttons.

She smiled at him as she dropped her blouse from her shoulders. His soon followed.

Blu reached down and unbuckled his belt, button, and zipper on his pants. He reached around behind her and unzipped her skirt. "You are the most beautiful woman I have ever seen." She smiled up at him as her bra fell to the floor. He took one of her bare breasts in his hand. "And these are fucking fantastic."

He pressed his lips to hers. Their tongues caressed and massaged each other as their breathing became erratic. "I need to tell you something before we do this."

Blu's eyes searched his for something, anything, to tell her what he was going to say. All she saw was love and desire. "Okay."

"I'm never going to be able to get enough of you. Even if I live to be 100, I will never get enough of you, of this." He pushed her skirt down her legs.

"Good." She kissed and nibbled on his neck, causing him to thrust his hips into her.

"I'll still want to play."

"With Everest and only Everest." It wasn't a question. It was her condition. She would never accept anyone else as a part of their relationship, male or female.

"No other women?"

"Not if you still want this pussy."

"You know I do. No other women, only Everest. But not all

the time. I am a greedy fucker and I want you to myself." He sucked on her neck. "Besides, I liked seeing him want what's mine and only be allowed to have a small taste."

"I can agree with that." Pax pushed his pants to the floor. Only their underwear between them.

"Are you going to continue to be my assistant?"

"Am I going to have to get rid of your weekly hookups anymore?"

"Never again."

"Then, yes, if you still want me."

"I do." He grabbed her underwear, ripping them from her body.

"Pax."

"What? They were in the way." He smiled as he slid two fingers inside of her, kissing her neck.

"Anything else?" He asked as he curled his fingers inside her, just like she liked.

"You are mine and only mine. I will not share you with any other woman, ever." She reminded him.

"Agreed, as you are mine, only allowed to play with Ev, when I am there."

"I can do that," she moaned as she sunk her fingernails into his back.

"You need to take the pill or the shot or something, I want all of you."

"Already taking the shot."

Pax swept his desk of everything on top. He lifted Blu and sat her on the edge, helping her to lay back. "I have wanted to fuck you on my desk for the last year."

Before she could answer, he slammed inside her, holding her thighs to keep her from sliding as he pounded into her, hard.

He leaned down, kissing her lips while he thrust in and out of her perfect body. Even though this was hard and fast, it meant more than any other time they had been together. He was claiming her as his own.

She was giving all of herself to him. It wasn't just sex this time. She scratched her fingernails down his back as she was getting close.

"I'm getting close, Pax. Please... don't stop."

He continued his movements, making her tighten around him. He could tell she was getting close to her release and he was happy about that because he was only seconds away from his own. "Come with me, baby."

She screamed out as her orgasm took over her entire body. Her whole body shook from the pleasure that Pax was giving her. Her legs wrapped tightly around his hips, her heels digging into his flesh. Pax sucked hard on her neck, leaving a mark for everyone to see. He wanted to claim her as his, he wanted no doubt as to who she belonged to.

He emptied into her as she tightened around him even more. He kissed her lips with a sweet kiss as they came down from their high together. While still inside her, he picked her up from the desk and carried her to the couch. He laid her on the sofa and laid down beside her. He pulled the new blanket from the back, since he threw the last one away, and covered them up.

"I need to get back to work." She mumbled as she cuddled into his chest.

"Not yet. The only thing you need to do right now is let me hold you."

She closed her eyes, his hand rubbing her back. He kissed the top of her head that was resting on his chest.

"Blu?"

"Yes?" She answered, her eyes still closed.

He took in a deep breath, "I love you."

Chapter 19

Blu opened her eyes. "What did you say?" She asked, hoping she heard what she thought she did.

"I love you."

"You love me?" She asked, unsure of what she heard.

He took her face in his hand, looked into her eyes, and said it one more time, "I love you, Blu Millar."

"I love you, too." He smiled at her as he crashed his lips onto hers. He rolled over onto her as he kissed her.

"Come home with me tonight?"

"I can't."

"Why not?" He asked nibbling on her neck.

"I need clothes for work tomorrow," she answered, wishing she could go home with him.

"I wouldn't mind if you worked naked." He chuckled into her ear.

"I need to get back to work now before my boss fires me."

He smiled at her. "I think he will forgive you, this time."

"He better, it's his fault that I'm late," she teased, kissing his neck.

"And the next round is going to be your fault if you keep kissing me like that."

He rolled back beside her, allowing her to get up and get dressed. He laid on the couch and watched her the whole time. Once she was dressed, she turned to find him watching her. "Perv."

"I can't help it that my girlfriend is so fucking sexy."

She stopped what she was doing. "Girlfriend?"

"What else would you be?"

"Um... I don't know."

"Exactly. Now get out there and keep everyone out so I can

get dressed because I need to get out of here on time tonight. I have to take my girlfriend to get clothes so she can stay with me tonight."

"I can't Paxton, I have to check on my house and the farm. I was gone all weekend."

He sat up on the couch, the blanket falling around his hips. She couldn't help but look at his chest.

"All weekend? You didn't go home yesterday?"

"No, I ended up staying at Zoe's."

He wrapped the blanket around his waist and came to stand in front of her. "I'm sorry, baby. Why did you leave yesterday?"

"I heard you."

"Heard me?"

"Yes, I heard you asking for forgiveness."

"Oh, baby. I am so sorry." He took her into his arms. "I was so scared. I was scared of loving you, scared of losing you, and just scared to tell you what I was feeling."

"And you aren't now?"

"I realized after a lot of whiskeys and a good ass-chewing from Everest, that if I didn't fight for you, I was going to lose you anyway. I couldn't let that happen. Everest told me yesterday that he was going tell you he wanted you if I didn't." He reached out to hold her in his arms. "And then he showed up here to take you to lunch. I was watching it happen right in front of me."

"I'm right here."

"Yes, you are and I'm more afraid of never holding you again than I am of telling you how much I love you."

"Well, that's good because I just about lost it when I saw that woman coming out of this office."

"I love jealous Blu."

"If that ever happens again you will see 'kick her ass' Blu."

"Mmm, that sounds hot."

"She'll be followed by 'kick YOUR ass' Blu."

"Mmm, I might like that, too."

Blu rolled her eyes, remembering what she saw in the club that night. "Yeah, you would." He chuckled.

"Get back to work, Blu. We will talk about what kind of things I might like later."

Blu laughed as she walked back out to her desk and took her seat. One of the women that worked on their floor walked by her desk and gave her a dirty look. She was too happy to be worried about that woman. She had a reputation for getting around the office and she was one woman that she knew Pax had never been with. She also knew that she would not be happy when she found out that Pax was taken. She had been working on him hard over the last year and Blu loved it that she never succeeded.

She sent Zoe a quick text to tell her that she had news. Her phone instantly rang. Blu answered, giggling like a schoolgirl. "I don't have long to talk, I have letters to get out and they have to go out today."

"Didn't he give them to you before lunch?"

"Yes, but I just now got back to my desk."

"OH… did you have some hot lunch date sex?" Zoe asked, excited for her friend.

"Not exactly."

"What happened?"

Blu told her about the woman coming out of his office and how he came into the women's bathroom and carried her to his office. She told her about the hot sex they had and…

Zoe squealed. "He told me he loved me." Blu laughed at her funny friend.

"And you?" She asked, hoping that she told him back.

"I love him, Zoe."

"Finally!"

"I have to go." Blu reminded her friend, looking at the stack of letters to go out.

"Okay, talk soon. Love you."

"Love you, too."

Blu jumped when Pax cleared his throat behind her. "And who is it that you are saying 'Love you' to on the phone, hmm?"

Blu turned to see him standing in his doorway. "Jealous much?"

Pax walked to stand beside her. He leaned down, his hands on the arms of her chair. "Who was on the phone?"

Blu smiled up at him. "It was Zoe."

He smiled at her as he leaned in closer to her face. "Okay."

"You were jealous, weren't you?"

"I can't say hearing you say 'love you' to someone else felt good."

She reached up and took his face into her hands. "I love you, Paxton Pascal."

Paxton started backing up, pulling her chair with him. She giggled as he got to his office door. "I love you and I would like to show you how much." He wiggled his eyebrows at her.

"You are such a perv."

He smiled at her. "You have no idea."

She wasn't sure if she should be scared or excited, but by how wet she just got, she was pretty sure excited was winning on this one.

The rest of the day went by fast. Everest texted her to find out how she was and what happened after he left. She gave him the clean version. He, of course, asked if he was still allowed to play with them. She told him he was, but not yet. She wanted some time with just her and Pax.

He said he understood and that whenever they were ready, just let him know and he would be there. She smiled at how sweet he was.

Pax didn't take Blu to his house that night. Instead, he stopped at his house, got an overnight bag, and went to her house for the night. He had never done that before. But he had not brought a woman to his house before, either. Not since her.

The rest of the week went well. Blu and Pax spent every

night together. They switched off between houses and each left some extra clothes at the other one's house.

Next week was a business retreat that most of the company was going to. Blu didn't go last year because she had just started working for Pax and he said it was okay if she stayed home. This year he told her she was needed and she had made arrangements at home for the farm to be looked after by the farm manager.

Zoe was over at Blu's house helping her pack for the retreat. "Are you nervous?" She asked as she picked out some sexy lingerie for Blu to take.

"Nervous? Why?" She picked up the sexy black nightie and held it up. "Why are you putting this in there?"

"Uh, your boyfriend is going with us. You think he won't be with you at night?"

It was true, Blu and Pax were both going but she had her own room. The reservations had been made months ago and everyone had their room assignments already. Blu and Zoe were sharing. "I'm in the room with you, Zoe."

Zoe put the nightie back in Blu's bag. "I wouldn't mind a room to myself."

Pax and Blu hadn't talked about staying together for this trip. They have been together every night since they said I love you, but they never talked about the trip arrangements.

"I don't think he's planning on me being with him every night."

"I am sure that he is. You've been together every night this week."

"Ever since that first day, we have kept things more professional at work. This is a work thing."

Zoe shrugged her shoulders. "Okay, but still take this, you know, in case."

Blu tossed the nightie in her bag, smiling at her best friend.

As they were finishing up Blu got a text.

"You coming over tonight, baby?"

She smiled at his text. She always loved hearing from him.

"Do you want me to?" She asked playfully.

"Is that even a question?"

She smiled again, knowing her answer before she even finished reading the first text. "Of course, baby. See you in a little while. Should I bring my suitcase for tomorrow or am I driving up with Zoe?"

"Bring it. Do you think I would let you drive up in any other car other than mine? Zoe can come with us."

Blu told Zoe what he said and she was happy that she didn't have to drive up on her own. "Told you. He isn't going to let you stay alone."

"I will tell Zoe we will pick her up in the morning. See you soon. Love you."

"Love you, too. Can't wait."

Blu put her suitcase in her car, said her goodbyes to Zoe, and drove over to Pax's house. He had dinner cooked and on the table when she got there. "Something smells good in here." She walked into the kitchen and saw Pax in only a pair of shorts, fixing their drinks. "And the chef is sexy as hell." She walked over to him and he took her in his arms. "Just don't tell my boyfriend I said so."

"You should see his girlfriend."

They ate dinner together and cleaned up together. It didn't matter what they did, it was always better when they did it together. Pax took her to bed that night and made love to her as he had done all week long. It wasn't the hot, hard kind of sex. It was slow and gentle. The kind that showed her how much she meant to him.

Making love with Pax was incredible and so was falling asleep in his arms. She wasn't sure how she would sleep if she wasn't with him this next week. She cuddled into his arms, her most favorite place to be, and closed her eyes.

"Baby?"

"Yeah," she whispered, almost asleep.

"Did Everest tell you that he was going to be there this week?"

Blu and Everest texted and talked on the phone over the last week but it wasn't a lot. He was busy with work and she was busy with work and being with Paxton. "He didn't."

"I know you are supposed to be with Zoe this week, but maybe... you could..."

She raised her head off his chest. "Are you asking me to stay the night with you?"

He shook his head no. "I'm asking you to stay the week with me... and Everest."

"The week, with you both?"

"Yes. I have a suite with two bedrooms and Everest is crashing in the second room. I... we... were hoping that we could talk you into staying with me, with us. You know... maybe..."

Blu laughed. "For someone so powerful, you sure do get tongue-tied."

"Oh, fuck it... Blu, Everest and I want you to stay with us and let us fuck the hell out of you this week."

Blu swallowed hard. "You want to play?"

He nodded. "Yes, we want to play."

"Same rules as before?"

"Yes. I don't want him kissing you and he cannot... well, you know."

"He can only fuck my ass?

"Fuck that dirty mouth of yours. I had almost forgotten how dirty it was this past week."

"Are you saying he wants to fuck my dirty mouth?"

"Holy shit, Blu. Would you want to do that?"

"You mean would I want to suck him off?"

"Yes."

"I don't know. Is that against the rules?"

"No. It isn't unless you don't want to do it, then it is. Anything you don't want to do or try is on the list."

"I hadn't thought about it, to be honest."

"I have two hard nos. No kissing on the lips and he cannot fuck *my* pussy. The rest we will have to see what we are comfortable with. So far everything has been okay, right?"

"Yeah, I don't want to do those things, either."

"Just remember, whatever you don't want to do, just say so. No one will ever try to make you do anything you don't want, okay? If we start something and you or I don't feel comfortable with it, we can stop."

"I know."

"That goes for toys, too, I will have some with me and there are some that he will bring, as well."

"Toys?"

"Yes, like you saw at the sex club."

"Oh, okay."

"So, is that a yes to staying with us?"

"If I said no, would you both want someone else?"

"No, he would just not stay with me. He would find someone else. No hard feelings if you say no, I promise. Either way, I want you to stay with me."

Blu nodded her head.

"This is going to be the best week ever. I love you so much."

"I love you, too."

Blu agreed, cuddling back into her place at his side, thinking about spending the entire week with Pax and Everest.

Chapter 20

The next morning Pax woke Blu by kissing on her neck and roaming his hands all over her body. She couldn't help but laugh thinking that this was probably the only time the whole week that she and Pax would make love, just the two of them and without toys. She showered and dressed for the several hours they would be in the car.

They picked Zoe and Owen up on the way. Blu didn't know that they were taking Owen, as well, but she was happy they were. Owen and Zoe seemed to be getting along and they had been out on a few dates. It turned out that Owen worked in the building with them and had asked about Zoe several times. That was the reason that Pax asked Zoe to come to the ball. Owen asked him to introduce them.

From what Zoe said, Owen was not into the playing that Pax and Everest liked. Zoe said she was happy about that because she didn't think that she could handle it.

"We're almost there," Pax announced as they turned off the main road.

"I'm glad. I'm tired of riding," Zoe always hated riding in cars, she said she didn't mind driving but she hated just sitting and riding.

"Have you girls been before?" Owen asked, taking Zoe's hand in his.

We both shook our heads no. "We have two virgins here, Owen."

Zoe coughed and laughed as she looked at Blu. "Yeah, right."

Pax chuckled, realizing that Blu told Zoe about their playtime. He smiled over at Blu, his eyes full of lust.

"You two are sharing a room, right?" Owen asked Zoe. Blu

saw her shake her head no and Owen smiled. "You're staying alone?" He asked Zoe, his face hopeful she was going to say yes.

She nodded, "Yeah, Blu is going to be staying with her boyfriend."

Owen looked between Blu and Pax and smiled. "I wasn't aware." He leaned in closer to Zoe as he whispered, "Care to have some company?" Blu knew that Zoe and Owen hadn't taken their relationship that far yet. It looked like it was going to be a good week for both of them.

They pulled into the resort and Pax and Owen got their bags out of the car. As Blu and Zoe were getting the things from the car seats, Blu felt a pair of hands on her hips, pulling her back into them. "Hello, beautiful." She stood, allowing her body to sink back into the strong arms.

"Hello, handsome." She felt his lips on her neck.

"Where's your asshole?" Blu laughed and Zoe looked up from the other side of the car.

"Holy hell, he's gorgeous." She accidentally let slip as she stared at Blu in the arms of the handsome Everest. Everest looked up, noticing Zoe for the first time. He smiled at her as he ran his hand up under Blu's shirt.

"Hello to you, too." Everest smiled at Zoe as he pushed his semi-hard erection into Blu.

"Zoe, this handsy fucker is Everest. Ev, this is my best friend Zoe." Zoe blushed at Everest's glance.

Owen quickly noticed her and went to her side. "Do you need any help, babe?"

Blu pushed back into Everest as she whispered to him, "Behave yourself, that's her boyfriend. "

He chuckled in her ear, "And they don't share?" He whispered back.

Blu shook her head no. "No, they don't. He doesn't know that we do, either."

"But she does?" He asked, intrigued.

Blu nodded. "She does, but she isn't interested."

"Too bad, I know someone that would love to play with them."

"You?" Blu asked him as he reached down, over her pants to rub between her legs.

"Not me, sweetheart. I've heard that I'll already be having what I want this week."

"Hands off my woman, Ev." Pax interrupted Everest's hands.

"Hey, asshole. I was wondering when you would ruin my fun." Everest teased back.

Everest backed off Blu and took one of the bags in his hand. "I've already checked us in. I'll help carry stuff up to our room," he winked at Blu.

Pax grabbed the rest of the bags. "I'll stay with Zoe until she gets everything to her room, then I'll be up," Blu told Pax as he grabbed the last bag.

Pax nodded. Everest handed her a key to their room, with the number on it. Pax leaned in and pressed his lips to hers. "See you soon, baby."

Zoe, Owen, and Blu went to check-in. It didn't take long. As soon as they heard they were with the Pascal party, the girl behind the desk sped up to get things done. She kept looking around the lobby as she finished up with Zoe. "Is he here?" She asked.

"Is who here?" Blu answered.

"Mr. Pascal. Everyone has been a buzz about him coming in today. All the girls have been fighting over who gets to check him in." She purred as she continued to look around the lobby.

Zoe looked at Blu and smiled. She knew that she was going to have some fun with this. "Can I get another key to my room? This one doesn't seem to be working." Blu dug out the key that Everest had given her to their room.

The woman behind the desk was quick to oblige, still looking for Pax. "Sure, ma'am, what room are you in?"

Blu placed the key to Pax's room on the counter, the girl's eyes getting big as soon as she saw the room number. She knew it was Pax's room. "If you could hurry, that would be appreciated. I left my boyfriends in our room and I can't get back in." Blu leaned in like she had a secret to tell her. "And they are both tied to the bed naked."

The woman's face turned into one of surprise and jealousy. "You are in his room?"

Blu nodded. "I am and I'm sure he's getting cold, being naked and all."

The woman couldn't make another key any faster if she tried. Her face was red and she didn't look up at Blu again. She just slid the key across the counter, excused herself, and Blu and Zoe laughed.

"You are such a bitch," Zoe laughed.

"Only to women that think it's okay to talk about my man like that in front of me."

Owen chuckled. "Remind me to never cross this one." He pointed to Blu.

"Don't worry, Owen. I'm sure you won't be hitting on my boyfriend anytime soon."

He shook his head. "Nope, just your best friend," he teased, smiling at Zoe. She returned his smile with a blush to her cheeks.

Blu walked with Owen and Zoe to her room. She carried some of Zoe's things and set them on the extra bed. Owen placed his bags on the bed beside Zoe's stuff. Blu smiled at the two of them, she was glad that Zoe wouldn't be alone for the week.

"We'll see you guys for dinner, right?" Blu asked as she was getting ready to leave.

Zoe looked to Owen and he nodded. "Yeah, I think we can do that." Zoe agreed.

"Okay then, I am going to get up to my room. I need to make sure the two of them didn't lose something of mine."

Blu left Zoe and Owen in their room and headed upstairs to her room. She used the new key and opened the door, laughing to herself as she walked inside. As soon as she walked in, she saw how big the room was. There was a huge living area with several doors off in different directions. She walked over to the balcony and looked out over the mountains. It was beautiful.

She felt large hands on her sides, sliding around to her breasts. "Oh, Ev, you know we shouldn't do this without Pax." She giggled as Pax groaned.

"You better be glad I love you so much, tease." Pax kissed on her neck, his hands kneading her breasts.

Blu turned around to face Pax, his arms around her back. "Yeah, well, I love you, too." Pax leaned in to kiss her, his tongue caressing hers with gentle strokes.

Blu moaned into the kiss as Pax backed them up until the backs of his legs hit the couch. He sat down, bringing her with him so she straddled his lap. His hands still under her shirt, unfastening her bra. One hand found a bare breast as the other pulled her hips into his, grinding himself into her.

Pax's mouth and teeth digging into her neck as both hands pulled her hips into his hardness. Two other hands came over her shoulders, down into her tank top, taking a breast in each hand. "Fuck, you are sexy when you ride my best friend," Everest moaned into the other side of her neck.

Blu leaned her head back, enjoying their touch, knowing they had to stop soon to make it to dinner. "We have to stop." She moaned out, not wanting to leave the room.

"Why?" Pax asked as he bit her neck.

"I promised to have dinner with Zoe and Owen."

"Ugh..." Everest groaned in her hair. He let go of her breasts and took a step back. Blu stood up in front of Pax. He spun her around and sat her back on his lap, her ass grinding into his hard member.

"Holy fuck, this feels good," Pax moaned as he worked her hips into himself. Everest stepped closer, holding her face in his hands.

"You are beautiful, isn't she, Pax?" Everest looked over her shoulder to his best friend.

Pax continued to rock her hips into himself as he answered,

"Incredible," he moaned, "Wait until you see those beautiful lips wrapped around your hard cock."

Everest smiled as he ran his thumb over her lips. "Am I going to see these lips around my cock, Blu?" Blu didn't answer him right away. She waited for Pax to tell her it was okay.

"It's okay, baby. You can tell him what he's missing seeing his cock going in and out of that perfect mouth."

"Am I going to get to fuck that beautiful mouth, Blu?"

Blu still didn't answer. Instead, she ran her hand over his pants, feeling how hard he was for her. She licked her lips, bringing the bottom one in between her teeth.

Everest looked down at her rubbing him through his jeans, a smile on his face. "I know what position I want tonight, what about you Pax?"

"Hell yes, I want it just like this." He ground his hard cock into her soaking wet center.

"Sounds perfect to me." Everest agreed as he stepped back. "But I am going to have to stop, for now. If not, she is going to have to give me that mouth now."

Blu leaned back into Pax's chest. His hands held her body close to his. "I love you."

"I love you, too, and I am going to go take a shower and get ready for dinner." She stood and walked towards the bathroom.

Pax yelled after her. "Wear a skirt tonight…" she smiled and nodded. "And no panties."

Chapter 21

*B*lu was almost done with her shower when Pax joined her. "Hi baby, I'm almost done."

"Good. I was hoping you would be."

"Why is that?" She asked as she finished rinsing her body.

"Because I'm trying not to take you before dinner."

Blu wrapped her arms around Pax's wet torso. "I'm so happy to be here with you this week."

"I'm so happy to have you with me this week. I know that Everest is, too." He smirked at her.

"Are you sure about this?"

"About what, baby?" He asked as he kissed her head.

"About what he wants to do tonight?"

He pulled back a little so he could look at her. "Are you having doubts?"

She shook her head no. "No, I just want to make sure that anything that happens doesn't affect us. I don't want to lose you, Pax."

"I'm not going anywhere. If things ever go too far or make me uncomfortable, I will speak up, okay?"

"Okay."

"I want you to do the same. If you ever feel like there is something you don't want to do, tell me or us. I want you to be comfortable, too." She nodded. "I love it that you are willing to experiment with this."

"I never thought I would."

"What changed your mind?" He asked curiously as to what made her decide that she would play with them.

"Because I love you and I know you like it."

"I do, but I love you more."

"I don't guess it hurts that Everest is hot, too." She laughed.

"He is, is he?" She nodded.

"He is." She smiled up at him, "But he isn't the one I love."

"I'm going to tell him you said that."

She laid her head on his chest. "If I ever don't want to do something, I will tell you, okay?"

"Okay. We have to be honest with each other. I know Everest and he will do anything we let him. We have to set the rules for what we can accept and what we can't."

"Like no other women?" He chuckled.

"You don't want to watch me lick another woman's pussy?"

She raised back from his chest. "No."

"Good, because I don't want another woman."

"Are you sure? Isn't it wrong for Everest to play with us and I don't want another woman around you?"

"The way I look at it is, I like watching him please you. I like watching you come with him. It is as much to please me as it is you. Watching him make you come makes me so fucking hard." He paused, kissing her head. "And I trust him. I know he would never do more than we let him do. He may ask for more, but he will never try to come in between us." Pax pulled her back to his chest. "I'm not jealous of watching him with you, but there are certain things I don't want him to do with you and he respects those things as off-limits. It isn't just about having another person with us to have one. I trust him, I trust you and I like how he pleases you. If having another woman with us wouldn't turn you on, then I don't want it. I don't need that, I only need you and need you happy."

"The thought of me giving him oral doesn't bother you?"

"Would it turn you on to do that to him?"

"Probably." She answered honestly.

"Then no, it won't. As long as I get to fuck you while you do it, I'm good with that."

"I wouldn't like seeing you with another woman."

"I'm glad. I have all that I can handle right here," he teased as he grabbed her ass.

"You know I would never be with him without you there, right?"

"I know. I trust you."

"I'm getting dressed now." She said as she stepped out of the shower to dry off.

"Do you have a skirt for tonight?"

She nodded. "I do."

He smiled. "Wear it."

"Okay," she smiled as she was stepping out of the shower, onto the rug.

"And, I meant it when I said no panties."

"Why no panties?"

"You'll see," he winked at her.

She dried off while he finished his shower. She dressed in her black skirt and as he requested, no panties.

They were both dressed and waiting in the living room area for Everest. He came out shortly after they did. "We all ready?" Everest asked as he eyed Blu's body.

"I am," she nodded. Pax stepped in front of her and placed his hand under her skirt. He rubbed between her legs and felt there were no panties.

"Yep, she's ready." She playfully smacked him as both men laughed.

As they were walking out of the door and into the hallway, Blu asked, "Baby? Why no panties?"

Everest looked at her and smiled. "Because at least one of us is going to fuck you with our fingers at dinner tonight."

Blu swallowed thinking about one of them having their fingers inside of her while they were at the table eating dinner. "You are going to what?" She asked as they got into the elevator.

Pax stepped up behind her, his hands on her hips. He whispered in her ear, "One of us, or maybe both of us," he shrugged his shoulders, "Is going to make you come at dinner with their fingers."

"Do you think anyone would notice if I went under the table and licked her until she came?" Everest asked, smiling at her.

"They might," Pax laughed. He pulled Blu back into his body, "Can you be quiet when you come, Blu?"

"I... don't know..." she answered as she swallowed the lump in her throat.

"This is going to be an interesting dinner," Everest chuckled.

The dining room was large and had at least fifty round tables. Blu recognized a few people that she knew from the office. Everest placed his hand on the small of her back to lead her to their table. Pax was busy answering questions from someone that worked for him as they walked. "This way, sweetheart."

She was glad that Everest was there to help her while Pax was busy with work. Everest led her to a table in the corner of the large room. Zoe and Owen were already seated at the table with another couple. Everest pulled out a seat for Blu that was completely in the corner, facing out to see the whole room. He took one of the seats beside her, leaving the one on her other side for Paxton.

They had lost contact with him during the walk to their table. She looked around the room but was unable to find him. "Don't worry, sweetheart. He's just talking business. He will be with us soon."

Blu tried not to be jealous, but it was impossible when it came to Paxton. He was the type of man that every woman noticed when he walked into a room. She knew that he hadn't been the type of man to hook up with his employees, but she also knew there were a lot of the women in the office that tried to get him more than once. She had also heard a few of them talking about trying to get with him during this week.

A few minutes of searching and she found him. Five or six women were standing around him, laughing at everything he said. She knew what they were doing and she also knew she would kick every one of their asses if they tried anything with him. They had not been flaunting their relationship around the office and it had been her idea not to. She didn't want people thinking she was sleeping with the boss to get ahead, but now she was wishing they were public. Maybe she would talk to him about that this week.

He looked over to their table and saw her watching him. He smiled at her, thinking about the comments she made to him earlier about not wanting to see him with another woman. He wasn't with any of these women, never had been and never would be. He had the woman that he wanted and had wanted since he laid eyes on her a year ago. He knew for a long time that he was in love with her, but he had been too scared to say anything about it. But that had all changed. She was his now and he wouldn't let any of these women mess that up.

He smiled at her and blew her a kiss. One of the women saw him do it and looked over to where he was looking. She looked down, smiling as she had just won the lottery. Everest saw what happened and he nuzzled his face into her neck. "Are you jealous of those women, Blu?"

She pulled her head up to see Everest looking at her, concern in his eyes. "I don't like seeing them all over him like that." It was true. She was jealous and she didn't like them being too close to him. She loved him and it was the time that they all knew it.

"You know he doesn't want any of them, right?" He asked as he made her look at him. "He loves you and has for a very long time. He only tried to ignore it by hooking up with random women. Now that he has you, he would not do that."

"I know." She believed Everest. She knew Pax was honest with her and she would have to trust him, but it didn't mean that she would have to like those women touching him.

"Do you want him to come back over here?" He asked, smiling at her with a mischievous glimmer in his eyes.

"And how do you think that is going to happen?" She asked as she watched another woman try to touch his arm.

"Oh, little one, you have no faith in how jealous of a man he can be."

"Jealous? I don't see him being jealous when he lets you... us... well, you know."

Everest nuzzled into Blu's neck, kissing and licking her skin. His hand pulled down the side of her blouse, leaving another area for him to kiss. "Ev, enough."

Everest chuckled as he whispered to Blu. "Told you. He's even more jealous over you than you are of him."

Pax took his seat beside Blu, grabbing her hand under the table. "What was that?" He whispered.

"He was just telling me how jealous my boyfriend could be."

Pax looked over to Everest. "Oh, was he?"

"He said you were even more jealous than I am."

Pax leaned in closer to her ear so he could whisper, "I'm a greedy man, Blu. I want everyone in here to know that you are mine, not his."

"I want that, too. I don't like seeing those women hanging all over you. I've already had to deal with the hotel clerk talking about fucking you."

"Then we need to do something about that." He took her face into his hands and kissed her. His tongue darting into her mouth to find hers. "Not one of those women could ever compare to you, no matter how much they tried. I love you, Blu. I want you for as long as you will have me."

"What if I want that to be a very long time?"

"I hope you do because that's what I want."

Blu smiled at him, holding his hand under the table tighter. "No more hiding us?"

"No more hiding us." He chuckled. "I'm so glad I can kiss you any damn time I want." He leaned in and kissed her again, short and sweet.

"Better?" Everest asked as he reached over and took her other hand in his.

She nodded as Pax kissed her on the cheek. Dinner was being

served and she had to let go of their hands to eat. After Pax cut up his food and he could eat with one hand, she felt him place his hand on her thigh. Her breath hitched as she felt his skin on her leg. His breath on her cheek. "I think it's my turn to please you, baby."

She coughed as he ran his hand up her inner thigh and dipped into her wetness. She grabbed her drink so she could try to cool down. She knew he had warned her that this was going to happen, but she had almost forgotten about it. She felt Everest's hand on her other thigh, pulling her leg over to him, giving Pax better access. His hand continued to trace circles on her inner thigh as Pax's fingers found her swollen clit.

Pax leaned in to talk to her. "You're always so wet for me, baby." She nodded, trying not to moan as he slipped his finger down further. "I can't wait for him to eat this pussy so I can fuck it."

"Pax..." she moaned as quiet as she could.

"Do you know how hard you make me, thinking about sinking into you while you suck on my friend?"

She shook her head.

"No?" He chuckled as he slipped his finger inside her. "I think you do."

Blu tried to hold herself together. She thought she was doing a good job until she felt Everest's fingers joining Pax's in pleasing her.

"Are you okay, Blu?" Owen asked as she took another drink of her tea.

"I'm fine, thanks." The boys chuckled to themselves as they stopped moving their fingers, allowing her to answer Owen.

Pax removed his fingers, wiping them on his pants. Everest removed his fingers, as well, after one last flick to her clit. "I think it's time to head back to our rooms," he suggested, hoping that others would want to leave, too.

Someone from the other couple that Blu didn't know said, "But you haven't had dessert yet."

Pax chuckled. "We have dessert back in our room."

"I bet you do," Zoe laughed as Pax, Everest and Blu excused themselves from the table. As soon as Pax had Blu standing in front of her, he took her into his arms and kissed her, in front of everyone. He took her by the hand and led her out of the room, Everest right behind them.

"Come on, love. We need you."

Chapter 22

Pax held Blu's hand as they walked to their room. Pax pushed her up against the wall beside the door and kissed her hard. He couldn't wait any longer for his lips to be on hers. Their kiss was hard and passionate. Blu bit Pax's bottom lip as he pushed his erection into her. "Unlock the fucking door before I fuck her in the hall," Pax ordered Everest. Everest worked the key, but the door wouldn't unlock. Blu giggled as he fumbled.

"I can't concentrate on the damn lock when you two are pawing at each other like that," Everest growled as he tried again.

"Concentrate? It's a fucking key." Pax growled back.

Blu pulled away from Pax. She reached out and took the card from Everest and turned to face the door. Pax groaned behind her. "God damn, open the door." She swiped the card and the light turned green. Pax pressed his body against her back as he turned the knob and pushed the door open. "Inside, now," he barked.

Everest chuckled at how desperate Pax sounded as he opened the door. As soon as they were inside, Pax had Blu in his arms again, kissing her lips like he couldn't breathe without her. Everest locked the door after he slammed it shut.

Pax's hands pulled her shirt over her head, only removing his lips long enough for her shirt and his to be removed. Everest threw his shirt off, unfastened her bra from behind her, and pushed her skirt down her body as Pax continued to kiss her.

Everest unfastened his jeans and pushed them down, leaving him in only his underwear. He kissed her back as he ran his hands around her waist and down between her legs. His finger slipped inside her wet slit, finding the pink pearl he was searching for. She moaned into Pax's mouth. Pax sucked her lip into his mouth in response. "You like that baby? You like him playing with *my* pussy?"

"Yes, I like it." Everest rubbed his erection against her ass, letting her feel how hard he was for her. Pax pulled back from her enough to push his pants down to the floor. He kissed his way up her leg as Everest worked her body with his fingers. Everest spread her apart with his fingers as Pax got closer to her center. He ran his tongue up through her slit, tasting what they had caused earlier while at dinner.

"Always so fucking good." Pax moaned his approval into her center. He slid a finger inside of her as he continued to lap her juices. Everest kept her spread open for him to gain better access while she was standing.

"I want to taste her," Everest said as he pushed into her again.

"What do you say, baby? Can Everest have a taste of *my* perfect pussy?"

Blu nodded, wanting Everest to do it, too.

Pax stood up and led her to the couch. He sat down and stood Blu around to face away from him. He pulled her back and helped her to sit down. She sat on his lap, his erection pressing into her back. "Is this okay?"

Pax kissed on her neck. "It's perfect, baby." She leaned back on Pax's chest, his hands fondling her breasts and erect nipples. He kissed on her neck as Everest got down on the floor in front of them. He took each of her legs and placed them over Pax's legs. Pax spread his further, holding hers open for Everest. Everest ran his hands up her inner thighs as he kissed up one of them. Once at her center he spread her open for him, sliding two fingers inside her. He flicked his tongue out to dart against her clit.

She moaned as she raised her hips, meeting his tongue. "Oh yes... Oh... that... shit..."

Everest worked her body into a frenzy as Pax kissed her

neck, biting at her skin. "Make her come, Ev. Make my girl scream."

Everest sped up his fingers and sucked her pink pearl into his mouth. Her hips lifted as she tried to make the feeling last. He slid his fingers almost out before he pushed them back inside. Pax's hands were on her thighs, holding her legs from closing in on Everest's body. She wiggled on top of Pax's lap as Everest made her come into his mouth. "Fuck that's hot." He said as he sucked on her again, making sure to get her through her whole orgasm. Her legs trembled from the strong orgasm that she had. She tried to put her legs together, but she couldn't, they were still being held by Pax. He pulled his erection from his underwear and stroked it a few times, letting her watch. "Do you like watching me stroke my hard cock?" She didn't reply. "I think you do, I noticed you that first night watching me." She nodded.

Everest stood in front of them, his erection in his hand. "Can you stand?" She nodded again as she started to stand up. "Not all the way, just enough to let Pax inside."

She stopped and let Pax remove himself from his shorts. He lined up with her entrance and helped her to sit back down, taking all of him inside. She moaned as he filled her. Everest stroked himself a few times as Pax helped her to move on him. He thrust up from underneath her, making sure he hit bottom every time. She rolled her hips as Pax moved in and out of her. "That's right, sweetheart. Ride that cock." Everest stroked himself with one hand and reached down to flick her clit with the other. As he leaned closer, Blu stuck out her tongue and licked his tip. He sucked in a deep breath, "Holy fucking shit, that tongue."

"What? Blu, did you lick him?" She looked back over her shoulder to Pax and smiled.

"I did."

"Fuck." Pax leaned over to the side a little bit and Everest stepped over to the same side. He knew what Pax wanted. He didn't just want to know that she was sucking on Everest, he wanted to see it.

Pax continued to help her move her hips, filling herself up with him every time. Pax could see Everest close to her lips. She hesitated. "It's okay, baby. You don't have to."

Everest looked down at her, his eyes filled with desire. His lips parted as he held himself in his hand, stroking slowly. "You don't have to, I can just…" Before he could finish his sentence, Blu leaned forward and took the end of his erection into her mouth. Her hand replaced his on his shaft as she stroked him. For a second, Pax stopped moving her hips. His lips parted as he watched Everest take a hold of her hair in his hands, helping her to take him in. "You were right, Pax. Those lips look incredible wrapped around my hard cock."

"Shit…" Pax moaned as he watched her take more of him into her mouth. "Suck it, baby. Suck it like you suck mine. You will have him coming in no time." Pax started to move her hips again, slowly, allowing her to get her rhythm with Everest. As she sped up her lips, her stroking and her suction, Pax thrust into her hard from below. Pax watched as Everest disappeared into her mouth, Everest's eyes on what she was doing.

"Shit," Everest moaned out as he threw his head back, pulling her mouth down on him further.

"Take it all, baby. I know you can." Pax's hand came around to rub her center, helping her to find her release as she was giving Everest his. "Suck it hard, baby. Make him come so I can fuck you."

"I am going to… shit…" Everest quickly pulled out of her mouth, stroked himself a few quick times until his orgasm took over his body, shooting it into the shirt that was lying on the couch. "Holy fuck, she's good at that."

Pax smiled as he raised her, only to slam her back down on him again. "I know."

He thrust into her a few more times until she came undone on top of him, his release coming quickly after hers. She collapsed back onto his chest, both of them breathing heavily. Pax helped her to raise off him and to sit beside him on the couch. He stood up, picked her up, and took her to his room. After a few minutes, she got up and went to the bathroom. She ran a hot tub of water and climbed inside. A few minutes later, Pax joined her and asked, "Can I get in with you?" She nodded and leaned forward. He stepped in behind her and held her body to his.

Pax enjoyed playing. He always had. When Everest first suggested that they try it one night, he thought that he was kidding. He had never done that before and he discovered he liked it. He trusted Everest and knew that he wasn't the type of guy that would ever hold anything against him. He wouldn't be jealous of Pax and they worked out a way to share a woman that worked for them.

Until that first time with Everest, Pax had never done it before. He was perfectly content being with a woman, just the two of them with no other influence in their relationship. Pax figured out that if he was able to share a woman with Everest, he didn't catch feelings for any of them. The trouble with that was that he fell in love with Blu well before he ever kissed her lips.

He once thought that he had found the woman that he could spend the rest of his life with. She turned out to be only using him and cheated. It was after her that he decided to try Everest's way of life for a while. It was easier that way. None of the women he was with expected a ring, even though they would call and harass Blu at the office to set up another hookup.

He never thought that Blu would ever be interested in playing like they did tonight. He wasn't sure she was into it as much as she let on, but that she was doing it because she thought that he wanted her to. He was happy that she was willing to do this to please him and this week was going to be good. He was going to enjoy it and he was going to let her explore Everest as much as she wanted, as long as Everest didn't kiss her or try to stick his dick inside her.

He also knew that after this week was over, he wasn't going to ask her to play anymore. Not that he wouldn't do it if she wanted to, but he loved that she was jealous of him. It was true, he didn't want another woman with them. After this week, he didn't want anyone with them.

He had already told Everest to make this week count because he was going to tell her soon. He knew that her family farm meant a lot to her and he had enjoyed the times he spent there with her. The house needed a little work done to it and he was going to find a contractor to do the repairs when they got home. Not because he needed to do it, but because he wanted to. He knew she would never ask him for such a thing and that made him want to do it even more.

He also told Everest that he thought he was going to sell his house. He liked his house, but he didn't love it, not as Blu did hers. He had planned to ask her to move in with him before they went home. He also knew that he was going to be asking her to marry him soon after that. They hadn't been together very long as a couple, but he didn't care. He had loved her for so long, it didn't matter how long they had been together. He knew she was the one for him and that he wanted her forever.

He just hoped that she felt the same way.

"Baby?" He whispered to her as he washed her in the warm bath.

"Yeah?" She answered quietly.

"More than anything else in this whole world, I love you."

Chapter 23

*P*ax and Blu were in the bathtub together and he had just told her he loved her more than anything in the whole world. She felt the same way. She loved playing with Everest when they did it, but she could do without it. She wasn't sure if Pax could, though.

She knew going into this relationship that he liked this lifestyle and she was willing to give it a chance. She just didn't know if she could continue it for a long time. Everest was sexy and he was a wizard with his tongue, but she loved Pax. She wanted to spend as long as she could with him. Even if that meant that her sex life would include Everest at times.

She was excited to spend this week with Pax, and she was happy that Everest was there, as well. She was attracted to Everest, but she didn't love him. She could have been just as happy to spend the whole week with just her and Pax.

"I love you, Pax, so much." She wrapped his arms around her body. They finished their bath, brushed their teeth, and headed to bed. Pax wrapped his arms around Blu, keeping her close to him. It was true, he loved her more than anything else in his life. He would give up just about anything to be with her.

He kissed her head and held her until they both fell asleep. The next morning, he woke up to an empty bed. He rolled over to look at the clock and saw that it was almost 7:00 AM. He laid back on his back, looking up to the ceiling, thinking about the night before. He smiled, thinking about Owen noticing that Blu was flush at the table while he was pleasuring her under it. Thinking of their night together certainly wasn't helping the issue he always had when he woke up in the mornings. He grabbed a pair of underwear, pulled them up, and went searching for Blu.

He heard some chatter when he got to the living area. It was coming from the small kitchenette that was off the living room. He smiled, hearing Blu and Everest talking. He stopped to listen to them talking.

Blu giggled as Everest whispered to her. Pax strained to hear what he was saying. "You are incredible, Blu. You know he will."

He will? Who will what?

"I don't know. What if I lose him? I don't want to lose him, Ev." He smiled at Blu's confession. She was telling Everest she didn't want to lose him.

"He loves you, Blu. You won't lose him. Just tell him."

Pax heard Blu sniffle. Was she crying? What happened to make her cry? He wanted to go to her and hold her. He wanted to comfort her. This was new for him. He had never felt the urge to comfort a woman before.

Blu sniffled again, "I'll tell him. Maybe when we go back home." What was it that she could tell Everest and not him? Were they closer than he thought? He trusted Everest and he trusted Blu, but they were hiding something from him and he didn't like it.

"Just sit him down and tell him. I promise you he'll be okay with it."

"I hope so. I love him so much. If he left me, I would just have to quit my job. There is no way I could go back to getting rid of those women again. Not after this. I could never go back to what it was before."

Pax heard a chair move and someone walking. It sounded like Everest was comforting Blu. He was glad that he was there for her and she had someone to talk to, but he wanted that person to be him. He coughed so that they would know that he was coming into the room and when he came around the corner, he saw Blu sitting at the bar and Everest cooking.

Pax walked over beside Blu, he could see that she had tears in her eyes. She quickly tried to cover them up, but it was too late, Pax saw them. It hurt him to know that something was upsetting her to the point she was crying. And that it had something to do with him made it even worse.

He put his arms around her and leaned in to kiss her. "Good morning, beautiful."

She looked up to him, a smile on her face. He could see that she was worried about something, but he was going to let it go, for now. She would tell him when she was ready and he would be there for her. He already knew that. He couldn't think of anything that would make him bail on her.

He kissed her lips and she melted into him as she always did. He was never going to be able to get enough of her, he knew this. He wanted things with her that he had never wanted before. Never thought of before and would have said no to if anyone asked if he would have it.

"I love morning kisses," she said as he pulled back. He kissed her again because he loved them, too.

"What are we doing today?" Everest asked as they sat down to eat.

"We have some team-building exercises for today. I don't know which ones are first. We will be put into different groups and switch stations at lunchtime."

Blu looked at him. "So, it's possible that I won't be with either of you?"

Pax nodded. "It is, but I will insist one of us has you with them."

She looked down at her plate, nervous about being without them. "Okay."

They finished up and headed over to the pavilion to get started. Everest stayed with Blu while Pax helped get things set up. She knew with him being the CEO that he was going to have to put in time without her, but she missed him when he was working without her.

The groups were being called and she was not with Pax. She was, however, with Everest. She watched as Pax and his group went to the second station, her group stayed at the first. The instructor told them they would need a partner, Everest was hers. They were instructed they were going to be blindfolded and given a rope. She saw the smile on Everest's face. He leaned over to whisper to her, "I have these back in the room. Maybe we can try them out tonight." He chuckled at her blush.

They were paired with another couple and each of them had to put the blindfold on and had a part of the rope. They were supposed to hold the rope and listen to a fifth person tell them where to move so that they made a perfect square with the rope in their hands. Everest put on his blindfold and grabbed towards Blu. He grabbed her breast and she squealed. "That certainly didn't feel like my rope." He laughed, along with anyone that saw what he did.

"Everest, you handsy fucker." Being blindfolded made Blu forget for a second that there was a group of people around her until they laughed at her comment.

"Be glad I only grabbed a boob."

The instructor laughed as he walked around helping the groups with their task. When he got to Blu, he smiled, happy that she couldn't see how he was staring at her. "Very good… keep going." He got a little closer to her, close enough that she could feel his body against hers. "This doesn't look like your first time in a blindfold." Blu startled at how close he was and what he said to her. She stepped backward, falling to the ground.

She removed her blindfold and looked up, the instructor standing above her, a smile on his face. He held out his hand to help her up. She took it and stood in front of him. "Thank you," she mumbled, not wanting to cause a scene.

He smirked at her, "If you would like to have more work with the blindfold and ropes, I would be happy to stay after everyone is finished to help you."

Blu backed up from him. He was attractive, any woman could see that, but he was a little creepy. "Thanks for the offer, but I think I've got it."

His eyes traveled her body. "You've got it…"

Before they knew it, it was time for lunch. She was hoping to get to see Pax during lunch. Everest came up to her, putting his arm around her shoulders. She jumped as soon as he touched her. "Woah, what's wrong?" Everest was concerned about how she reacted.

"It's good. I'm just jumpy." Blu didn't want to make a big deal out of it and the session was almost over. She was sure that she could avoid him for the rest of the day. As they were finishing up, Moon was taking all the supplies from them. When he took the things from Blu, he grazed her hand with his, causing her to pull back quickly.

Everest was standing right beside her and he saw her reaction. "What the hell was that, Blu?"

"Nothing, just drop it, okay?" Everest put his arm around her, pulling her into his chest.

"Don't lie to me."

"Just drop it, okay. It's nothing, I promise."

"That wasn't nothing. You jerked your hand back when he touched you like he burned you."

"He was just making comments during the session that made me uncomfortable. It's nothing. I'm fine."

"If you were uncomfortable with what he was saying, that is not okay. What did he say?"

"He offered to help me after everyone else left."

"That isn't so bad. Is that all?" Everest asked as he kissed her head.

"He said I looked like I had been comfortable with a blindfold." Blu shivered at the thought of the way he looked at her body and how he touched her. "I didn't like the way he was staring at me or touching me."

Everest's body tensed. Blu wasn't his girl but while Pax was not there, he would treat her as if she was. He would look out for her like Pax would if he were here. "What did you tell him?"

"I told him that I was good and didn't need any help. We are going to lunch now and then to the other session. He will be gone."

"He won't. We keep the same instructor for the whole day. He will be with us again after lunch."

"I have to see him more today?" Everest nodded.

"Pax is not going to like this."

"I'm not going to like what?"

Chapter 24

"Nothing," Blu lied as she stepped away from Everest, letting Pax take her into his arms.

"Don't lie to me. I don't like being lied to." Pax stood back from her, his hands on her arms. The conversation he heard earlier playing in his mind.

"I don't mean to lie to you, but I don't want to make a big deal out of it. I just don't like our instructor." That was true, she didn't like him. She just did not want to tell him why.

"Why not?"

"For fuck's sake, tell him. Or I will," Everest huffed.

"He just makes me uncomfortable."

"How? What did he do?"

Everest chimed in. "He was making comments to her about being in the blindfold and how she looked like it wasn't her first time. He was staring at her body and touched her, asking her to stay after for private sessions."

"Touched you how?" Pax was pissed. Blu could see how mad he was getting.

"Just my hand but he creeps me out. I don't like him."

"Then you are coming with me. We will get the two of you in our group."

"We can't do that, Pax. We have already done this exercise. We have to move to the next one."

"Not with him, you aren't. That one is much more hands-on and he will not be touching you." Pax looked around where they were standing. "Where is he? We need to talk."

"Please don't make a scene. Please, Pax." She begged him to not make a scene about her.

Pax pulled her to him. "Fine, I won't… yet. But he is not

going to be hitting on my girl. End of story. I won't put up with that shit."

Blu laid her head on his chest as he rubbed her back. She loved how protective he was of her.

Everest chuckled, "You should know, I grabbed her boob." He laughed. "It was an accident, this time."

Blu laughed, "You're a handsy fucker."

Pax growled at Everest. "You are a handsy fucker when it comes to my girl."

Everest shrugged his shoulders. "What can I say? I like touching her body."

"Fucker," Pax kissed Blu's head.

They went to lunch, the three of them together. Pax held her hand the whole way to the cafeteria. He wanted to make sure that her instructor knew that she was his. Not only could he be a greedy man, but he was also a possessive man. Not to the point that he would limit what she did, he had proved that with sharing her with Everest. But he was possessive when it came to some random man hitting on her and making her uncomfortable. That shit wasn't going to go over well.

As they ate lunch she started to feel more at ease. She knew that she wasn't in danger, there were people everywhere, but that man made her skin crawl. She couldn't explain it, but he made her feel uneasy and unsafe.

The guys were talking when she blurted out, "It was my first time you know." Both guys looked at her and smiled.

"What was your first time?" Pax asked his hand on her thigh, rubbing circles.

"The blindfold. It was my first time wearing one."

"I told her I brought mine. I also have some rope," Everest smirked at her.

"Hmmm, would you want to wear another one?" Pax asked, his hand closer to her throbbing center.

"With you?" She smiled at Pax.

He glanced at Everest. "With us?"

Everest added, "Tonight."

"Will there be rope, too?"

"Fuck, she's got me hard already," Everest admitted as he adjusted himself in his pants.

"Yes, there will be, baby. If you want there to be."

"What do you plan on doing to me?" She asked, innocently.

"Holy shit, she's going to make me come in my fucking jeans." Everest chuckled.

"Easy, Ev." Pax laughed at how turned on his friend was getting by just talking about tying her up and blindfolding her.

They were talking about what they would be doing if she agreed when someone walked up to their table. "Can I talk to you?" She looked at Blu, "Alone."

Blu immediately recognized her. It was the woman from the office that she knew had been trying to get with Pax the whole last year. The one Blu was sure that he had never been with.

"We are having lunch. Can it wait?" He asked as he took another bite of his food.

"Pax," she insisted. Blu did not like her calling him Pax. She knew that other people in the office called him by his first name, but she did not like this woman doing it. "We need to talk about tonight."

"What about tonight?"

"Our dinner."

Blu could tell that she was making this up, she was in charge of his schedule, even here, and she knew that he was not having dinner with anyone tonight.

"We have things we need to talk about, in private." She stated, again, looking at Blu.

Paxton noticed her continuing to look at Blu and it was starting to piss him off. He looked at Blu and smiled before turning his attention back to the other woman. "You know Blu, right? My assistant?"

"Of course, we all know her." She frowned at Blu.

Everest mumbled, "Not like we do." He and Blu laughed.

"Do I have any dinner meetings tonight, Blu?"

"I haven't seen one on your schedule." She smiled at the woman.

"Good, then you are free and we can…"

"I'm sorry if I gave you the wrong impression." Blu paused for the woman to say her name since Blu did not know what it was.

"Missy. My name is Missy."

"Of course, it is," Everest let out a small laugh as Blu was staking her claim to Paxton. Pax just sat back and watched Blu take care of it. Truthfully, all he could think of right now was taking her back to their room and having his way with her. She was turning him on.

"I didn't mean to give you the wrong impression. While he does not have dinner reservations, he is most definitely not free. I'm afraid he will be tied up all evening."

Everest couldn't hold it in any longer. He did the whole fake cough, speaking thing. Cough, "tie you up," cough.

Blu saw Pax adjust himself out of the corner of her eye. She smirked at Missy as she continued. "He is not free tonight, or any other night for dinner with you. Or any other of the women in this damn company that thinks they have a chance with him."

"Excuse me, exactly who do you think you are? You are an assistant and you may know his schedule, but you don't control it."

Blu had just about had enough toying around with this skank that thought she was going to be having dinner with Paxton.

Missy looked at Paxton again. "I can come by your room if that is easier."

It was all Blu could do not to stand up and smack her. She knew that they had said last night that they were not going to hide their relationship anymore and this was as good of a time as any to make it clear to this woman exactly who Paxton Pascal belonged to.

"I get it, Missy." Blu looked at Pax for effect. "He's sexy as hell. Every woman in the office wants to be with him." Blu looked up and down her body. "You are nowhere near enough to satisfy him. And as far as coming by OUR room, I wouldn't advise it."

Missy looked between Pax and Blu when she said OUR room. "You have your assistant staying with you?"

"Not that it is any of your business, Missy," she spat her name, "but he has his girlfriend staying with him." She ran her hand down Pax's chest and stopped at his belt. "Isn't that right babe?" Blu batted her eyelashes at him and he just smiled at her.

"Do you even know how fucking hot you are?" Pax asked as he grabbed her hand from his pants.

"Fuck yeah, she does. Why do you think she does that shit? She knows what it causes," Everest answered.

"I love it when you claim me," Pax announced before he crashed his lips onto Blu's. His hands in her hair, holding her still while he devoured her lips.

Everest looked up to Missy. "You get used to it eventually. They can't seem to keep their hands off each other." Everest looked at his best friend kissing his woman. Pax's kiss moved to her neck as he bit and licked her sensitive flesh, causing her to moan slightly as he continued. "But you can't blame him. She is hot as hell and such a little tease." Everest smiled as he ran his hand over her breast, circling her hardened nipple with his finger. "Watching them makes a man want to fuck the hell out of her."

Everest ran his hand down between her legs, sliding up and down like he knew she liked. Biting his lip as he looked up at Missy, still standing there. He smiled widely at her as Blu moaned into Pax's neck. "I know I sure as hell do."

Missy stood there, her mouth open, as Pax kissed Blu with everything he had while Everest played between her legs. The three of them glad they were in the back corner of the room.

"I can't wait until you are tied down tonight. Ev is going to eat that pussy so good until you scream for my cock."

"Fuck yeah, I want to eat it now." They both mumbled into her neck. Blu opened her eyes to see Missy watching them. She winked at her as she said, "I told you, you couldn't handle him."

"Us baby... she can't handle us." Everest added.

The three of them laughed as Missy closed her mouth and stormed off. The boys pulled back from her, both of them hard and wanting to continue.

"I'm going to tie you up tonight," Pax stated.

"And I am going to eat that pussy so good that you are going to be begging to be fucked."

Blu reached both hands out, finding their growing bulges. She stroked them both through their pants as she whispered, "I can hardly wait."

Chapter 25

They finished up their lunch with smiles on their faces. Blu couldn't stop thinking about what tonight would be like with the both of them. After she finished eating, she excused herself to head to the bathroom before the next part of their day started.

"Can I talk to you?" Everest asked with a serious expression on his face.

"Sure, what is it?"

"Are the rules going to apply for the rest of the week?"

"What do you mean?" Pax asked, wondering what his friend was asking.

"I know that I'm limited in what I can do with her, and I know that you are all up in love, but…" Everest looked over to where Blu was walking to the bathroom.

"But what? What is it that you want, Ev?"

Everest smiled as he watched her turn the corner. "I want all of her."

Pax looked over to where Blu was. "Yeah, I get it. She's incredible."

"She is. I have never wanted a woman as much as I want her."

"I don't know, Ev. She isn't just sex for me, man. She's it. She is the one I want to stay."

"Fuck. I know that. That's why I never said anything before now."

"Why now?"

"Hearing about that ass hitting on her pissed me off. I wanted to kill him for touching her or even looking at her."

Pax chuckled. "Well, fuck man. You have feelings for my girl."

Everest shrugged his shoulders. "I think I do."

"I'm not giving her up, Ev. Ever. Not for you or anyone else."

Everest smiled at his friend. This was the first time he had ever heard him talk about a woman like this. It made him very happy for his friend, but he also was jealous that Pax had all of her. "I know. I wouldn't ask you to give up anything. Just..."

"You want to share her?"

"I want to be with her... too." He paused. "I want her to be mine, too, not just playing with her."

This was the first time that Pax had ever heard Everest want to be with someone for more than just a quick lay. Pax was happy that his friend had finally been able to develop feelings for a woman, but he wasn't sure he liked that it was Blu.

"I don't know man. Have you talked to Blu about it?"

"Talked to me about what, baby?" Blu asked as she sat back between the two men that she felt the most comfortable with.

"Nothing important," Everest offered, pleading with Pax not to tell her what they were talking about.

"Just talking about the last half of the day, baby," Pax lied.

Pax knew that he would have to talk to Blu about what Everest asked but he felt like he needed to figure out what his feelings on it were first. He knew that Blu would ask him what he thought about it and he needed an answer to that and right now, he didn't have one.

"Okay. I trust being with Everest. He will take care of me, won't you?" She looked at Everest and smiled. He took his hand and placed it on her cheek, smiling back at her.

"Like you were mine," Everest promised. He leaned in and kissed her cheek as she closed her eyes, enjoying his touch.

Pax watched as she leaned into Everest. He knew that she loved him, and he knew that Everest was developing feelings for Blu. What he didn't know is if he could share all of her with Everest, including her heart.

The rest of the day went by quickly. Pax made sure that Everest took care of Blu while they were separated, just like he knew that he would. Everest had told Pax that he was developing feelings for Blu and that he wanted to be with her. They had already shared so much of her, could he share the rest of her? He wasn't sure.

"Paxton, I need to talk to you," his thoughts were interrupted by Missy.

"Missy, what can I help you with?"

"Are you sleeping with that slutty girl?"

"Absolutely not!" He exclaimed.

Missy smiled, knowing that Blu had to be lying. "I knew you wouldn't sleep with your assistant."

"I think I'm confused." He looked at her, confusion in his eyes.

Missy ran her hand down Pax's chest. "I knew you couldn't possibly be sleeping with your assistant."

"Oh, now I see where the confusion lies. You asked if I was sleeping with a slut, and I'm not. However, I am sleeping with Blu, who is nowhere close to being a slut."

"But... She was letting that other man touch her at the same time as you were kissing her."

Just as he was about to answer, taking up for their relationship, another one of their colleagues yelled for Pax to come settle an argument. "Sorry, I need to take care of this," he answered as he walked away from Missy.

She knew something was going on and she was determined, more now than ever, to find out what it was.

Pax handled the issue with the other team and was just about to go and find Everest and Blu when he heard her laughing. He turned to see her and Everest walking towards him. He smiled as he watched them talking and laughing together. He knew they were becoming closer than they had before and he knew that was going to continue as they spent more time together this week.

As soon as Blu and Everest reached Pax, she jumped into his arms. "Hi, baby." She smiled before kissing him. He held her close to him, kissing her back with everything that he had in him.

"Hi, sexy." He lifted her, her legs going around his waist. When Pax pulled back, he saw Everest watching them. He saw the look in Everest's eyes. It was similar to the look that he had when he looked at her. It was then that he knew that Everest was falling for his girl.

"I'm ready to go back to the room," she whispered into Pax's ear. He smiled at her, pulling her body into his as he held her.

"Our girl is ready to go back to the room. What do you say, Ev?" Pax set her back on her feet, her body still pressed up against his.

Everest smiled when he heard Pax call her "our girl". That was the first time he had ever heard him say anything other than "my girl." He stepped up behind her, pressing his own body into hers.

Blu glanced around the woods to see if there was anyone else close by. Everyone else had already headed back to the resort, leaving the three of them alone in the wooded area.

She reached behind her and pulled Everest into her as she pulled Pax into her from the front. Pax's hands on her hips as he kissed her lips. Everest reached around her waist to get under her shirt. His hands found her breasts as he ground his erection into her from behind.

Pax pulled back from the kiss to look at Everest. "You ready?"

"Fuck yeah, I'm always ready when it comes to her."

Blu giggled at the two of them. "You do know you have to feed me first, right?"

Both men growled as she laughed at them. "Food. I need food."

"Pax, what are we going to do with her? We are offering her dick and she wants food."

Blu slid her hand between her and Everest, grabbing onto his fully erect bulge. "If I'm going to be able to keep up with this... I need food first."

Everest picked her up from behind, laughing. "Then what are we waiting for? Let's get the girl some food." He turned her around and slung her over his shoulder and took off towards the resort. Pax laughed and followed behind them.

They went to the dining room and sat down for dinner. They sat in one of the rounded booths so that they would sit close together. As they were sitting in their seats, Owen and Zoe appeared. "Hey girl, we have missed you." Zoe smiled. She knew what was going on with the three of them, but Owen didn't. The three of them slid around in the booth so that Pax was on one end and Zoe and Owen slid in beside Everest.

"Did you two get into the activities today?" Blu asked, glad to have caught up to her friend.

Blu and Zoe talked with Everest in between them. Owen and Pax carried on their conversation.

"Today was amazing. We went to the pool area and did some water exercises." She looked at Owen, "What was it called babe?"

Owen stopped talking to Pax long enough to answer Zoe, "I don't remember, it was something to relieve stress."

Everest chuckled, rubbing his hand along Blu's thigh. "Stress relief is important when you work for Paxton." He smiled at Blu, "Isn't that right, sweetheart?"

"Fuck off, Ev," Pax chimed in, laughing as he placed his arm around Blu's shoulders. He pulled her over to him so he could kiss her lips. "Do you need stress relief baby?"

Blu nodded and smiled, squeezing Pax's leg with her hand. "I do."

"I love you," he whispered as he took her lips in a kiss. Everest took her other hand and placed it in his lap, holding it in his hand.

The waitress came to take their order. She eyed Pax like he

was on the menu. Blu was used to women looking at him like this. She was proud to be with him. "What do you want, baby?" He asked her, paying no attention to the waitress' glances.

Blu smiled at him calling her baby. She noticed that the waitress's glance went to Everest and Blu found herself not being happy about that. Everest noticed and leaned closer to Blu. "She wants a nice juicy burger, isn't that right sweetheart?" He answered the waitress, his eyes on Blu. Blu nodded and Everest smiled at her.

The waitress took the rest of the orders and left the table, her face red with embarrassment. Owen looked at the three of them with a smile on his face. "Are you three… uh…?"

Everest smiled at Blu while he waited for one of the other two to answer what they were. "We don't have a label, yet." Pax offered, looking at Everest and Blu. He saw that look of love on Everest's face again. Pax knew he was either going to have to let Everest be with Blu, if she wanted it, or Everest was going to have to not be with them anymore. He was getting attached and Pax could see it as plain as day. The conversation he was dreading was going to have to happen soon.

Chapter 26

They ate their dinner, the five of them talking, laughing, and enjoying their company. No one mentioned what was going on between Pax, Blu, and Everest again for the rest of the evening. For the rest of dinner, they kept things PG and family-friendly. Pax and Everest both took their chances to touch Blu as often as they could, but they didn't try to take it too far.

After dinner, the boys decided they wanted to have a drink. Blu and Zoe said they would go along with them. The music was thumping through the dance floor, bodies all over each other. Pax grabbed onto Blu's hand and led them all to a VIP section. "This way," he said as they walked to the roped-off area. Pax showed them his card and all five were seated right away. The waiter came to take their drink orders.

"This place is incredible," Blu leaned over to talk to Pax.

"It is." He cupped her face in his hands. "It's even better with you here."

She smiled as she licked her lips, inviting him for a kiss. Pax glanced at Everest and saw him watching them. Pax knew that Everest wanted to kiss her, too. For some reason, it was turning Pax on to think of Everest kissing her. He took her lips with his, his tongue entering her mouth to explore her. Her bottom lip in his mouth as he sucked on it, causing her to sigh. His kisses moved to her neck and up to her ear. "Everest wants to kiss you."

She pulled back, looking at him with surprise. "He does?"

Pax nodded. "He does."

"What about the rules?"

"Do you want to kiss him, baby?" Pax asked, already knowing the answer. She shrugged her shoulders. "It's okay to tell me the truth." He smiled at her, knowing that she was thinking about it.

"Maybe, I don't know."

Pax leaned into her again. "If you want to, you can."

"Do you want me to?"

Pax nibbled on her ear, "The thought of you kissing him is making me hard."

"Really?" She asked, surprised.

He nodded. "Yes. It is."

"But…" She started. Pax took her face into his hands.

"If you don't want to, you don't have to. If you do, I would be okay with it." He chuckled. "I would like to watch it though."

She laughed, "Of course, you would."

He laughed with her before he kissed her again.

Their drinks came and the five of them took their first shots. "You want to dance?" Owen asked Zoe. She smiled as they took off to the dance floor.

"How about you, baby? You want to dance?" Pax asked, holding his hand out to Blu. She nodded and took his hand, standing to follow him to the dance floor. Everest sighed as the other two stood to go dance. Before they left Blu held out her hand to Everest. "Come on, sexy. You're coming, too." Pax chuckled as Everest took Blu's other hand and the three of them went to the dance floor.

Pax took Blu into his arms as a slow and grinding song played. Their bodies moved together to the music as she felt another set of hands on her hips. She was sandwiched between these two men and there was no other place that she would rather be. Pax was in front of her, holding her close to his body while Everest massaged her from behind. Pax grabbed her hips and pulled her close to him. "I love you," he mouthed before he kissed her, deep and needy.

She felt Everest push into her more as Pax kissed her. After Pax pulled away from her, he turned her so that she was now facing Everest and Pax had taken his place grinding into her from behind. Pax wrapped his hands around her waist as he hugged her from behind. Everest smiled at her as he fondled her breasts over her shirt.

She felt Pax's breath on her neck as she stared up at Everest. Blu smiled up at Everest and she pulled him down to her. She pressed her lips to his as she felt Pax grind into her ass. It took Everest a moment to realize what was happening. As soon as the shock wore off, he grabbed her face with his hands. His tongue demanded entrance into her mouth, Blu giving him access. "Fuck," she heard Pax groan into her hair as Everest took over the kiss.

Everest was a good kisser. It was different than Pax, but Blu liked it. She especially liked that it was making Pax hot.

Blu's hands found Everest's hair as he continued to kiss her lips. He had never kissed her before, and he wasn't sure he was ever going to be able to do it again. He was going to make this one count in case it was his one and only.

His lips moved over hers, his tongue massaged her own and his heart was beating out of his chest. He knew that he had been feeling something for her and this was going to make those feelings even stronger. He didn't know what was happening, but he was taking full advantage of this kiss.

Everest finally pulled away from Blu's lips with a smile on his face. "God damn that was hot." He looked over her shoulder to see Pax watching them. Pax smiled at him and nodded to the table. Everest smiled and followed them back. They drank a little more, danced a little more, but Everest didn't kiss her again. They were all getting a little drunk. Owen and Zoe had joined them back at the table and were well on their way to being drunk, as well.

"I have to pee," Zoe announced as she laughed. Zoe and Blu left the table to go to the bathroom. As they were on their way back, Blu saw some woman talking to Everest and Pax. She was just drunk enough not to care what she was about to do. "Oh shit," Zoe mumbled as she saw the woman hitting on Pax and Everest.

Blu walked up to the table, a smile on her face. "Hi, baby."

Pax looked up at her, a smile on his face. "Mmm, my gorgeous woman is back." Blu giggled at his drunken talk.

Blu leaned down and kissed his lips. "That's right and it's about time that these bitches in here figure out that both of you are mine."

Pax grabbed her face and kissed her hard as his hand wandered up to her thigh. She moaned into the kiss as he reached her ass. "I have one small thing to do and then I want you to take me home." Pax nodded as she pulled back from the kiss.

She looked over to see Everest watching her kiss Pax. The woman at his side, trying to get his attention. Blu smiled at the woman as she approached Everest's chair.

"Hi, baby." He looked up to her and smiled.

"Hi, beautiful." Everest reached his hand out to her and she took it. She sat in his lap and pulled his face to hers. As soon as their lips touched, they both felt it. Blu pushed her tongue into his mouth, their tongues danced together. His hands all over her body as she wiggled her ass into his groin.

"Take me home," she mumbled into their kiss.

She stood from Everest's lap, taking his hand in one of hers. She reached out to Pax, taking his hand in the other. She looked at the woman and smiled. "If you will excuse me, I am taking my boys home."

Pax and Everest laughed as she led them out of the club and back to their room.

Once at the door, Everest unlocked it with his key. The three of them stumbled into the room, Pax's hands all over Blu. "I love you so fucking much." His lips on hers in a needy and passionate kiss. Watching Everest kiss her tonight turned him on. Pax grabbed her shirt and pulled it over her head. His lips on her collarbone, sucking the sensitive skin. Everest was behind her, his hands on her waist, pulling her into him.

Clothes were flying off and onto the floor. Hands were all over each other and bare skin was pressed to bare skin. It was hard to tell where one ended and the other began. Pax lifted Blu and carried her to his room, Everest behind them. "You are going to have to tell us if you don't want us to do something." Pax reminded Blu.

She nodded. "Rules?"

Everest looked at Pax as Pax smiled at Blu. "There are no rules tonight."

"No rules?" Blu asked as she ran her hands down Pax's chest.

"No rules. Nothing is off limits tonight."

Everest growled as he kissed on Blu's neck, her hand reaching back to take his hardness. Her other hand caressing and stroking Pax. Pax kissed her lips as he backed them up to his bed.

Pax laid back against the headboard. His hard cock in his hand, stroking slowly. Blu climbed up onto the bed on all fours, licking her lips as she watched him please himself. She replaced his hand with hers as she licked his tip. He watched her take him into her mouth. "That's it, baby, suck it in." Pax held her hair up out of the way, as he caressed her face. The love he felt for her was more than he ever imagined possible. He knew that she was the one for him. That no matter what happened or didn't happen tonight, she would forever be his.

She laid flat on her stomach as Everest pushed her down by her ass. He slapped her ass as he climbed over her legs. "Suck that dick, sweetheart," he ordered as she lowered her mouth onto Pax even further.

Everest spread the cheeks of her ass with his hands as he straddled her legs. He grabbed himself with one hand, rubbing his condom covered tip through her wetness as he stroked. "It's right there." He moaned as he circled her entrance. "One little push and I would be balls deep in this perfect pussy." He circled her again.

Blu raised her ass to him slightly. Everest glanced up to look at Pax. He was asking permission to have her, the way he wanted. Pax looked down at his perfect girl. She was licking and sucking on him just the way he liked. He knew that he wanted her to have whatever she wanted and if that was Everest, he would find a way to give it to her.

He pulled her back from him to get her to look at him. "Baby?"

She looked up at him as she bit her lower lip. "Yes, sir?"

He groaned. "Fucking hell, don't do that right now."

She smiled as she looked up at him through her lashes.

"Tonight there are no rules, no limits." She nodded. "Ev is asking for permission to have *my* perfect pussy." Pax glanced up at Everest, watching him rub Blu while he stroked himself. "It's up to you, baby."

She glanced over her shoulder at Everest. She wasn't sure if it was her wanting him or if it was her drunken state, but she nodded at him.

"Are you sure?" Everest asked as he leaned down over her back.

She nodded again before she took Pax back into her mouth. Pax leaned his head back as she took him into her mouth as far as she could.

She felt Everest's body resting on her back. His tip at her entrance. She adjusted herself so she could take him in. He lowered his body, his tip pressing inside her.

She moaned out as he entered her, vibrating on Pax. "Damn, baby. I am not going to last long like this."

Blu worked Pax's body as Everest pressed into her. He groaned as he filled her. "She's perfect."

Pax grabbed Blu's hair and helped her down onto him as he watched Everest take her from behind. Everest thrust in and out of her as he kissed her back. His hand reached under her to find her sensitive nub. He rubbed circles around her, making her squirm under him. Her hands were on Pax as she pleased him with her tongue. Everest's thrusts became more erratic as he was reaching his climax.

One last thrust into her caused him to spill into the condom inside her. She sucked hard on Paxton as her own orgasm ripped through her body, quickly followed by Paxton's own. Everest pulled out of her, going to discard the condom in the trash. Pax pulled Blu up to him, her straddling his lap.

His lips were on hers in an instant. He didn't need a needy, rough kiss. He needed her to know how much he loved her.

She pulled back from the kiss and smiled at him. "I love you, Pax."

"Move in with me."

Chapter 27

*P*ax just asked Blu to move in with him and she could not believe what she heard. Before she had a chance to answer him, Everest was back in the room. Everest came over to where Pax was sitting up against the headboard with Blu in his lap. He leaned down and quickly kissed her cheek before saying goodnight. "Goodnight, beautiful."

Blu smiled at Everest as he turned to leave the room. "Night, asshole." Pax shook his head as Everest left Pax and Blu alone in his room.

"So, back to what I asked you." Pax smiled as he rubbed his hands up and down her back.

"You are drunk."

Pax nodded. "I might be a little drunk, but I know what I want. I want you to live with me."

"Ask me that when you're sober and then we will talk about it."

He chuckled as he pulled her closer to him. "Deal."

Blu climbed off his lap and laid down in the bed. She cuddled into Pax's side as he wrapped his arms around her. "Being sober isn't going to change my mind about you living with me. I think we've wasted enough time over the last year. I don't want to waste anymore."

"We will talk about it when we get home."

He nodded. "Okay."

They cuddled into each other's arms, falling asleep quickly. The next morning Blu climbed out of bed and headed to the bathroom. She showered, dressed and went to fix some breakfast. She made her way into the kitchen to make Pax his coffee. On the counter beside the coffee maker she found a piece of paper. She picked it up to read what was written on it.

Dearest Blu & Asshole,

Blu giggled at the nickname that Everest always called Pax.

Last night was incredible, you are incredible. You are the most incredible woman that I have ever met. Before what happened last night, I told Pax that I was developing feelings for you. It's true, I have feelings for you.

I see how much Paxton loves you and how much you love him. I don't want to intrude on that. I don't know if I am in love with you, but I know that I could be. I decided to go home and let the two of you have time together. Maybe I shouldn't have come here this week, but I will never regret our time together, even if it ends. I hope neither of you regret last night, or any of our time together. I never will.

I never thought I had it in me to fall in love. I never gave it much thought, until my time with you. Now it's all I can think about. Have a great rest of your week and I hope to see you guys when you get home. Oh, Pax, man up and ask her what you want to ask her. Blu… say yes.

Love,

Ev

Blu reached up to her cheek to wipe away the tear that had fallen. She felt two arms come around her from behind. "What's wrong, baby?"

She handed Pax the letter that she found. He took it from her hands and read it. "He left," Blu said as she cuddled into Pax's chest, his arm wrapped around her after placing the letter back on the counter.

"Are you okay?" Pax asked as he held her close to him. He knew that there were feelings growing between Everest and Blu and that him leaving would upset her.

"I guess. Do you think he regrets what we did last night?"

Pax turned Blu in his arms so that she was facing him. "No. I know he doesn't. I think he is feeling more for you than he knew he thought he could and I'm sure it scared him."

"Do you regret it?" She asked, concern in her eyes.

"I never thought that I could share you like that. I love you more than any other person in this world. But I see what's going on."

"What's going on, Pax?"

"I see the way he looks at you. He looks at you the same way I do. The same way you have started looking at him."

"Pax."

"It's okay. I was so caught up in how I felt about you and how much I love you that I didn't realize how he was feeling. He always said he would never fall in love and I just never thought it would go like this. He's never had any feelings before."

"What are we going to do?"

"I don't know, baby," he reassured her as he kissed her head. "I don't know. I never thought I could share you, and if it were anyone other than him, I couldn't. The only thing I do know is how much I love you. I don't ever want to be without you in my life." He pulled back to look her in the eye. "I think he is feeling the same thing."

"I'm sorry."

"Sorry? For what?"

"I didn't mean to have any feelings for him. What I am feeling for him doesn't mean I love you any less."

Pax chuckled. "I know. It's my fault. I should have known that this would happen. How could he not fall for you?"

"You're not mad?"

"Why would I be mad?"

"Because I just told you I am having feelings for him, too."

"Do you love me any less?"

She shook her head. "No, never."

"We will figure it out when we get home."

She nodded, "Okay."

Pax let go of Blu so that she could finish making their breakfast. While he was sitting at the table, he sent Everest a text.

"We need to talk."

A few moments later, Pax got a reply from Everest. *"You two okay?"*

"Yeah. She got your note and cried."

"Fuck, Pax. I didn't mean to make her cry. Last night was so good, I couldn't take it if she woke up and regretted our time together."

"You know I love her, right?" Pax smiled as he sent the message, listening to her singing as she cooked.

"I know.... So do I."

Pax took in a deep breath. "Then you need to fix this."

"How?"

"I don't know, Ev. I know how much she loves me and I think she just might love you, too."

"Fuck, Pax. I don't want to hurt her. I thought leaving was the right thing to do."

"I know. This is all new to me. I have never had feelings for a woman that we played with." Pax admitted as he smiled at Blu.

"Me either. What do we do?"

"Honestly, Ev, I don't know. I know that I will never leave her. I want her forever. Even if that means that she wants to be with you, too."

"You mean the three of us, together?"

"I don't know what I mean. I just know that this whole thing with the three of us started out as some fun, like always. I knew I wanted to be with her, but I didn't expect her to have feelings for both of us. No one else has."

"Yeah, well, neither of us have ever had feelings for any of those other women, either."

Blu sat a plate down on the counter in front of Pax. He smiled up at her. "Tell Ev I said that we don't regret last night and we miss him."

Pax laughed as he typed out her message to Everest.

He got back a reply quickly, *"Tell her that neither do I and I miss her already."*

Pax relayed the message as Blu was making her own plate of food. She sat beside him at the table and laid her hand on top of his.

"No matter what happens, I don't want to lose you."

Pax reached over and kissed her lips. "I am not going anywhere, no matter what happens in the future."

"Promise?" She asked, hopeful that he meant it.

"I promise. Besides, I have plans for us."

"Oh?"

He smiled at her as he took a bite of his food. "Yes, now eat so we can get going. We have things to do today and then I plan on bringing my girlfriend back to my bed and showing her exactly how much I love her."

"Oh?"

"Yes."

Blu and Pax finished breakfast, while Everest and Pax continued to send a few text messages back and forth. Blu understood why he left this morning, but she wished he hadn't. She felt much better now that she knew that neither of them had regrets about what happened last night.

She didn't know exactly what the future held for the three of them but she knew that she wanted them both in her life, forever.

Chapter 28

*T*he rest of the week went along quickly. Everest, Pax and Blu texted a lot throughout the week. They had a group text going and Everest told Blu that he missed her and he apologized again for leaving that morning after they were together.

"What are you doing in there?" Pax yelled through the bathroom door as Blu was still inside.

"I'm almost done," she yelled back, laughing at his impatience.

Pax had asked Blu to live with him a few days earlier. They had not talked about it again since then. "Hurry up, babe. We are going to be late."

Blu opened the door and as soon as Pax saw her, his jaw dropped. He took the few steps to stand in front of her, taking her into his arms. "Now we are going to be really late." He said just before he took her lips, kissing her hard. Her fingers ran through his hair, tugging lightly as he bit her bottom lip.

Blu giggled as Pax's kisses moved to her neck and exposed skin on her shoulders. Blu was wearing a beige flowered sundress. The shoulder straps were wide and hung off her shoulders, allowing Pax to have mostly skin to kiss.

"Paxton. We have to go. You can't be late to your own party." She smiled, knowing he was going to be wanting to take her dress off her.

Pax had been insatiable since Everest left. He can't seem to get enough alone time with her. Last night, Blu was on a video chat with Everest when Pax walked into their suite.

Video Call:

"Show me what you are wearing tomorrow night." Everest

demanded while Blu was in their bedroom, packing a few things. They only had two more nights at the resort before they left to go home.

"It's just a dress. Nothing special."

"Show me, baby girl."

Everest had taken to calling her baby girl when he was feeling frisky since their last night together.

"It's just a dress. I can't show you before Pax sees it." She teased as she tossed a few things into her suitcase.

Everest shrugged his shoulders. "Then just show me something else."

"I don't have anything else. I'm packing up what I don't need for tomorrow or for the ride home."

Everest chuckled. "Good, I was hoping for no clothes."

"Ev."

He raised his eyebrows at her. "What? It's been days since I have seen that gorgeous body." He adjusted himself on the couch he was laying on. "I want to see your body, Blu."

"Fuck off, Ev. If you hadn't left you could see it," Pax teased as he stepped up behind her and kissed her neck, "and taste it."

"Fuck, I'm coming back." Everest adjusted his hardening member in his pants as he watched Pax's hands cup Blu's breasts.

"Mmm, she feels so good."

"Ass." Everest growled as Pax's hands moved down her body.

"Good suggestion." Pax laughed as he ground into her ass.

"Dammit, I am getting in my car and coming back. I miss that tight little body."

"We'll be home day after tomorrow." Pax reminded him.

"I can't wait that long. Come on, show me something. If I am going to have to take care of myself, at least give me something to look at while I do it."

Blu giggled as she pulled up her shirt, flashing Everest her bare breasts.

"Fucking hell, show me that pretty pussy."

Pax laughed as he ran his hands down between her legs. "She's so wet." He smiled at Everest as he slipped his fingers between her legs.

"Okay, we have to go, Ev. I'm going to have to be buried..." The phone went dead as Pax pulled her back into him. "I love you."

Blu wrapped her arm around the back of Pax's neck, pulling his head down to kiss her as she turned to face him. "I love you, too." She whispered against his lips.

"Then you should have picked a different dress." He laughed as he found the front buttons and started to remove her dress. Blu backed up and fastened it back.

"We're going to be late."

Pax groaned into her neck as he left one last open-mouthed kiss on her sun-kissed skin.

"I don't care." He murmured into her neck as he kissed her again. "Fuck the party."

Blu stepped back again. "Come on, baby. We have a party to attend and you have to perform your CEO duties. We have spent all week up here, building our team. How would it look for its leader to not show up?"

"It would look like he was making love to his girl." He sighed, "I wish Everest was here to watch over you while I was doing those duties." Blu smiled thinking about how Everest would be with her when Pax had things he had to do during these events.

"I can take care of myself."

"I know you can. I just don't like leaving you alone. Maybe you could come around to meet people with me?"

"Paxton, you know that isn't how this works. Just do what you have to and when you are done, I will be there waiting for you."

"I know. Maybe you can hang out with Zoe and Owen?"

Blu smiled at Paxton and how concerned he was about her. It really made her feel special and cherished. She'd be lying if she said she wasn't missing Everest, too. She had come to rely on him when Pax was off doing what he did. She was going to have to pull on her "big girl panties" tonight and make it on her own.

That is if she were wearing any. She'd save that little secret for later.

Blu finally got Pax out of their room. She had to promise to do anything he wanted when they got back. They didn't play much with the items that he had brought with him. She told him that tonight he could use whatever he wanted.

Once they arrived at the dining hall, they saw most of the team had already arrived. It wasn't a formal affair. It was more of a celebration for making it through the week as a team and a farewell until next year.

Since that first day, Moon and Blu had become friends. He was not as bad as she had thought at the beginning. Pax said that he didn't have a talk with him, but she wasn't so sure that he didn't. Moon backed off with the flirting and was a nice guy. He showed Blu how to do yoga and how to be mindful. She was doing it every day and found that she was more relaxed than she had been. Moon gave her some tapes that she could play to help her get into the meditation state when she went home.

"I have to make my rounds. You sure you are going to be okay?" Pax leaned in to ask, making sure she was going to be okay on her own until she found Zoe and Owen.

"I'm fine. Go be incredible and come back to me as soon as you can."

Pax smiled at her, knowing that he wanted her by his side for the rest of his life. He leaned in and kissed her lips. "I love you."

"I love you more. Now, go. The sooner you go, the sooner you can come back."

He kissed her again before he turned to leave her. Blu was so happy that they had decided to not try to keep their relationship a secret. She wondered if Everest was added into their relationship, would he be comfortable in public with them like this.

"Hey girl. Your man making his rounds?" Zoe asked as she hugged Blu.

"Yep." She looked over to see him charming some of the

older women of the company. They were smiling and laughing as he talked to them.

"Where's Ev?" Owen asked.

"He didn't come back." Blu answered, again wishing he was here with them.

"Are you okay with that?" Zoe wondered.

"I am. I don't know what is going to happen when we go home."

"You miss him, don't you?"

It was true. Blu was okay on her own while Pax did what he needed to do for his company. She was also okay hanging out with Zoe and Owen while Pax worked and took care of his employees. It was his concern with the happiness of his employees that made him such a great boss and boyfriend. However, she would be lying if she said that she didn't miss having Everest with her while Pax was busy.

"I do. You know me too well, Zoe."

"It doesn't take a genius to see that you have feelings for two men, Blu." She laughed, "Even Owen noticed."

"Hey!" Owen gave Zoe a fake look of hurt as he took her into his arms.

This last week had done wonders for Owen and Zoe. They made their relationship official this week. Neither one of them were seeing anyone else, but as of this week, they were an official couple.

It had been almost an hour since they had arrived at the party and Blu still hadn't been able to be with Pax. She had seen him on and off, but she wasn't sure where he was right now.

She was looking around the crowd, trying to find him when two arms wrapped around her waist. She closed her eyes as a smile drifted across her face. "What are you doing?"

"Holding my girl," his deep voice whispered into her ear.

"Your girl, huh?"

She felt his breath on her skin, goosebumps rising down her body from the small contact.

"Dance with me," he whispered as he kissed on her ear.

"I didn't think you liked to dance much at these things," she teased as she leaned back into his arms.

"That's only because I didn't have you in my arms before."

"Then I guess we should do a little dancing." She smiled, taking his hand in hers and leading him to where a few of the others were already dancing to the music playing.

"How did you get back, Everest?" She asked him as he pulled her closer to him.

"Our car service is on call twenty-four hours a day. It only took one call to bring me back to you." The music played as he wrapped his arms around her waist. "You're beautiful."

"Thank you."

"How am I supposed to keep my hands to myself when you look like this?" He pulled the shoulder strap down from her shoulder, giving him a place to kiss. He leaned down and pressed his lips to her skin.

The song that played was a reggae remix of "Someone You Loved" by Melo and Lambada Francesa. His hands ran up and down her back as their bodies moved to the music, her hands loosely draped over his shoulders. He moved his hands down to her ass, pulling her into him as they swayed to the music.

"You are a really good dancer."

"It's all you, baby girl."

Blu looked up into his eyes and smiled. She felt another set of hands on her hips as a hard body pressed into hers from behind. "I think it's time we take this back to our room."

"Now, that's the best idea I have heard in days."

Chapter 29

"Not so fast, boys. It's not very often that I get you both like this."

Everest kissed on her neck. "I can think of some other ways you could have us."

Blu leaned back, stopping Everest from kissing her neck. "Mmm, I can, too, but I want to dance more."

Pax backed up from her. "Okay, I'll go…"

"No. I want you both."

"How much have you had to drink baby girl?" Everest asked, making sure that she knew what she was asking for.

Blu smiled as she answered, "Enough to not give a fuck who knows that I want you both. That you both are mine."

Everest smiled at her, getting what she was asking for. "You want us both to dance with you? Here?"

Blu nodded. Everest glanced over her shoulder to Pax and smiled. "You know if we do this, everyone is going to know?"

Pax nodded at him. "I know." Pax stepped back up to press his body against Blu's back. He leaned in to whisper in her ear, "Are you okay with everyone here knowing that you belong to us?"

Blu glanced around and saw a few people watching them. A few of the men looked like they were getting excited by the display and the women looked jealous. "Do you love me, Pax?"

Pax started swaying his hips to the music, causing Blu to move with him. "You know I do. More than anything in this whole world, I love you." He kissed on her neck as their bodies moved to the music. "I want every piece of you." She leaned her head back and allowed herself to enjoy his touch. She opened her eyes and looked at Everest.

"What do you want, Everest?" She looked him directly in the

eye as she continued to move against Pax, feeling him becoming aroused with her movements.

Everest stepped forward, pressing his body against hers, allowing her to press harder into Pax. "Fuck, baby. You keep rubbing that ass on me and I'm going to come right here, in front of everyone." Pax rubbed his hands up and down on her hips and thighs.

Blu ran her fingernail down Everest's chest, stopping at his belt buckle. Again, she asked, "What do you want, Ev?"

Everest took her face into both of his hands. His glance dipped to her lips before resting back on her eyes. "You, Blu. I want you." He leaned down and kissed her, his lips gentle on hers as he tasted what he had desired for so long. Blu pulled him closer to her, his body against hers. His tongue asking permission to dance with hers.

Blu was so into the kiss that Everest was giving her that she didn't realize that Zoe and Owen had joined them on the dance floor. "Holy hell, Blu."

"Am I the only one that is getting hella turned on with this?" Owen asked, watching Everest kiss Blu as Pax pressed his hips into her.

Everest pulled back from the kiss, a smile on his face. He glanced over Blu's shoulder to look at Pax. "Rules?" Everest asked as he still held her face in his hands.

Pax rubbed Blu's shoulders and down her back and to her hips. "No more rules. Whatever she wants is hers."

Everest smiled as he leaned down and placed his hands under her ass, lifting her straight up. Her arms wrapped around his neck as his lips crashed onto hers, his tongue demanding entrance into her mouth, eagerly finding hers. He turned toward the door and carried her out. Pax chuckled, shook his head and turned to follow. He glanced at Zoe and Owen. "See you two tomorrow."

"Yeah... Sure... uh..." Owen stuttered as Zoe put her arms around his waist.

"You take care of her, okay?"

Pax nodded, "Of course, we love her." He assured Zoe as he followed Everest and Blu out the door.

Everest carried her to the elevator, only setting her down long enough to back her up against the side of the elevator after it closed. "I can't control myself around you any longer," Everest moaned into her neck as he bit the sensitive skin just above her shoulder.

Pax pushed the button for their floor and he tapped Everest on the shoulder. Everest backed up a small step, turned so that his back was against the elevator wall and pulled Blu's body into his. "I am not done with these lips yet," he moaned into another hot and hard kiss.

Pax pressed his body against hers as his hands roamed her skin under her skirt. "Fuck, baby," he said, discovering her little surprise. "You don't have on any panties."

"I was planning on taking you in the bathroom later." She giggled.

"Hmmm, next party I will take you up on that, baby," he said as he pressed into her.

Everest groaned into the kiss, "Is she wet?"

Pax slipped a finger in between her legs. "Soaking fucking wet." He moaned into her neck as he rubbed circles around her clit.

Everest slid two fingers inside of her as Pax worked her with his fingers. "Fuck me, please." She pleaded as the doors opened. Pax stepped back from her, removing his hand from between her legs. Everest pulled his fingers from her body and sucked them clean before crashing his lips on hers again. He lifted her and kissed her as he walked down the hall, allowing her to taste herself on his tongue. Pax opened the door and Everest carried her inside, shoving the door shut with his foot. Pax locked the door and tossed his jacket onto the couch. He unbuttoned his shirt as he watched Everest kiss Blu, her legs now wrapped around his waist.

"I want this pussy." Everest moaned as he rubbed her up and down on his growing erection. Pax removed the rest of his clothes as he watched Blu unbutton her dress. Everest set her down onto her feet so she could step out of her outfit, leaving it in the other room as they went to the bedroom.

Pax turned her to face him as Everest removed his own clothes. "I love you."

"I love you, Paxton."

Pax smiled at her. "I will give you anything you want."

"I want you both tonight."

Pax smiled as he leaned in to kiss her. His kiss was different than what Everest gave her earlier. Pax's was full of love, desire, passion and promise. She knew he meant what he said. He would give her everything.

While Pax kissed her lips, Everest took himself in his hand. He stoked himself a few times before he stepped up behind Blu and rubbed his tip into her wetness from behind her. She moaned into the kiss with Paxton and he sucked her lip into his mouth.

"Can I have her a minute?" Everest asked as he grabbed onto her hips, his hardness still between her legs.

Blu looked up to Pax, asking him for permission. Pax nodded at her. "Anything you want is yours."

Everest pulled her away from Pax and laid her onto the bed. Pax took a seat at the side of the bed and watched as Everest crawled over Blu's body. "Tonight you are mine, too." He growled as he laid down on top of her body, his lips taking hers in a delicate kiss. One hand on her breast, pulling her nipple in between his fingers. His other hand rubbed his tip through her wetness. His tongue drew circles around her nipple before taking it into his mouth, sucking hard. Her back arched as he flicked her with his tongue.

Blu glanced over to the side of the bed to see Pax watching them with half closed eyes, his hard member in his hand. Her attention back to Everest when his head dipped between her legs, his tongue pushing into her slit. "Oh, God." She screamed out as Everest's tongue flicked at her clit, his fingers delved inside her.

"That's it, baby girl. Scream for me. Get Pax hard so he can fuck that ass tonight," he groaned. "Because this pussy is mine."

Hearing Everest claim her for the night, made her body shake and her orgasm fly through her. Her legs shook, her back arched and her breathing fast. "Yes, fuck me." She yelled out as Everest raised from between her legs.

"Fuck yeah. I want you to tell Pax how good my cock feels inside this perfect tight pussy," he demanded as he slammed himself inside her.

After a few thrusts, Blu dug her nails into his back, causing him to bite her breast. He flipped them over so that Blu was straddled on top of him. Her hips continued to move as she looked over to Pax. "I need you, baby."

Pax smiled as he stood and walked over beside the bed. He leaned down and took her face in his hands. "You will always be my girl." His lips were on hers, showing her who she belonged to.

"Please, Pax. I need you."

"You've got me, baby. Forever."

Pax let go of her face and went to the bottom of the bed. He climbed on his knees in between Everest's spread legs. Pax ran his hands down her back, pushing her forward before he spread her ass with his hands. He grabbed himself with one hand and pushed the tip against her ass. "You look sexy with Ev's cock going in and out of *my* tight pussy."

She moaned as he pressed himself into her ass. "Fuck, that's tight," he growled as he pulled back out again. Everest continued to help her move her hips on him as Pax took her from behind. Pax found her sensitive bud and helped her to find her climax while they both filled her. Pax came right after Blu, filling her ass. He leaned down to kiss her back as he felt Everest slam her down onto him, moaning out from his own orgasm.

"Holy fuck, that was good." Everest laughed as he felt Pax roll over to the side of the bed. Blu followed behind him, lying in between the two men on her back. Everest turned to face her on one side, Pax on the other.

"That was…" Pax started.

"Incredible," Blu agreed.

"Amazing," Everest added, "When we get home, we need to talk."

They all agreed that when they got home, they were going to have to have a talk and figure out what they were doing. Blu had thought a lot about what Pax had asked her earlier in the week, about living with him. She knew what her answer was going to be. What she didn't know was…

How Everest fit into this picture.

Chapter 30

Sleep quickly finds the three. When morning came, Blu woke with an arm thrown over her chest and the head from the same person buried in her neck. On the other side she found a leg over hers and his hand just above her already aching center. She squirmed a little, needing to get up to use the bathroom.

The hand that was close to her center started to move. She giggled as she shoved Pax's hand away from her. "Stop. I have to use the bathroom." She gently removed Everest's arm from across her chest, causing him to groan and turn over, facing away from her.

Pax slid his fingers in between her legs, finding her warm and wet. "But this would be so much more fun." He whispered as he nibbled on her shoulder. "Buried deep inside you is the best way to wake up. I am sure Ev would love to wake up to watch me deep inside you."

"Would you like to wake up to see me riding Ev?" She asked, smiling at him as she moved in the bed.

"Fuck yeah. As long as I can join you, I'd love to wake up seeing his cock buried deep inside you."

"Of course, you can, baby. You know how much I love you." She shoved him back again, laughing as she straddled his legs. "And your cock, but right now, I need to pee, Paxton."

He grabbed her waist as he rubbed his erection between her wet folds. "Mm, baby, you feel so good." Blu leaned down and kissed him, getting him to remove his hands from her hips. As he moved his hands, she jumped off the bed and giggled all the way to the bathroom. After she was done, she walked back into the room to see Paxton leaning up on one elbow, the sheet pooling around his thighs. "Come here, baby, lets wake Ev." He patted the bed beside him, eyeing her naked body like she was a present he had been waiting for all year.

"We need to get dressed, Pax."

"The fuck we do. I need to be buried in you." He jumped up and grabbed her by the waist, lifting her up. He stepped over to the dresser and set her on top, stepping between her legs. His lips on hers before she could object.

He only pulled back when he heard Everest behind him, laughing. "And to think I almost slept through this."

"She's denying me, man." Pax huffed.

"Well, we did kind of fuck her hard last night," Everest said as he stepped up closer to the two of them. "Are you sore, baby girl?" Blu nodded at him. Pax moved over slightly to allow Everest to approach her, as well. "Want me to kiss it and make it better?"

She smiled at Everest as she thought of what to say. "I do." He smiled at her, thinking he'd won, as he went to lean down between her legs. "But we need to get dressed." Pax laughed as Everest groaned.

"Fuck, she shot me down, too."

"Has that ever happened to you before?" Pax asked Everest, his hands still on Blu's legs.

"Fuck no, it hasn't." Everest looked to Blu with a cocky smile on his face. "It's a damn good thing I love that pussy so much."

Blu giggled as she pulled Everest closer. "What would you do, Ev? Would you stop fucking me with your friend?"

"Hell no!"

"Is my pussy all that you love, Ev?" She inquired as she ran her hands up his bare chest.

Everest took in a deep breath. He had never told a girl he loved any part of them, much less that he loved them. "No."

Her lips pressed to his for a hot and sexy kiss. Pax groaned beside them. "You have to stop that shit."

Blu pulled back from the kiss, a look of concern on her face. "Is it not okay if I kiss him?"

Pax smiled at how she was still concerned about him not approving. "Not unless you want to get fucked this morning. I can't watch that shit and not be inside you."

Blu smiled, knowing that it was okay to kiss Everest. "You interrupted my kiss, Paxton," Everest growled at him.

"You interrupted me trying to fuck her on this dresser," Pax shot back, smiling at how flustered Ev was getting. "I was just saying. She keeps kissing like that this morning," he glanced down, "and I am going to fuck her."

Everest glanced down at his own morning wood and chuckled. "Right there with ya man." Everest smiled at Blu. "Go get dressed, baby girl. Otherwise, we are going to be finding places to put these." He gestured to their erections. Blu licked her lips as she glanced at them. Truth was, she wanted them both. She had already fallen in love with Pax and she knew that if things continued the way they were, she was going to fall for Everest, as well.

Blu didn't plan on this. She had feelings for Paxton for quite some time that she never expected to act on. When Everest told her what they were into, she just figured that was it. She would never actually get to fully act on her feelings for him. Then, one night in Pax's house, she decided that she wanted to explore with them. She wanted to see what it would be like to have them both.

Falling completely in love with Pax was not part of the plan that night. She thought it would be fun to let herself go, just that once. Let herself experiment with something she had never dreamed of doing before with a man that she already had feelings for and his best friend that she was attracted to.

Now, here she sat, on a dresser in a hotel suite. The two most gorgeous men that she had ever met standing in front of her, naked and ready to please her. All she could think of was how she wanted to kiss them both, make love to them both, please them both and let them both please her.

That's the thing about life, relationships and love. What you thought you were getting in the beginning wasn't always what you ended up with. A few weeks into whatever this was that they were doing and not only was Blu head over heels in love with Paxton, but she had feelings for Everest, as well. He always said that it would only be sex and playtime for them, but Blu was having a hard time not wanting more with him. More from him.

Blu glanced down, afraid that what she was feeling would show if she looked at them. "I need to get dressed." She jumped off the dresser, grabbed her clothes and went into the bathroom.

"What was that?" Everest asked, concerned he had done something wrong.

"I'm not sure," Pax answered, looking at the door that she went into. Both men put on some boxers and got dressed and ready to check out. "Maybe this is all too much for her."

"You think so? I... dammit Pax."

"What?" Pax asked concerned.

"I don't want to lose her man. I'm... fuck, Pax. I have feelings for her."

Pax chuckled. "Join the club. I love that woman more than anything. I would give her anything she asked for, even if that was that she wanted to be with you and not me."

Everest glanced at the door to the bathroom. They heard the shower running. "I think... fuck Pax, I think I love her."

"Well, hell. Are you going to tell her?"

Everest threw his clothes from last night into his bag. "I don't know. I don't know if she could ever love me. Not like she loves you." He sat on the edge of the bed. "I can't tell a woman I love her for the first fucking time and have her not feel the same because she's already in love with my best friend."

"I think she has feelings for you, too." Pax sat on the bed beside Everest. "Maybe not to the extent that she does for me. We have known each other for over a year, but I think she is feeling it."

"You think?" A smile crept up on his face.

Pax took a deep breath. He knew that Blu was starting to have feelings for Everest. It was one of the reasons that he agreed to let them explore their relationship. He didn't want to lose her and it did get him off to watch them together. "I do."

"What are we going to do? Are we always going to have to be a threesome?"

"What do you mean?"

"I mean are you always going to have to be there when I am with her and me there when you are with her? Do either of us get alone time with her?"

"Shit man, I don't know. I have never done this before. Not with someone I loved." Pax answered honestly. "We need to talk about things. See what she wants."

"What do you want?" Everest asked, eyeing his friend for any signs he was upset.

"I want time with her, alone." Pax looked at his hands. "I love her, Ev. I want her for the rest of my life. I want everything with her. Do you want that, too?"

Everest glanced back at the door, the shower still running. "The whole fucking thing."

"Then we are going to have to figure out something."

"A schedule?" Everest chuckled, trying to make the mood lighter.

"A fuck schedule?" Pax chuckled.

"Do you trust me with her? Do you know that I won't ever try to come in between the two of you?"

Pax nodded. "I do."

"Will it be hard for you to know I am making love to her when you aren't there?"

Pax sighed. "Maybe. I don't know. But if I want time with her alone, then it's only fair you get that chance, as well, if we are going to do this."

"We will still play, though, right?"

"Fuck yeah," Pax answered, getting turned on again thinking about taking her in the shower. "I do love seeing you with her.

That face she makes when she's coming all over your tongue... shit, that gets me going." He chuckled. "I told her this morning that I would love waking up one morning to see her riding the hell out of you like I was going to do to her this morning."

"I get it. Watching her suck on you while I was fucking her got me so fucking hard, I lost my shit. And watching her ride the hell out of you when I woke up... fuck, the only thing better would be the one getting ridden."

They both laughed. "We're fucked up, aren't we?" Everest asked amused.

Pax shook his head, "We might be, or we just fell in love with the same damn woman."

Everest slapped Pax on the back. "That we did, bud. That we did."

Chapter 31

Blu dried off and got dressed. She wasn't ready to go home because she knew that it was going to be different at home than it was in their little love and sex bubble that they had the last week. She was so happy last night when Ev came back. She had really missed him. She was falling for him, as well as Pax. She didn't want Pax to think that wanting to have Everest with them was in any way saying she loved him any less.

She walked back into the room to see Everest and Pax sitting on the side of the bed. They both stood and walked to her side. Each leaning in to kiss a cheek. "Are you okay?" They both asked at the same time.

Blu smiled at how sweet her boys were. She knew that any girl that ended up with either of them would be lucky. "What are we doing?" She asked, almost afraid for them to answer.

Pax took her hand in his. "We need to have a talk when we get home."

Everest took her other hand in his. "Yes, we do."

Blu tried to smile and not show how nervous she was about this talk. She knew that it needed to happen, but she also knew it was going to change everything.

The three of them drove home in Pax's car. The ride was a little more quiet than Blu expected it to be. She couldn't take it any longer. "Oh, for fuck's sake. Paxton, pull over."

Pax looked at her, concerned something was wrong. "What's wrong baby? Are you sick?"

"Baby girl, are you okay?" Everest asked from the back seat.

"I can't stand all this quiet. Can you pull over at the next gas station?"

Pax saw a gas station coming up ahead. He looked at Everest

in the mirror and gave him a look. He hoped that this whole thing wasn't about to blow up in their faces.

Pax pulled into the parking lot and Blu got out as soon as the car stopped. She went inside the station and the boys stayed in the car.

"What was that all about?" Everest wondered out loud as he tried to see her through the front windows.

"I don't know, but I am about to find out." Pax got out of the car and walked inside the station. He saw Blu back beside the bathroom doors, looking in the cooler for drinks. He walked back to where she was and wrapped his arms around her waist. "Baby?"

She stepped forward. "Don't baby me, Paxton Pascal. Why are the two of you so fucking quiet? Are you leaving me?"

Pax was shocked at her outburst. Not because she was upset, but because she thought that he might want to leave her. He pushed his body into hers and pushed her into the ladies' room. He pushed her up against the wall, under the window. He took her hands in his, raising them over her head and pinning them to the cold glass. His foot shoved her feet apart so he could step in between her legs.

His voice was gruff and coarse, "Do you think I'm leaving you, Blu?" She nodded. "You think I don't want you anymore?" She nodded again. "Why do you think I would want that?" He mumbled into her neck.

A tear fell down her cheek. "Because I am falling for your best friend."

Pax bit her neck and sucked the skin in between his lips. "Is that all?"

"Isn't that enough? I didn't mean for it to hap…" Pax crashed his lips to hers, taking her breath away with the desire in his kiss.

"I love you, Blu. That doesn't change because you have feelings for Everest."

"It doesn't?" She asked surprised.

"No, it doesn't." He leaned his head on her forehead. "Do you love me any less because you have feelings for him?"

Blu shook her head vigorously. "No. I could never love you less." She tried to look away, but he wouldn't let her. "I don't know what is happening."

Pax sighed. "You are in love with two men, Blu."

"I have never loved two men before." She whispered honestly.

He chuckled. "I have never shared the woman I love with another man that loves her, either."

"What?"

"It isn't my place to tell you what he is feeling, Blu. But I can tell you that neither one of us wants to leave you."

"You don't?" She asked, a smile on her face.

"No. We don't." She smiled at him as she kissed his lips again. He pulled away from the kiss. "We better get out of here before I bend you over and…" She giggled, pushing him back.

"It's nasty in here."

He looked around for the first time. "Eww, it is. Let's go." She nodded. "You okay?" She nodded again.

They bought some snacks and drinks and walked back out to the car. Before getting in the front, Blu opened the back door and leaned in. "Thank you." She pressed her lips to Everest. He wrapped his hands into her hair as he shoved his tongue into her mouth. His lips moved on hers with perfect rhythm. He pulled back from the kiss, panting, closing his eyes as his forehead touched hers. "Pax, can you drive while I fuck her in the backseat?"

Blu giggled as she grabbed the bag of snacks. "Have some chips, Ev."

Everest reached up and held her breast in his hand. "I will take a snack, but what I want to eat isn't in any of those damn bags."

"Fuck," Pax groaned from the front seat. "You drive and I'll get back there with her."

Blu giggled again and pulled back from Everest. "Pax, you drive. Ev, you eat… snacks," she winked at him. "I'm sitting back in the front seat."

Everest groaned as Blu climbed back in the front. "Don't mind me back here… I will just fuck myself." He laughed as he adjusted himself in his jeans.

They drove the rest of the way home teasing and flirting with each other. Blu was much happier now that she knew she wasn't going to lose Pax. She was just hoping she wasn't going to lose Everest, either. She wasn't ready to give him up yet.

Pax took all of Blu's bags into his house when they arrived. "Can you stay tonight?"

She nodded. "I just need to call Raphael and make sure everything is okay at home." Pax nodded and he took her bags up to his room.

"What kind of farm do you have?"

"We have wheat fields that we grow our own hay and then we have cattle."

"Wow, I didn't know that. How long have you had that?"

"My parents…" she paused, remembering her family. "I grew up there. It was awesome. Raphael takes care of the day to day operations now that my parents are gone."

"You have that farm and still work for Pax?"

She nodded. "I needed some money when my parents died last year. He paid well and I was able to get the farm caught up and we are almost making a profit again."

Everest followed her over to the couch.

"Are you going to stay with him after your farm makes money again?"

Blu shrugged her shoulders. She had never thought about that. She just needed to get the farm to make money again and she was almost there. Her parents didn't take care of the finances too well and with all the cost from their funerals, she was in danger of losing the farm after they died. "I never thought about it. I have just been too busy trying to save it to think about making enough money to live with just the farm."

"Your parents would be proud of you, keeping it in the family."

"It was the best to grow up there. We used to have horses and all kinds of farm animals. Now, we only have cattle. I hope to have the animals there again and one day..."

"One day what?" Everest asked taking the seat beside her.

"I would like to raise my own family there."

Everest put his hand on top of hers, intertwining their fingers. "You are an incredible woman, Blu." Everest leaned over and kissed her sweetly. His other hand on her cheek as he claimed her lips. Everest pulled her over onto his lap, her legs on each side of his on the couch. Their kiss heated up as he ran his hands down her sides, cupping her ass and pulling her into him. "I need you, Blu."

"Ev."

He ran his hand up under her shirt and cupped her breast in his hand. "I have never needed a woman like this before."

"Ev..." She moaned as she laid her head back, allowing him access to kiss and suck on her neck. Everest grabbed her shirt and pulled it over her head, exposing her lacey bra to him. His eyes darkened as he unfastened her bra and pulled the straps from her shoulders. He took one of her breasts into his mouth, sucking and nibbling on her. Her hands in his hair, holding him close to her.

She felt another set of hands on her shoulders, massaging her neck. She looked up and saw Pax, standing behind her. "Baby?" She looked at him with all the love she had for him.

Pax leaned down and took her lips with his. As he pulled away from the kiss, he whispered. "It's okay baby, let him love you."

Pax removed his hands from her body and stepped back from her and Everest. Everest took her lips with his once again, this time in a hard kiss. He pushed her gently back and off his lap. He unfastened his jeans and pushed them down and off his feet. He then reached up and pulled Blu's shorts and panties down from her body. She stepped out of them and straddled his lap again. Everest took her in his arms and helped her to lower herself onto him. She moved her hips while his hands guided her movements.

He helped to raise her up and down on him until they were both panting, each of them chasing their own high. Blu came first, quickly followed by Everest. She remained on his lap, him still inside her as he kissed her again. "I can't give you up."

She laid her head on his shoulder as he gently rubbed her back. "I can't give you up, either, Ev."

A little later, Everest and Blu were dressed and sitting back on the couch. Neither knew where Pax had gone until he came back down, his hair wet from a shower. He joined them in the living room, taking Blu into his lap.

"Hi baby," he whispered in her ear as he kissed her neck.

"Pax…"

He kissed her lips. "Shhh, baby. It's okay." He chuckled. "I took care of myself in the shower. It was really quick thinking about you riding Everest down here."

"I love you, Pax."

"I love you, too." He smiled, kissed her lips and said, "I think it's time we had that talk now."

Chapter 32

Blu let out a deep breath as she snuggled into Pax's chest. He kissed her on the head as he wrapped his arms around her. "I think we need to talk." He looked at Everest and saw that he was looking at the two of them. "The three of us."

Blu and Everest both nodded. Blu knew that this talk needed to happen, but she was scared. She knew she loved Pax so much and she would never want to lose him. She knew that she had feelings growing for Everest, too, but if it meant she would lose Pax, she wasn't sure she could do it.

She nuzzled into Pax's arms, her face buried in his neck. Some may think that it was weird for her to be nuzzled into Pax when she had just had sex with Everest a few minutes ago. A few weeks ago, she would have agreed with them, but they weren't living her life. They weren't having real feelings for two different men.

She was.

Pax sighed, pulling her into him even more. "Okay, I will start."

He glanced at Everest and Ev smiled back at him. They had already talked and knew that they both wanted to be with her. They also agreed that if she loved one of them and not the other, the one that she didn't love would bow out. "Over the last year, I have watched you. I have thought about what it would be like to be with you." He pulled back to look her in the eye.

"I never thought that you would accept my life and the things that I have become accustomed to."

"You mean I wouldn't want to play with you?"

Pax chuckled. "Yes."

"I never thought I would do that, either." She glanced at Everest, saying sorry with her eyes. He smiled back at her.

"I asked you to the ball because I wanted to find out what your interest would be… in being with me."

"Did you want me to play?"

"Yes. I did. I wanted to have you, but I wanted to watch Everest please you, too."

"Did you set us up to meet?"

"No. I wanted you to meet him, but I wanted to build up to that." Pax chuckled at Everest. "But he isn't exactly subtle about things."

"Hey, I couldn't help it. I mean look at her. She got me going with that sassy mouth of hers that very first night," Everest admitted with a smile on his face.

Pax continued, "I wanted to be with you. I wanted you to play with Ev and myself, but after the ball, before you were at my house for the weekend, I couldn't keep my hands off you." Blu smiled thinking about making out with him in his office. "I took you to my house that weekend to be with you. I had no intentions of playing that weekend. I wanted to be with you, playing or not."

She giggled, "Until I dressed in your robe."

Everest adjusted himself in his seat. "That was fucking hot."

"It was," Pax agreed. "You asked for us both and hell, who was I to say no to that? A sexy as fuck woman in my robe, asking us to fuck her. I mean, come on."

"So, I was just someone to play with?" Blu asked disappointed.

"I was starting to have an attraction to you that I had never had before and that weekend I wanted to explore it with you. I was planning on it being just the two of us, I swear."

Everest interjected, "He was. I was going to leave until I saw you in that robe. Holy shit you were sexy." He smirked at her. "You still are."

"Somewhere along the line, I fell in love with you."

Blu looked up to him and smiled. "I love you, too."

"The week that we were going away, I invited Everest to be with us to play some more. If you wanted to."

"I did." She smiled at them both.

Pax took a deep breath. Before he could speak, Everest spoke. "After that first night, I freaked the fuck out."

"Why? We have played before."

"That night, I didn't want to leave you. It wasn't just that night, that day and that guy Moon hitting on you. It pissed me off."

"It did me, too, I was ready to beat his ass." Pax chuckled.

Everest continued, "I said something to him later that evening."

"You did?" Blu asked, sure that it was Pax that said something to Moon.

"I did. It was then that I realized…" He paused.

"What Ev? What did you realize?"

Everest got up and came to sit beside Pax and Blu, her still on Pax's lap. "It was then that I realized that I had feelings for you. You weren't just someone that I wanted to get ready for Pax to fuck." Blu reached out and touched his hand.

Pax ran his hand up her thigh. "We talked about that night and about him leaving, after he left."

"You did?" She asked, confused.

"Yes, we did." Ev admitted. "He asked me why I left and I had to tell him that I was falling for you and I…"

She took Ev's hand and put it on her lap. "What?"

"Fuck, Blu. Are you going to make me say it?"

Blu nodded. "Yes."

Everest looked at Pax and he nodded at him.

"I fucking love you. I don't want to just play with you and get you ready for Pax. I want to be with you, too. I want to be a part of this relationship. I want…"

Blu leaned over and kissed Everest. "Ev."

"Don't get me wrong, I still want to be with you with Pax. It's hot as hell to eat that pussy while he watches. It almost makes me come just knowing how much you both like it."

Pax nibbled on her neck as Everest was talking.

"But I also want time alone with you, too. I want to make love to you all night long and sleep next to you, just us."

Blu looked to Pax. He smiled at her. "I want that, too. I want time where it is just us, as well as times where I watch him please you, I want him to watch as I fuck the hell out of you, and I want us to both have you at the same time."

Blu took a deep breath. This was not exactly what she expected to hear but she wasn't hating it. "So, we would all three be together?"

Both guys nodded. "Yes," Pax said as he pulled her close to him.

"Yes," Everest agreed.

"What about the two of you?" She asked with a smirk on her face.

"What do you mean?" Pax asked.

"Will you two be… together?"

Everest laughed. "Are you asking if I plan on fucking my best friend?"

Blu giggled at Ev's bluntness. "Yeah."

They both answered at the same time, "No."

Everest chuckled. "The only ass I am fucking is yours baby."

Pax chuckled. "Agreed."

"I have a couple of questions."

Pax encouraged her, "Go ahead, baby."

"How will this work? I mean, we are all three in different houses. Would I spend nights with one and then the other? How would we be together, the three of us? Would either of you see other people? I…"

"Woah, baby." Pax chuckled. "We haven't thought of everything yet. I liked last night, both of us waking up with you."

"Me, too. I'm into that whole waking up with you riding the other one. That would be fucking fantastic." Everest chimed in.

"Oh, yeah. I agree." Pax smiled. "And no, I will not see anyone else."

"Really?" She asked Pax.

"Yes, really. I am in this, Blu. I love you and I don't want anyone else."

"Me, either. After I left you guys that morning and spent a little time alone. I didn't play. I have offers to come play, there was even a party being held that night that I came back. I only wanted to be with you. I had to come back. And… asshole over here said you missed me."

"I did."

"The three of us would be only with each other?" The guys nodded. "Okay."

"But we also both agreed…" Pax looked to Ev to finish.

Everest took in a deep breath. "We also agreed that if you didn't love one of us but did love the other…"

"The one you didn't love would step back from our relationship and let the other two be together, if that is what you wanted."

Blu laid her hands on both men's cheek. "What if I love and want you both?"

They both smiled at her. "Then you have us both." Pax smiled at her.

"Fuck yes, you have us both."

Blu smiled at Pax and leaned in to kiss him. Her lips pressed against his as he licked her bottom lip, begging for access into her mouth. She gave it willingly. She sucked on his tongue as Everest moved his hand up her thigh. His hands in her hair, deepening the kiss as much as he could. His lips roughly kissing hers as he hardened underneath her.

She pulled back from the kiss and leaned over to kiss Everest, lifting her ass from Pax's lap to reach Everest's lips. Pax took full advantage as he rubbed her ass with his hand. His hand slipped between her legs, finding her soaking wet. After she kissed

Everest she sat back on Pax's lap. "What is the plan for tonight?" She asked, smiling at them both.

"What do you want to do?" Pax asked as he rubbed her hip, pulling her into him.

"I already planned on staying here, with you." She saw the look on Everest's face.

"I can go home."

"Pax, baby?"

"Yes, love?" He smiled at her calling him baby.

"Can Ev stay with us?"

Pax chuckled. "I guess since he finally told you that he loves you, he should stay with us tonight. Tomorrow you are only mine."

"Yes. I agree." Blu smiled as Everest leaned in to kiss her one more time.

After he pulled back from the quick kiss, he said, "I love you, Blu."

"I love you, too, Ev."

Ev stood and helped Blu to stand off Pax's lap. The three of them cooked dinner together. This was the first time that she got to see Pax really cooking. If she hadn't already loved him, this would have made her fall. They put the lasagna in the oven and decided that they would go out to the hot tub since it was going to take about two hours to be ready. Blu went up to Pax's room to get her swimsuit on. She put on a bikini that had ties on each side of the bottoms and on the top, too. Both guys went in the water in their boxers.

Blu leaned back and let the jets hit her back. "This feels amazing." The guys agreed. They spent the next half an hour talking about the retreat and what it was like to have everyone together.

"That Missy chick is a desperate fuck, isn't she?" Everest asked, amused at the look on Pax's face.

"She's a bitch," Blu blurted out.

Both men chuckled. "Why is that baby?" Pax egged her on.

"She was looking at you like a piece of meat and it pissed me off."

"Is our girl jealous?" Everest teased.

Blu huffed. "I will beat her ass if she thinks she can touch either one of you."

Everest looked to Pax and smiled. "Am I the only one that wants to skip dinner and just go upstairs? I get what's so hot about her claiming you now."

"I told you."

"It's not hot. It pisses me off that she thinks she can fuck you."

Pax moved closer to her, laying his hand on her thigh. "I want no one other than you, baby. I swear."

"You better not, or I will cut if off."

Pax smiled and Everest grabbed his junk. "Damn, am I the only one getting a fucking boner right now?"

Pax laughed hard at Everest. Blu reached over between Everest's legs. "He's not lying. He's hard as a rock."

Pax laughed even harder. "I will take your word for it, babe."

Blu giggled. "You can see it. Show him, Ev." Blu teased as she rubbed him through his boxers.

Pax pulled her closer to him. "Babe, I've seen it before. The last time it was being buried in that perfect pussy of yours."

"But it's really hard right now," she teased again.

"Babe, I love you and I am glad that you are enjoying yourself, but the only way I want to see his 'hard as a rock' cock is if it's in your mouth, your ass, or in that sweet pussy."

"Where do you want it tonight?" Blu asked as she rubbed them both. "Hmm, baby. You're hard, too."

"Wherever you want it. But if you keep rubbing me like that, I am going to pull you over here and…"

Blu laughed as she stood up in the hot tub. "You are going to what, baby?" Pax teased her back.

"Fucking hell," Everest moaned out as he watched Blu

straddle Pax's lap and kiss him hard. He rubbed himself over his boxers. "Go ahead, baby girl. Fuck him in this tub."

Blu pulled back from the kiss. "It's time for dinner, boys."

She stood and got out of the tub and walked into the house, stripping as she went.

Everest looked at Pax. "Fuck man, is she dinner?"

"Hell if I know, but I am sure as shit going to be finding out."

Chapter 33

Pax stood and hopped over the side of the hot tub. He slid his boxers down as he went in the house. "Fuck man, wait for me." Everest yelled after him, also hopping over the side and stripping before he entered the house.

Once inside, Pax saw Blu bent over, looking in the oven at the lasagna, bare ass in the air. "God damn woman."

Blu took out the lasagna and placed it on the stove top. As soon as she set it down, Pax was against her body, pressing his naked, wet body into hers. His hands slid around her stomach and dived into her wetness. "Wanna come before dinner?"

Blu reached back with her arm and hooked it around the back of his neck. "Dinner first, boys." Everest was already there and had latched his mouth onto her bare breast.

"Fuck lasagna, I want you for dinner," Everest mumbled around her hardened nipple. Everest slid his hand down past Pax's fingers that were circling her clit and he shoved two inside. "Pull her back from the stove, Pax. I want to fuck her with my tongue."

"Dinner first, boys," she repeated. She turned away from both of them and walked over to where the towels were. She wrapped one around herself and threw the other two to the boys. "Put these on and after dinner we can go to the playroom."

The two of them looked at each other. "The playroom?" They both asked at the same time.

She smirked at them. "Yes. The playroom. You boys wanted to tie me up before and we didn't get to. I think it's time to try some of the toys in there."

"Holy fuck, I think I just came in this towel," Everest said as he stared at Blu.

Blu walked over to him and rubbed her fingers across his

chest. "I sure hope you can come again tonight, baby." She leaned up and pressed her lips to his. He cupped her ass in his hands as he deepened the kiss. She felt Pax against her back as she pulled away. She turned to face Pax and kissed him just the same.

When she pulled away she fixed their plates and sat them on the table. "Come and eat, boys."

Everest looked at Pax with a smile. "I hope she says that again in the playroom."

They all sat down and they ate their dinner. Blu was able to get their minds off sex for a little while. Sex with them was great and she loved every second of it but being with them was just as good. She watched the two of them as they talked about work and what was coming up this week. She smiled as she listened.

She cleared the table and was putting the dishes in the dishwasher when she felt two hands on her waist. She felt his breath on her neck before she heard his voice. "I want to make love to you," he whispered in her ear.

"Just us?" She asked.

"Tomorrow you are all mine, tonight you are ours," he whispered in her ear. "Come with me." Pax took her hand and led her to the room at the end of the hall. Everest was already inside holding a pair of leather handcuffs in his hand.

"You ready for this?" Everest asked as he dropped the towel. His hard cock sprang free and she bit her lip, seeing how hard he was again. She reached behind her and took Pax into her hand.

"I am ready for both of you."

She walked over to Everest and held out her hands. He placed one cuff on a wrist and smiled at her. "On the bed, baby girl." Blu laid on the bed, her heart racing. Ev raised her hands above her head and ran the chain connecting the two pieces of leather around the rail of the headboard. He fastened the other to her other wrist as she lay on her back.

Everest hovered over her body. "If you need us to stop, you

just have to say so, okay?" She nodded. "I need words baby girl."

"Yes," she agreed.

"Good." He laid on top of her body, his lips crashed to hers as she fought against the cuffs, already wanting to hold onto him. "You aren't gonna break those baby girl."

She glanced over to see Pax digging in his closet, naked and ready for her. "What's he doing?" She asked as she watched Pax.

Everest chuckled as he kissed down her body. "Looking for a toy." Everest spread her legs apart with his hands and her center apart with his fingers. "I want a taste," he stated before he licked from her entrance to her clit, stopping there to suck on it.

"Mmm…" she cried out.

"That's it baby, I want you to come on my face," he demanded as he continued to suck and flick at her with his tongue as he entered her with his fingers. He curled them inside as he moved them quickly. She turned to see Pax was beside her head, his hardness in his hand. He turned her head so she could take him into her mouth. She gladly opened for him. She knew how much he liked it in her mouth.

She licked his tip with her tongue as Everest worked her body into a panting mess. She wanted to stroke Pax like she knew he liked but she couldn't get free. She sucked on him as he thrust in and out of her mouth until her orgasm took over and she had to let go to scream out.

"Oh… God…" Her orgasm rushed through her body as Pax leaned down to kiss her, pinching her nipple with his fingers. He thrust his tongue into her mouth, massaging hers as he kissed her hard.

She heard Everest groan between her legs as he continued to finger her. His tongue lapping up what he had caused. "We are going to get another one, baby girl." He increased the speed of his fingers and his tongue, causing her second orgasm to crash into her harder than the first. "God damn, I gotta fuck this pussy." He said as he hovered over her body.

Pax took her nipple into his mouth as Everest grabbed her legs and pulled them apart. He took himself in his hand and lined up with her entrance. He pushed himself inside. "I love being inside you," he growled as he thrust in all the way.

Pax rubbed her clit with his fingers as he watched Everest thrust in and out of her. His other hand stroked himself. "I love watching him fuck this pussy." He stroked harder as her legs shook with her third orgasm from his words.

"She's so tight when she comes," Everest boasted, thrusting faster. He pulled out of her. "Flip her over," he ordered as he flipped her over to her stomach. He pulled her hips up and slammed back inside. He thrust hard and fast as Pax stopped over her back. He held himself in his hand as he pushed into her ass from above. Both of them claimed her body as they thrust in and out of her.

Blu had one more orgasm flood through her as Everest came right after her. Still inside of her, Pax came, as well. Everest pulled out first, Pax soon after. Blu's body collapsed onto the bed as Everest unbuckled her wrists. Pax helped her on her side as he slid in behind her, wrapping her body with his and kissing her shoulder. Everest laid in front of her and caressed her face. "I love you," he whispered before he kissed her lips.

She smiled at Everest and held onto Pax's arms before closing her eyes. "I love you both."

The next morning, she had Pax on one side of her and Everest on the other side. This was the second morning she woke up with both of them touching her somehow. Pax had his arm over her waist and Everest had his face buried in her hair. His breath tickled her neck as he snored lightly. She needed to get up to use the bathroom. It was on Pax's side of the room. She decided to climb over his body to get out. She was halfway over him when he grabbed onto her and pulled her down to his body.

"Morning, beautiful."

She smiled at him as she quickly kissed his lips. "Morning handsome, I have to use the bathroom."

He chuckled as he rubbed her back. "I love you." He kissed her lips again.

"I will love you more if you let me pee."

He slapped her ass as she got out of the bed. Once she was done in the bathroom she came back to his room. He was still lying in bed as she approached. "I need to get a shower. Do we have anything planned for today?"

He shook his head. "No, Ev and I may have a little work to get done before tomorrow."

She nodded. Pax patted the bed beside him. "Come here."

She smiled as she sat down beside him on the bed. "Are you going to stay tonight?"

"Do you want me to?" She asked as she climbed back over him and laid down.

"I do," he whispered, careful not to wake Everest. Pax reached out and grabbed her in his arms, pulling her into him. "I want you right here tonight."

"I'm going to have to go home eventually."

"About that..."

"What about it?"

"Did you forget what I asked you last week?"

She smiled up at him. She hadn't forgotten, but she wasn't going to bring it up. "No, I haven't."

"I want to wake up with you every morning." He said as he kissed her.

"I can't live here, Pax. I have to be on the farm."

"Okay."

"Okay what?" She asked, confused.

"Okay. We will live on the farm."

"You'll move to the farm?"

He kissed her cheek as he pulled her closer. "I would live anywhere you are. I meant it when I said I am in this, Blu. This isn't something I ever want to end."

"Never?"

He chuckled. "Never, Blu. I want to marry you one day, I want the whole thing. Home, kids, a life together."

Blu wiped a tear from her cheek. "You want to marry me?"

"I do. I want there to be no doubt that you're mine and I'm yours. I want little Blu's running around, causing trouble. I want to grow old with you and watch our grandchildren grow up. And if that means living on your farm, then that is where I will be." He paused. "If you will have me."

"Are you asking me to marry you, Pax?"

He chuckled. "Not yet. I am telling you that is what I want for our future and I hope you do, too."

"What about our talk last night? What about our time with Everest?"

She felt another set of hands touch her back. "I love you and I do want to be part of this relationship, but we talked about it. He will be the one to marry you."

"But if we live out on the farm, how will we ever see you?" Blu asked Everest as she took his hand and pulled him into her back.

"I will see you all the time. I just rent my house and I'm not partial to it. I could stay with you as much as you wanted. When the time is right," he whispered as he kissed the back of her shoulders.

"Are we really doing this?"

Both boys leaned in to press kisses to different parts of her body.

"Yes," they whispered against her.

Chapter 34

It had been a month since Pax, Everest and Blu decided to be together. Things had been going very well. "Do you have everything you need?" Blu asked Pax as he packed up the last of his clothes from his bedroom.

"I do. The rest will be coming next week," Pax said as he grabbed the bag of clothes that he just finished packing.

Everest popped his head into the bedroom. "Hey baby, asshole. We ready?"

"Fuck off, Ev," Pax joked.

Everest walked over to Blu and took her into his arms. "You should just ditch him and keep me."

"I could never ditch my fiancée." She smiled as she looked at the ring on her finger. A week after they decided to move in together and the three of them be together, Pax officially asked her to marry him. The three of them went out to dinner, each of them teased and kissed her all night. At the end of the night, Pax got down on one knee and asked her. She, of course, said yes and they were planning a wedding in about six months. They asked Everest to be a part of the ceremony, making sure that he knew he was with them, too.

"Just remember, it's my turn to sleep next to you tonight, baby."

Pax rolled his eyes at Ev's reminder that he and Blu had plans for the night. "She remembers."

Everest teased, "Are you jealous?"

Pax and Everest often teased each other about their times with Blu without the other one, but neither of them were jealous. They spent more time as a triad than they did apart.

"Not jealous one little bit. I know she loves me." Pax stepped up to Blu, still in Everest's arms and pressed his body against her back. "You want to fuck one last time in this room, the three of us?"

"I would love to," she admitted as she grabbed onto Pax's hardness that was pressing against his jeans. "But we'll be late."

"We can be late. No one will care." Everest pressed, wanting to take her now.

"I will care. It's our party, you know?"

They both pulled away from her, reluctantly. Pax slapped her on the ass. "Okay, let's get going." He adjusted himself in his pants. "I'm going to need a cold shower if I can't have any pussy tonight."

They all laughed as they took the bags to the car. Once they arrived at the farm, Blu excused herself to the bathroom to get a shower and ready for the night. Pax put the rest of his clothes in the closet, beside Blu's. This would be their first night officially living together. Pax put his house up for sale the day after they decided to do this. It was closing at the end of the month.

Blu was done in the shower and was wrapping the towel around her body when the bathroom door opened. "Damn. I was hoping to catch you in the shower."

"Paxton."

Pax walked over to her and took her in his arms, kissing her neck. "Do you know how much I love you?"

"I do." She leaned back, allowing him to suck on the spot that drove her wild with desire. "Baby…"

"I want you, baby." He moaned into her neck.

"I have to get dressed."

Pax groaned, knowing that she was right. People would be arriving soon and it was important to them to have their friends with them tonight.

Everest had decided that he was not going to move in. He stayed there more nights than he didn't, but he hadn't officially decided to move in yet. Blu wanted him to be there all the time, but she and Pax told him that when and if he wanted to move in, he was welcome. Pax put Blu's old bed in a guest room and bought them a new king size bed. It was big enough for all three of them, when they all slept in the same bed, which they did at least half of the week.

They were getting dressed when Everest came into the bedroom. "Hey guys, Zoe and Owen are here. She wants to know if you need anything?"

Blu took both of their hands in hers and pulled them into her. "I have everything I need, right here."

Everest leaned in and kissed her, whispering on her lips. "I love you so damn much."

"I love you, too, Ev," she whispered back as he kissed her.

"Well, fuck. I'm hard again." Pax mumbled into her neck as he rubbed his hardness on her ass.

Everest chuckled. He knew what it was like. He'd never had so much sex in his whole life. Just one look from her had him ready to go. Throw in watching how much Pax wanted her and he was ready all the time. Each of them got off on watching the other please her or her please them. It was almost as good as when they were the one pleasing or being pleased. They didn't usually plan time alone, but if they happened to be alone with her and things led to mind blowing sex, so be it.

He and Pax had talked earlier in the day and Everest told him that he wanted to stay there with them. He was not jealous about Pax spending every night with her because he was there more than he wasn't, but he missed her too much when he wasn't with her. Blu thought that she was going to be alone with Everest tonight, but she wasn't. He was going to tell her he wanted to stay. He even had his clothes in his truck.

Pax also had a surprise tonight. Everest was the only other person that knew about it. It was going to be a night full of surprises, love and desire for the three of them.

They made their way out of the room and down the steps. There were a few more people there and everyone was drinking and talking. When they reached the bottom of the steps, everyone turned to look at the three of them.

"Thank you all for coming tonight to celebrate our love." She took Pax's hand in hers. "And to celebrate with us on our first night together."

"Finally," Zoe yelled out. Everyone laughed.

"I also wanted to tell everyone thank you for being here." He looked at Blu with such love in his eyes. "When I met you that first day, I knew there was something special about you." He pulled her closer to him. "I just didn't know that I had met the love of my life that day." He leaned down to kiss her. "I tried for a long time to not fall in love with you, but it was impossible not to."

Everest stepped up to them and handed Blu an envelope. She looked down at it "What's this baby?" She asked Everest.

He leaned in and kissed her lips. "Ask him."

Pax smiled at her. "As you all know, we," he pointed to Everest and himself, "we love this woman more than anything in the world."

"We do," Everest chimed in, wrapping his arm around her waist.

"We know that what we have isn't considered a normal relationship. It took some of you a little longer to accept us, but by being here tonight, you do." He kissed her cheek. "Ev and I wanted to give you something. Something that we know means the world to you."

"Open it, baby girl." Everest said as he smiled at her.

Blu opened the envelope and pulled out some legal looking papers. She read it and started to cry. "Pax." She looked at him with tears falling.

"We love you, baby. You don't have to worry anymore."

She hugged and kissed Pax. She pulled back from him and turned to hug and kiss Everest. "You did this?" She asked him just before she kissed him.

"We did." She turned to hold up the deed to the farm to show everyone. Pax and Everest had paid off the mortgage on the farm. Blu was now the free and clear owner. Everyone cheered as she cried.

Everest leaned in and whispered in her ear. "There's more, baby girl."

"More? I don't think I can take anymore."

"We all know that's not true. We know exactly how much you can take."

Blu blushed at Everest's words. She playfully slapped him on the chest. He chuckled. "I will remember that tonight when I slap that ass."

Blu grabbed his shirt and pulled him in to kiss her. He took her into his arms and kissed her back.

"Get a room," Owen hollered at them.

Everest pulled back, chuckled and smirked at her. "That is exactly what I want to talk to her about."

Blu looked at him with confusion.

"I want to move in, Blu."

Blu didn't know what to think. She looked at him with surprise. She then turned to look at Pax. He smiled at her, "It's true baby. He has clothes in his truck."

She turned back to Everest. "You're staying?"

He nodded. "I am. If that is okay with you."

She jumped into his arms, kissing his face. He laughed as she hugged him tight.

Everyone was looking at them, not sure what was going on.

"Ev is moving in, too," she announced to the group. They all clapped and said their congratulations.

Everest set her back on the ground in between them. She put her arms around each of their waists, each of them holding onto her, as well.

"I can't believe it. I have my boys."

They each leaned in and kissed one side of her face.

They had the best evening with all their friends. Everest and Pax had introduced her to a few other couples that liked to go to the sex club. None of them were anyone that either Pax or Everest had played with and Blu was happy about that. One of the women told her how lucky she was to have them both. Apparently, they were the most sought after and most elusive at the same time.

They had become close friends with another triad. Josh, Lewis and Cindy had been together for a few years now. She helped Blu when she wondered how they were going to make things work for the long haul. Blu experienced some guilt after they had agreed to be a triad about not wanting another woman in their group. She knew that she could not share either of them with another woman.

Cindy told her that it was okay to feel that way and that she did, as well. She encouraged Blu to talk to the guys about it and she did. They assured her that they were not interested in another woman in or out of their group. Everest explained it the best when he told her, "I love watching you with Paxton and he loves watching you with me. We are both comfortable with you showing the other person affection and love, but we don't want you to be with anyone else, either." It turned out Blu's boys were just as jealous as she was at the thought of anyone else other than the three of them being in their group.

Sometimes Blu forgot that fact because they were never jealous of each other.

Cindy also reassured her that she could keep two men satisfied, sexually. Both Pax and Everest had healthy sex drives and she had also been worried that she wouldn't be enough for them. So far, that had not been an issue because Blu wanted them as much and as often as they wanted her. They spent more time together than apart.

Tonight would be no exception to that. Pax had already moved in and Everest had his clothes in the truck. Now she understood why Pax took part of the room next to Blu's room to make a bigger walk in closet. It was going to have to house three people's clothing.

The party was over and everyone had left, but not before offering their congratulations to them.

Blu watched as Everest and Pax closed and locked the front door as they ushered the last person out and Everest had brought in one of his bags. She started removing her clothes while the two of them were talking about the party and how it was such as success.

Everest turned around first, seeing that Blu was completely naked, standing behind them. "Holy fuck." He licked his lips.

"What man?" Pax asked as he turned around. "Shit."

"You boys ready for bed?"

"Fuck yes." Everest panted as he grabbed Blu and slung her over his shoulder.

Blu looked up from her upside-down position over Everest's shoulder to smile at Pax. "You coming?"

Pax chuckled as he followed behind the two as Everest carried Blu up the stairs. "Soon, love. Soon."

Chapter 35

Once inside their room, Everest set Blu onto her feet, his lips on hers as soon as she got her balance. Pax turned on some music as Everest kissed Blu. The soothing saxophone music played in the background as Pax watched Everest taking what was his. What was theirs. Everest's hands caressed her body as his kisses moved down her neck.

Pax smiled at the two of them. He knew this was what was right, no matter what anyone else thought about their relationship. He knew that they all three were where they needed to be. Together.

Blu glanced over to where Pax stood, watching the love of his life. She smiled at him, asking him with her eyes to come kiss her. He smiled back at her as he walked to where the other two were standing. "Hi, baby," Pax whispered in her ear as he stood behind Blu.

She laid her head back onto Pax's shoulder, granting Everest more access to her neck. Pax kissed just below her ear as he whispered to her again. "I love you." She turned in Everest's arms so that she was facing Pax, her hands around the back of his neck.

"Make love to me," she whispered back.

She felt Everest's kisses along her shoulder blade as he ran his hands down her sides. Pax pulled her closer to his body as Everest skimmed her back with his fingers. "You're beautiful." He mumbled onto her back as he kissed her hot skin. "I can't believe you were naked under that dress." Everest growled as he ran his fingers along her silky skin.

Pax gave her one more kiss before he stepped back from a confused Blu. "Tonight is supposed to be Everest's night, baby." Blu smiled up at Paxton as he turned her back to Everest.

She looked up to Everest with the same love in her eyes that she had for Paxton. He caressed her face with his hand, his eyes darted between her eyes and her lips. "I love you, Blu." She pulled him down to kiss her lips. His hands cupped her ass as he kissed her. He looked over her shoulder and saw Pax ready to leave the room. "Don't leave." He looked down to Blu. Everest carried Blu over to the bed, kissing her the whole time. He laid her onto the center of it, staring at her naked body. He glanced over to Pax, who stood at the door, ready to leave them alone. "She doesn't want you to leave, do you baby girl?"

She shook her head no. She didn't want either of them to leave. She had been with each of them at times without the other one, but it wasn't usually planned. It would just happen. She preferred to be with them both, even when one watched while she was with the other. "No, I want him to stay." Everest crawled up her body, leaving kisses as he went. Pax continued to watch as Everest lowered his body onto hers. He smiled as he took the steps to the bed. He laid down beside Everest and Blu as Everest kissed her.

"I love to watch him love you," Pax rumbled as Everest devoured Blu's perky breast. Blu turned her head to see Pax beside her, stroking himself as he watched Everest's tongue dance across her nipple. Everest groaned his approval as his kiss continued to the apex between her legs.

Everest kissed her inner thigh as he spoke softly to her. "I need to taste you." He plunged his tongue into her wetness as his fingers entered her. Her back arched off the bed as Pax took her nipple into his mouth. She dug her hands into Pax's hair as he lightly bit her skin.

"How does she taste?" Pax asked as he watched Everest lick her sensitive bud.

"Fucking incredible," Everest moaned out as Pax rubbed her clit with his finger. He placed his wet finger into his mouth as he maintained eye contact with Blu.

"Mm." The sound vibrated through his chest. After cleaning

his fingers, he grabbed his erection in his hand. "God damn, Ev. Please fuck her."

Everest chuckled as he sped up his tongue and his fingers so she would come for him. Blu's legs shook around Everest's head as her orgasm took over her body. Pax kissed her, swallowing her screams from the orgasm Everest gave her. "Fuck her," Pax demanded, needing to see Blu's body take him in.

Everest raised up and positioned Blu's legs over his shoulders so he could go deep inside and let Pax watch. Everest lined up with her and slammed inside. She cried out as Pax watched his friend disappear inside the woman they loved. "Fuck, that's hot," he said as he stroked himself faster.

"She's so wet for us." Everest bragged as he thrust in and out of her. Pax took Blu's hand and replaced his own. She stroked him hard and fast as he circled her clit with his finger.

"Yes, baby. Stroke my cock while we make you come," Pax ordered as he gave her the second orgasm of the night. Everest and Paxton were quick to follow. Everest collapsed on the bed beside Blu while Pax got a wet rag to clean her off.

The three of them cuddled together as they drifted off to sleep.

The next morning, Blu woke before both men. After her trip to the bathroom she returned to the bed. Pax was lying on his back with the covers barely pulled over his hard shaft. Blu licked her lips as she took him in her hand. She licked his tip before she took him into her mouth. He started to stir as she sucked on him. "Fuck, I love it when you suck my cock," Pax groaned in his sleepy whisper voice.

Blu kissed up his stomach and neck until she reached his lips. "We are going to give Ev a little surprise for his first night with us."

"What surprise is that baby?"

She raised up and sat down on him. He slid in easily as she rocked her hips on him. It was a few minutes before they heard Everest stir. "What the hell is…" he started until he saw Blu riding Pax. "Oh... fuck yeah, baby girl. Ride that cock." Everest threw the blankets back. Blu glanced over to see him take himself into his hand. He watched them for a moment before he got up and came over to their side of the bed. Blu grabbed for him, taking him into her mouth as she worked her hips on Pax.

"I want to wake up like this every morning," Everest admitted as he thrust into her mouth. He watched as Pax pulled her down onto him, bottoming out every time. "I'm getting close," he warned so she could decide where she wanted him to come. She took him further in as Pax came underneath her, her own right after. She worked her hips slowly on Pax as she took Everest as far as she could. His orgasm shooting down her throat as he threw his head back.

Pax chuckled as Blu let Everest go. "Watching you get your dick sucked is almost as good as getting mine ridden."

"She sucks it so fucking hard. I've never come so fast." Everest agreed as he kissed her while she still had Pax inside her. "I love you, baby girl."

"I love you, too, Ev." She kissed him again before she looked down at Pax. "I love you, too, Pax."

Pax smiled at her, "You are my world and I cannot wait to make you my wife."

It had been four months since they all moved in together. They all slept in the same bed together every night. There were times they were with her without the other one, but none of the three of them preferred that. Just a few nights ago, Everest made love to Blu. Pax was there the whole time and kissed or touched her when he could, but he felt comfortable enough to let them have their time together, as well as getting his own.

Everest knew that this relationship was not something that everyone would understand or approve of, but he didn't care. He had never been in a relationship before and being in one with

Pax and a woman was not exactly how he thought it would happen.

Some of the guys that they used to see at the club asked him once if he was in a relationship with Pax, as well. They knew that he was never into guys and he still wasn't. He and Pax were never intimate with each other, at least not in that sense. Being with Blu at the same time had given them a comfort level with each other that was new to the both of them before this relationship.

Blu had been in the bathroom throwing up for the last fifteen minutes. Zoe was over that morning and both guys were at work. Blu had stayed home sick and Pax sent Zoe over to check on her. "Blu, you really sound bad. Are you sure you don't want to go to the doctor?"

Between hugging the toilet, Blu answered. "I'll be fine. I must have eaten something that didn't disagree with me."

Blu flushed the toilet, brushed her teeth and washed her face. Zoe came into the bathroom as she was drying her face. "Here," she said, sitting a box down on the counter.

Blu picked up the box and read the outside. She looked at her best friend. "A pregnancy test?"

Chapter 36

"Why are you giving me a pregnancy test?" Zoe laughed as she took the test from her friend and opened the box. "Really? You have two hot, sexy men and you tend to have lots of sex." She sat the test on the counter beside Blu. "Pee. I want to see if am going to be an auntie."

Blu laughed as she took the test from the counter. "Then get out of here."

Zoe went back to their bedroom and sat on the bed. Blu took the test from the box and took it. She laid it on the counter as she waited for the second hand on her watch to click off another minute. Another minute closer to find out if she was going to be a mother.

Blu made an appointment for later that week. Zoe was the only person that she told about the positive test result. She didn't want to be alone, so she asked Zoe to go with her.

Sitting in the doctor's office, waiting for her to come back with the conformation of what she saw after she peed on the stick, was taking forever. Everything around her seemed to be moving in slow motion. She saw the other women, some of which were in different stages of pregnancy, reading magazines, talking with their significant other, or staring at their phones.

"Blu?" Blu shook her head as she tried to focus on Zoe. "Are you okay?"

Am I okay? Do I want a baby? Will they be happy about having a baby? Will the man who the baby doesn't belong to, get jealous? Blu nodded to her friend that she was okay, afraid that trying to speak would give away the nervous feeling in the pit of her stomach.

A few minutes later the doctor entered the room that she had been put in after the nurse took her blood. "Good afternoon, Ms. Millar."

"Is it?" Blu asked, trying to smile like she meant it.

The doctor returned her smile. "I guess it is if you want to be pregnant."

The doctor talked about what to expect for the next visit and Blu could only think about how she was going to tell the two men in her life that she was going to have a baby. She knew she needed to go and see Paxton right away and hope that Everest was close and she could tell them at the same time.

"Paxton, your meeting for this afternoon is canceled," Missy announced as she walked into Pax's office. She closed the door behind her as she walked over to his desk, his eyes on the papers in front of him. "Pax, did you hear me?"

Pax looked up from the papers he was reading to see Missy standing in front of his desk, unbuttoning her shirt. "What are you doing?" He asked, angered by her display.

"Come on, Pax. I know that you are sharing a woman with Everest." She walked around the side of his desk as she slipped her shirt off her shoulders. "You don't have to share me." She reached out to touch his face as the door opened.

"Pax, baby, I need to talk to you…" Blu stopped short as soon as she saw Missy without her shirt on standing beside Pax's desk. "What's going on in here?" Blu asked, ready to lose control on the woman standing bedside Pax.

"Isn't it obvious?" Missy replied, smiling at Blu.

Pax slid his chair back from his desk and stepped around the front and close to Blu. "Baby?" He reached out to grab her. She swatted his hand down from her hips.

"Don't." Blu turned to look at Missy, the smile on her face grew, thinking she had won. Blu bent down in front of Missy and picked up the shirt she had dropped to the floor.

Blu shoved the shirt into Missy's stomach causing her to take a deep breath. Blu could hear Pax behind her, trying to get her attention. "Stop Pax. Missy and I need to have a discussion and then we can."

Pax watched Blu with desire in his eyes. He was always turned on when Blu claimed him and this was going to be one of those times.

"I don't know who you think you are messing with here."

"You are no good for him," Missy interrupted.

"Did I give you the impression that I was done talking? No? I didn't think so." Blu stepped forward, causing Missy to step backwards. "You see that man standing over there?" Blu glanced back to Pax, smiling at him adjusting himself from what she was causing. "That man is mine."

"Fuck me," he mumbled as he watched his woman.

"That is my man, not yours." She looked back to Missy. "I'm not sure what brand of stupid you are to continue to throw yourself at a man that has turned you down... every... single... time."

"Hell," Pax growled as Blu continued.

"Are you really that desperate to get my man that you need to strip to try to get his attention?" Blu chuckled. "If he was interested in your skank ass, he would've taken you up on your many desperate attempts to fuck him." Blu looked to his desk. "He would have already had you bent over that desk."

Blu felt hands slide around her stomach and Pax's hard body press against her back. "I need you," he whispered into her ear.

"I suggest you get your shirt on, leave this office and never look at him ever again. Because the next time I see you trying anything with either of my men," Blu stepped closer one more time, pushing Missy into the arm of one of the chairs in the room. "I won't hesitate to fuck you up. Do I make myself clear?"

Missy looked over Blu's shoulder to see Pax with his face buried in Blu's hair. "Are you going to let your little tramp talk to me like this?" Missy asked as she buttoned her shirt.

"Get out!" Pax growled as he pulled Blu's body into his. Missy stood there, looking at him like she wasn't sure what to do. "Unless you want to see me fuck the hell out of my woman, I suggest you leave."

Missy groaned as she turned to leave. Before she reached the door, Pax called out her name. "Missy?"

She turned to see Pax unbuttoning Blu's jeans from behind her. "Lock the door on your way out…" He slid his hand into her jeans as he continued. "And… you're fired."

Missy walked out of the office and slammed the door behind her. Pax shoved Blu's jeans down her legs as he pushed her closer to the desk. "What was that you said about being bent over this desk?"

"Pax." Blu whispered as she bent over, pushing her ass into Pax. She heard him unbuckle his belt and unzip his pants. She felt one of his hands on her back as the other lined him up with her opening. "Please, Pax…"

Pax slammed into her with one quick thrust. "God, I love you." He panted as he thrust in and out of her, holding her hips still. She felt his hand slide around her hip and find her swollen clit, circling it as he continued to slam into her. The only sounds in the room were the grunts and heavy breathing coming from them both.

Pax chuckled as Blu pushed the ringing phone to the floor, letting whoever called hear their love making. "Fuck, baby… I am so fucking close." Pax panted, leaning over her back to get a different angle.

"Oh… Pax… Please…"

Pax gave her one more thrust, sending them both over the edge. His body collapsed onto her back as they both caught their breath. Pax kissed her back as he pulled out of her. "I think we gave someone a show." He chuckled as he picked up his cell phone that had lit up. He read the text message on the screen and chuckled.

"At least now I know that hearing you fuck our girl is just as much

a turn on as watching you fuck her. Thanks for the boner at work. I wish I would have heard all of it because now I am going to have to take care of myself."

Pax chuckled as he showed Blu the text from Everest. Blu giggled, "At least it was Ev."

They dressed and Pax took Blu into his arms. "What did you want to talk to me about?"

She smiled at him as she laid her head on his chest. "It can wait until tonight."

Later that night, Blu had planned dinner for Pax and Everest. She cooked their favorite meal; bacon wrapped scallops, Beef Wellington and roasted baby vegetables. She planned on telling them that she was pregnant and hoped that they both still wanted to stay.

Pax was the first one through the door. "Hey, baby." He stepped up behind Blu as she was getting the Wellington out of the oven. "Dinner looks really good."

"But not as good as she looks," Everest added as he entered the kitchen. Blu kissed each of them before she shooed them away and to the dining room table. "What's the occasion, baby girl?"

"You will find out soon, just sit down and I will bring the food to the table." Each of the guys grabbed a plate or bowl of food and took it to the table for her. They ate dinner, both men trying to get out of her why the special dinner.

"Are you ready to tell us what's going on now, Blu?" Pax asked as he took her hand into his.

She nodded as she pulled out a box from beside the table and handed them each one. The two of them looked at each other and smiled.

"What's this?" Everest asked as he shook the box in his hands.

Blu giggled at him acting like a child, trying to guess what's inside. "Just open them."

Both men opened their boxes, pulling out a sonogram picture. "Baby? Is this what I think it is?" Pax asked, looking at Blu with a worried look.

Blu nodded at him.

"We're having a baby?" Everest asked with tears in his eyes.

She nodded again. She was afraid to say anything, knowing that she would cry if she spoke.

Everest jumped up and took Blu into his arms. "I love you."

"I love you, too, Ev." Blu hugged him back.

When she pulled away from him, she glanced over to Pax. He was staring at the picture, tears falling down his face. He looked up to see her watching him, still in Everest's arms. "How far along are you?"

"About three months." She answered quietly. "I went to the doctor this morning and she confirmed the test I took earlier in the week."

"Before you came to my office?" Pax asked with a smirk.

"Yes."

"Do you think you will be ready to marry me in two months?"

"Two months?"

"Yes, I want you to be my wife when our baby comes. Is that okay?" He asked, looking at Everest as well as Blu.

"That's good for me." Everest agreed as he kissed Blu's cheek. "I think it's a great idea."

"Are you happy about the baby?" She asked Pax, still unsure how he felt. He stood and walked to stand in front of her.

"I have never been happier in my whole life. I never knew that I could love like this," he glanced at Everest. "I never knew that being a part of a relationship like this would be where my life would take me, but I am so happy it did."

Pax kissed Blu and pulled her into his chest. Everest pressed into her back and ran his hands up and down her sides. "Shall we take this celebration upstairs?"

Blu nodded, Pax picked her up and carried her up to their room, Everest right behind them.

Four months ago, Pax and Blu got married. Because of the nature of their wedding, they only invited people that knew about the three of them. Pax and Blu were legally married and they also included Everest in their ceremony. The three of them still together and going strong.

"Baby girl?" Everest greeted as he walked in the door.

Blu looked up from her bed to see him walk into the room with pink carnations and balloons in his hand. "Are you talking to me or her?" Blu asked as she glanced at the swaddled baby in her arms.

Everest sat the vase on the bedside table and kissed her forehead, "Are my girls ready to go home?" He asked as he took the baby from Blu's arms. "Hi, sweet girl. Are you giving your momma a hard time?"

Pax joined them from the bathroom where he was packing up the rest of Blu's things. "They are both perfect."

"My angel," Everest cooed as he cradled their daughter in his arms.

The day that Blu went to Pax's office and got Missy fired, she wanted to tell them that they were going to have a baby. They decided that they didn't want to do a paternity test. Even though they didn't test Angel, Blu knew exactly who she belonged to. As soon as she was born, they could all tell who she belonged to by how she looked just like him. Pax teased Everest as he held Angel's fingers. "Is Uncle Ev giving my girl a hard time?"

Everest flipped Pax off. "She may not be my biological daughter, but I will never be Uncle Ev." Everest handed Angel to Pax. Pax handed a slightly fussy baby back to Blu to feed her.

"Maybe the next one will be mine." Everest sat on one side of the bed while Pax sat on the other side.

"Don't worry Angel. You will get used to your daddies and their silly ways." Each man leaned in to kiss Blu on a cheek.

"I love you." Everest whispered against one side.

"I love you." Pax whispered against the other side.

Blu smiled at them both before looking back at their daughter.

"I love my boys."

ABOUT THE AUTHOR

Aimee Stone is an emerging author of young adult romance. This is Aimee's first book.

Aimee Stone is an emerging author of romance novels. This is Aimee's first book to be published outside of the interactive reading app where she got her start. All of her titles will be transformed into print as well as ebook copies.

It has been a life-long dream to become a published author and to tell the stories of her imagination to anyone and everyone that wants to read them.

Follow her on social media to keep in contact with her, find out what's next and for the most current release dates and titles.

You can look forward to all of your favorites, coming soon!

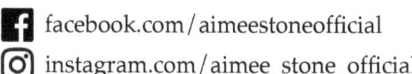

facebook.com/aimeestoneofficial
instagram.com/aimee_stone_official

Lightning Source UK Ltd.
Milton Keynes UK
UKHW012249250920
370542UK00001B/79